MW00772992

SAVED BY THE
SINGLE DAD

SINGLE DADS OF SEATTLE, BOOK 3

WHITLEY COX

Copyright © 2019 by Whitley Cox

All rights reserved.

No part of this book may be reproduced in any form or by any electronic or mechanical means, including information storage and retrieval systems, without written permission from the author, except for the use of brief quotations in a book review

ISBN: 978-1-989081-19-8

For Author Jeanne St. James. A friend, a mentor,
a sounding-board, my alpha-reader,
and a fucking phenomenal writer. You are an inspiration
and I am so thankful to have you in my life.

xoxo

1

MITCH BENSON'S jaw dropped open, and his balls tightened in his shorts. The woman dancing on stage was one of the most spectacular things he'd ever seen. He was supposed to be taking pictures of the performers, but at the moment, he was stunned. Paralyzed by the vision on stage.

Not only was she fucking stunning, with dark, chestnut hair piled up high on her head in a ballerina bun, but the way she danced was incredible. Every emotion she felt came through in the way she moved. The focus on her face and the raw feelings in the way her body reacted to the rhythm and tempo of the music were unlike anything he'd ever seen before. She was perfection.

He thought the dance following the children's performance was supposed to be the adult contemporary group, but when she stepped out nibbling on her bottom lip and with apprehension in her light brown eyes, he was struck dumb. He hadn't taken a single photo.

She'd been introduced as Paige McPherson, a beginner adult dancer in Violet's contemporary adult class. She must have danced Wednesday nights when he was home with Jayda, otherwise Mitch would remember meeting her. He'd remember meeting Paige.

Paige.

Paige?

Paige!

Holy shit!

This was Adam's wife.

Ex-wife, he corrected.

This was Adam's ex-wife. Mira's mother.

Holy fuck.

The clearing of a throat behind him brought him out of his stupor.

"Shouldn't your camera be making more *clicking* sounds?" It was Zak, Adam's brother and one of the fellow Single Dads of Seattle Mitch played poker with every Saturday night.

Mitch swallowed, nodded and focused his gaze back on the screen of his camera. His finger pressed down on the button, and he began to snap shots of the woman on stage.

"She's beautiful," Zak said matter-of-factly. "Adam filled you in on their split?"

Mitch nodded. "Yeah. Sad."

"Yeah, it was. You can tell that she's pouring all of her pain into her dancing. Just look at her face, her movements. They're so precise, so driven, so focused."

Mitch's finger paused on the button, and he turned to face the big, beefed-up, tattooed, redheaded man, who stood at least three inches taller than Mitch's six-two frame. "You, uh ... you interested in her?"

Zak shook his head but didn't smile. He also didn't look down at Mitch. His blue eyes, the same shade as Adam's, remained focused on Paige. "No. Not interested in anyone. Sworn off love for a bit. Sworn off women."

Mitch's shoulders relaxed. Why had they been tense?

"Taking a page out of Liam's book? Love is for suckers?"

Zak shoved his hands into his pockets and rocked back on his heels. "Something like that, maybe. Just taking a breather." Finally, he dropped his gaze down to Mitch. The intensity of his stare was unnerving. "Adam can't say this because Paige is his ex-wife and it would come across as possessive. Plus, what he and Violet have right now is good, and I know he wouldn't want to fuck that up. But I can say it."

Say what?

Zak's mouth crooked up into a lopsided grin. "I've been watching you for the past several minutes. Your reaction to Paige on stage is visceral. You're attracted to her."

Mitch shrugged, hoping his demeanor came across as cavalier. "She's beautiful, not going to deny that."

Zak nodded. "That she is. She's also hurting. She's in a lot of pain. So just tread lightly if you're going to pursue her. She deserves to be happy. We all do. But just be careful. She's been through a lot."

Mitch's back straightened, and he stood up to his full height, squaring off with the big muscly man. "We all have. I lost my wife. I lost my father. My daughter lost her mother. I don't need a lecture or a warning. If anybody knows to tread lightly, it's me. I'm allowed to think someone is attractive, *be* attracted to them without immediately asking them for a date or jumping into bed with them. I'm a grown-ass man, not a fucking teenager. I have some fucking self-control."

Oh fuck.

The lady doth protest too much, methinks.

He could just hear the words of Melissa, his late wife, echoing in his brain. She loved Shakespeare. Loved quoting it and reading it. She'd dragged him to many a play in their years together, swooning over the costumes and sonnets. She came by it honestly though. She was an English lit major and had only just started teaching at the University of Arizona when they met.

God, how he missed her.

Zak's dark red hair glinted like a brick-colored helmet in the warm July sun. They were all in Magnolia Park, celebrating the Fourth of July by enjoying the Arts Council of Seattle's Art in the Park. Jayda, Mitch's six-year-old daughter, had just performed on stage with her dance class, and before that, Mitch's sister Violet and her boyfriend, Adam, Zak's brother, had performed. All of The Single Dads of Seattle were sitting on the grass with their children, enjoying beer, food and the afternoon sun. This was what summers were made of. Friends, food and festivities.

The two men simply stood there, staring at each other. But finally, something passed behind Zak's blue eyes, and his face split into a grin. He reached out and slapped Mitch on the back. "All right then. Good chat." He nodded at Mitch's camera. "Best get back to work there, camera jockey, before your muse runs off stage." Then he spun around on his heel and sauntered his big frame back to the cluster of blankets and single fathers and children, all while earning more than a few ogles from female admirers.

Mitch fought the urge to flip him the bird and instead turned back to his camera and the captivating woman on stage. He started snapping photos again, the camera—and Mitch—loving the way Paige's body gracefully moved about the floor. She used her hands and arms in a way he'd never seen before, at least not in contemporary dancing or in North America. It was reminiscent of his time spent in Bali, photographing the Balinese dancers, decked out in heavy makeup, gold and tapestry. Where had she learned to dance like that?

He couldn't remember Violet ever doing such moves, and he'd been watching his sister dance for years.

Paige leapt across the floor and fell to her knees. She was close to where Mitch stood down on the grass near the edge of the stage. Her head popped up, and they came face to face. She stared into his eyes, into his soul. He knew he should smile, encourage her to dance, let her know he enjoyed her performance, but he couldn't.

He was stunned.

Stunned by the lone tear that slipped down her cheek and the pained expression on her face. She really was dancing with every emotion right out on the surface for all to see.

As if acting of its own volition, his finger pressed down on the button, and he took a picture. That must have snapped her out of whatever moment she'd been having, because her eyes left his and dropped down to his camera. Mitch followed her gaze, then glanced back up at Paige, but she was gone—standing at the front of the stage, bowing to the roar of applause from the audience. Mitch let the camera swing down around his neck and began to clap as well.

PAIGE MCPHERSON RAN off stage to the thunderous applause from the city of Seattle. Her heart pounded just as loud as the crowd. She couldn't believe it. She'd danced in front of hundreds of people on stage all by herself.

And it felt good.

A warm arm draped around her shoulder, and she could smell her ex-husband Adam's cologne. "Great job, Paige! We knew you could do it."

Violet, Adam's new girlfriend and Paige's dance instructor, stood next to Adam and was all smiles. "Thank you so much for going on. You danced beautifully." She wiped away a tear from beneath her eye and laughed. "See, I told you your dancing brings people to tears. Your solo was inspiring."

Paige's face got hot, and she quickly averted her gaze down to her feet. "I messed up at the end there. When I was supposed to slide down on to my back, I missed a few beats." She didn't want to add that she'd missed a few beats because she'd been stunned by the man standing at the edge of the stage with the camera. The man with piercing green eyes, the same color as cedar boughs, with dark hair, a close-shaved beard and full lips. Very full lips.

When she'd lifted her head at the corner of the stage and come face-to-face with him, she'd forgotten what she was doing. Forgotten about the crowd, about the music and her dancing, and instead got lost in the way the lighter yellowy-green around the center of his eyes seemed to swirl in the sunlight.

She was about to open her mouth and excuse herself, go find Mira and her parents, when the man with the camera, the man with the eyes, the man with the lips, appeared around the corner.

He seemed to laser right in on her and walked directly up to where Paige stood with Adam and Violet. He stuck his hand out, waiting for her to take it. "Mitch Benson. Your dance was amazing."

Mitch Benson.

Violet's ... ?

"This is my brother," Violet confirmed, having obviously noticed the confusion on Paige's face. "He's a professional photographer."

Paige took his hand with a careful curiosity. It was warm and big, and even though she hadn't been overly keen on shaking his hand, now she didn't want to let it go.

His smile was wide and genuine, showing off perfectly

straight, white teeth. And those lips. Good God, those lips. Full and totally kissable. Yum.

"Nice to meet you," she finally said, swallowing down the sudden lump in her throat and having to look up a fair bit to reach his eyes. The man was tall. Taller than Adam, and Adam was over six feet.

"Likewise." He pulled his hand back and winked. "I took some pretty great shots of your dancing. I'll let you know when I've edited them so you can take a look for yourself. Let me know if you want any printed, and I can mail them to you."

Insecurity dug her fire-engine-red harpy talons into the back of Paige's neck, and she felt her shoulders slump where she stood. "I don't think I'd like to see any pictures of myself dancing. I wasn't that good."

Was that confusion that flashed behind Mitch's eyes? Either way, they darkened, and his smile dropped. "You were incredible. Don't sell yourself short. Take the compliment. You'll be getting a hell of a lot more of them when you head down to the blankets to go sit with the girls."

Paige needed to get away from him. She couldn't handle the praise. She couldn't handle the pressure that someone thought she was good at something. Couldn't handle the pressure of living up to their warped idea of her, that she wasn't a complete and utter failure.

Taking a step back, she pulled out of Adam's arm and away from Mitch and his scrutinizing stare. "I'm going to go find Mira."

Mitch's smile was back. "I'll come with you. I'm headed that way to find Jayda anyway. We'll walk together."

"No."

Adam, Violet and Mitch all shared confused looks with one another.

The palpitations in Paige's heart made her chest ache,

and the pulse pumping in her ears was deafening. "Wh-what I mean is ... I have to go to the bathroom first and get changed. I'm sweaty and gross in all this Lycra. Then I'll go find Mira. No need for you to wait for me. Go. Go on your own, and I'll catch up." She didn't wait for them to offer to hold up for her or to say they'd follow her to the bathroom. She just sprinted down the metal grate stairs at the back of the stage and turned the nearest corner. Took the quickest exit away from Mitch Benson and his full lips, his compliments and the fact that she wanted his hand back in hers. She wanted his hand all over her body.

2

TUESDAY AFTERNOON, Paige walked into work. Like every Tuesday, she worked from two in the afternoon until nine o'clock at night at the very popular Narcissus restaurant, not far from the Space Needle. She'd been at the restaurant for almost eight years and had worked her way up from line cook to head pastry chef.

Classically trained at one of the most prestigious culinary schools in France, Paige was just an up-and-coming chef when she'd met Adam. They dated, fell in love and then got married. He'd been a grad student at the time, so they lived modestly, scrimping and saving where they could. Her dream had always been to open up her own restaurant—The Lilac and Lavender Bistro—because they had always been her favorite flowers and she thought it was not only a hip but also chic-sounding name. Hipsters could abbreviate it to the *LLB* or something kitschy like that.

When Adam graduated, they made plans to start socking money away for her restaurant.

Only life had other plans, and now, five years later, there

she was, still at Narcissus. Still working for someone else. Still not her own boss.

"How's it going?" Jane, her apprentice and a pastry chef student, asked as Paige tied her apron around her waist and washed her hands in the big stainless-steel industrial-size kitchen sink.

Paige dried her hands with a paper towel. "It's okay. Where's Tristan? I didn't see his car out front." It was not at all like the manager of the restaurant to not be at work by two in the afternoon. Sometimes the staff swore the man lived in his office upstairs, he was there so much.

Jane's mouth dipped into a frown. "You haven't heard? Did you not get my message?"

Paige shook her head. "Heard what? What message?" What the heck was going on?

Jane rolled her sky-blue eyes. "Shit, that's right. You weren't here yesterday. The owner sold the restaurant, and the new owner fired Tristan. Says she wants to manage the place herself."

Paige's eyes nearly popped out of her head. "What?"

Jane nodded, then blew a strand of blonde and purple-streaked hair off her forehead. "Yeah. According to Jill, Tristan's already taken off down to Mexico to lick his wounds. No word when he'll be back. Or *if* he'll be back."

Holy shit. Why hadn't Tristan called her? Paige thought they were friends. She'd been at Narcissus for eight years. Had that not meant anything to him?

Reeling from the news, she shook her head as she asked, "Who bought the place?"

Jane's lips pursed. "A woman by the name of Marcelle Thibodeaux, and from what I've heard, she's a real cow. I've only met her once though, so I can't say for certain if that rumor is true, but the fact that she canned Tristan isn't working in her favor to counter that rumor."

Marcelle Thibodeaux.

Why did that name sound so familiar?

Jane leaned in and brought her voice down to nothing more than a whisper. "Rumor has it she owned a bunch of other restaurants all over Seattle and is in the habit of running her staff ragged and doesn't believe in the after-shift drink."

Now it was Paige's turn to purse her lips. She liked Jane, but the woman was still quite young and very much into the partying scene. She would often start her evening out at the restaurant bar after her shift, imbibing her after-shift free drink, and then taking advantage of her staff discount. Most of the time it wasn't a problem, but once in a while a friend or two would join her, they would have one too many drinks, and things would get a bit loud. Never out of hand, but Narcissus had a certain reputation for being an upscale dining experience. The last thing customers, or the owner, wanted was a group of twenty-somethings getting carried away and disrupting someone as they ate their $49 rack of lamb with their $57 half-bottle of malbec.

"I'm sure she's not that bad," Paige said, grabbing the tub of flour from off the counter and carrying it over to the enormous stand mixer. "Maybe just runs a tight ship. But that probably means her restaurants are successful." She began to measure out flour in a five-cup measuring cup.

Jane made a face that said she wasn't convinced, and her lips flattened out. "I don't think that's it. There's tight ship and then there's tight ass, and I think she's the latter. She fired Tristan, don't forget." A throat cleared behind them, and Jane's hand flew to her mouth to cover a gasp. "Marcelle, so lovely to see you again."

Paige's head snapped up from where she'd been messing around with the *on* switch for the mixer only to come face to face with a woman from her past.

Correction, a *bitch* from her past.

Marcy Thibodeaux. The bane of her entire elementary, junior and senior high school existence. The girl who made Paige's life an absolute nightmare for twelve fucking years.

"Paige!"

"Marcy!"

Marcy's face pinched, and her cold blue eyes squinted. "It's *Marcelle.* I go by Marcelle now."

Paige swallowed. "Okay then."

Marcelle *clickety-clacked* her high-heeled black slingbacks across the tiled floor of the kitchen. "Didn't Janie tell you? I'm the new owner."

The new owner.

Marcy Thibodeaux, the meanest of mean girls from Villa Academy and then Lakeside School, who had tormented Paige from their days playing puzzles on the floor in kindergarten to when they both tried out for the cheerleading squad their freshman year, was her new boss.

Deep breaths. Deep, deep breaths.

Marcelle smiled, though it would be obvious to everyone that there wasn't an ounce of genuineness behind it. "I thought I recognized your name on the schedule. But then I thought it wasn't possible little Paigey McFatson was a *cook.* I thought you got married and had a bunch of kids."

Paige fought the urge to duck from all the passive-aggressive barbs being thrown her way.

"I'm a pastry chef, and I have a daughter."

Marcy's nose scrunched. "Just one? I thought I heard through the grapevine you were pregnant again?"

Paige swallowed. "I *was.*"

Understanding quickly flashed across Marcy's face, but, just as Paige expected, not an ounce of compassion or pity showed in her eyes.

Paige didn't want either from this woman. She didn't want to even be in the same room as her, let alone work for her.

Marcy's long, pointed, shiny black nails tapped on the back of the electronic tablet she held against her breasts. "Well then. I'm going to go up to my office. I'll be meeting with each and every staff member in the coming days to discuss productivity, scheduling and expectations." She reached out and wiped a counter, her finger coming away with what was obviously a thin layer of flour. Of course it would. She was in the fucking pastry section of the kitchen and right next to the mixer. Flour flew. But that logic was lost on Marcy, and she fixed Paige and Jane with a disgusted look. "Things need to change around here. Tristan was more concerned with being your *friend* than he was with being your boss." She lasered in on Paige. "And I have enough friends already."

Lackeys who feared you were not the same as friends.

Though Paige wasn't sure Marcy would be able to tell the difference now, as she certainly hadn't back when they were in school.

Paige and Jane waited until Marcy left before either of them let out a breath or even dared to move. Then Paige counted to twenty in her head, the time she knew it took the average person to walk from the kitchen, up the stairs and then down the hall to the manager's office, before she shuddered.

"Why the hell didn't you tell me about the new boss before now?" Paige said with a hiss, her whole body trembling. "What happened to us being a *family*?"

Jane's eyes went wide. "I did. I texted you on Saturday when Tristan introduced us to her. I told you I messaged you." She pulled out her phone, her fingers flying across the screen. "See—oh shit!" Guilt dashed across her face. "I forgot to hit send. Fuck!" Her hands fell, and she slapped the sides of her legs. "I'm so sorry, Paige. I thought I'd given you the heads-up. I was wondering why you weren't replying, but then I remembered you had that dance thing, so I figured you were just busy with that." She wandered over to the big mixer and turned it on, filling the kitchen with the low whining sound of the paddle in the bowl mixing the batter for Paige's famous white chocolate pound cake. "How the hell do you two know each other?"

Paige was still shaking. She was trying to measure out the white chocolate chips into the double boiler, but her hand wasn't steady enough, and chips spilled out onto the floor.

Jane rushed over and grabbed the measuring cup from her, then switched off the stove. "Come here." She took Paige's hand and led her down a small corridor to the walk-in fridge. This was one of the only places in the building they knew there was a blind spot for the security cameras. It was the only place they could talk in total privacy. They'd figured it out when Tristan discovered one of the dishwashers and one of the liquor distributors were having a torrid love affair, getting jiggy with it in the fridge in the one corner nobody could see them.

Jane shut the door behind them, and Paige immediately wrapped her arms around herself. Even though it was July, hot outside and the kitchen was usually an absolute inferno, a chill had clutched her bones the moment she came face to face with the she-devil from her past.

"Okay, dish!" Jane crossed her arms in front of her chest. "What is she to you?"

Paige swallowed. "My absolute nightmare."

TUESDAY NIGHT, Mitch tipped back his beer as he sat at the cramped desk in the corner of the kitchen. He and his sister

Violet had bought the small three-bedroom house a little less than a year ago, after they'd both lost their spouses and moved back to Seattle. Violet was helping him raise his six-year-old daughter, Jayda, and they were all trying to start over in the city Violet and Mitch had grown up in.

With a dull ache in his neck, he cocked his head side to side in an attempt to relieve some of the pain. He hated working in such busy and confined quarters: a small desk with a folding chair shoved into the far corner of the kitchen, where the lighting was terrible. This was no place for a professional photographer to be working.

The *scuff-scuff* sound of his sister's slippers grew louder behind him. Then he felt her hand land on his shoulder. "Is that Paige?"

Shit!

He'd been staring at one of the images he'd snapped of Paige for a good five minutes. He'd adjusted the lighting around her a bit, reduced the glare on her cheek from the afternoon sun, but otherwise he hadn't had to touch up the image at all. He hadn't had to touch up Paige one bit. She was perfect.

"She's beautiful," Violet marveled. "Look at the way she gets her leg up like that. You'd never know in a million years that she was a beginner and had only been dancing for a couple of months."

Mitch swallowed. "Yeah."

"That's a great shot. Cool that she was able to get right down on the stage close to you. She's even looking straight at the camera. You don't get many of those. Usually doesn't work, either. Looks fake and cover-modelish. But this works."

Hell yeah, it worked.

He doubted Paige took a bad picture. The woman was made for the camera. Her bone structure, her build, her expressive eyes. Photographers went years, if not lifetimes, in search of somebody so photogenic, so natural in front of the lens.

And she'd practically fallen right into his lap.

"What's her hair like?"

Oh fuck! He hadn't meant to say that out loud.

Her hair had been tucked up in a high and tight ballerina bun, as was mandatory at the dance school. But he would bet money that with her hair down, Paige was a million times hotter. And the woman was *smokin'* with her hair up. That long, slender neck. Creamy skin.

"Why?"

"Why what?" He turned around in his seat to find his sister giving him a raised eyebrow and a skeptical look. Her green eyes, the same shade as his, burned bright with curiosity.

"Why do you want to know what her hair is like?" Violet asked, cocking a hip and tossing her sandy-blonde hair behind her shoulder. "You like her or something?"

Mitch lifted one shoulder before turning back to the computer screen and Paige's face. "I don't know her."

"But you'd like to."

"I'd like to photograph her again. Get her to let her hair down. It looks like it's curly."

He loved curly hair on women. Especially when their hair reflected their personality—wild and untameable. And although he didn't quite get the *wild* vibe from Paige—yet— he could tell a lot about a person by the way they photographed, and with Paige he could see she had wounds that ran deep. Wounds that she hid behind, that muted her fire, but deep down she was a fierce spirit with incredible passion. She wasn't as mousy as she feigned; she was simply hurting, and that made her duck into the corner. She was a wounded tigress, but still a fighter, still alive and slowly healing.

He'd never liked a predictable woman. Never liked one who toed the line every minute of every day. He preferred women who weren't afraid to break the rules once in a while. Weren't afraid to take off their shoes and go dancing in the fountain.

His heart constricted inside his chest. God, how he missed Melissa.

For an English lit major on the shyer side, she'd had a wild streak to her as well. More than once they'd let loose, throwing caution to the wind, not letting their inhibitions get the better of them.

A small smile tugged at the corner of his mouth at the memory of their skinny dipping adventure just shortly before Melissa's accident. Their neighbors a few doors down from where they lived in Arizona had an outdoor pool, and when they knew Rich and Rhonda had gone to bed for the night, Melissa and Mitch made a detour on their way home from date night. They parked in their own driveway, ran down the road and then hopped the fence, taking a clothing-optional dip in the dark.

It had been one of the best, and most memorable, nights of their lives.

"It is curly."

Violet's voice behind him pulled him back to the present, his heart still hurting from remembering the past. Even the good times and all the wonderful moments they shared hurt to think about.

"Her hair is just like Mira's. You going to print that off and give it to her?"

Mitch nodded casually. "Yeah. She should definitely have it." Despite the fact that she didn't think she was any good and had brushed off his offer on Saturday. The woman obviously didn't know how beautiful she was or how incredibly well she danced. Mitch needed to show her.

"I can give it to her tomorrow during dance class," Violet offered.

Mitch zoomed the screen in on Paige's face. On her expressive, light brown eyes and the glinting of gold just around the pupils. She wasn't smiling. No. There was sadness. Pain and an ache he could feel through the computer screen and deep in his chest.

"I'll give it to her," he said quietly. "I want to talk to her."

3

_____

IT WAS a warm and muggy Wednesday night. A few forest fires toward the south had blown their smoke northward, and the entire city was blanketed in a thick, yellowy fog. Mitch felt like he'd been living in sepia mode all day, and his lungs weren't too happy about it either.

Emmett, one of the other dads from poker night, had shown up at Mitch's place with his daughter Josie, or JoJo as they all called her, with the offer to take the girls for ice cream. Jayda and JoJo had played very well together at Art in the Park on the weekend, so Jayda was very excited to get a later bedtime and go grab ice cream with her new friend. Mitch took the opportunity of his sudden child-free evening to head to the dance studio where he knew Paige would be.

There was a scattering of vehicles in the parking lot, including his sister's Fiat. He glanced at his watch. Class ended in five minutes.

Slowing his pace so that it didn't look like he was lying in wait for Paige, he shoved his hands in the pockets of his shorts and strolled along the strip mall where Violet's dance studio was located. That's when he noticed the two _For Lease_ signs tacked up in the front window of two adjacent store fronts.

He peered inside, cupping his hands around his eyes and pressing his nose to the glass. It was a deep space, with what looked to be a storeroom and what he could only assume was a bathroom. It held good lighting, getting all the afternoon sun, and there was a door connecting it to the vacant space next to it. He took a few steps to the side and peered into the next unit.

It had been an old restaurant.

A smaller space than the first vacancy, but that didn't mean it still wasn't a decent size. A big industrial-size kitchen took up the right side along one wall, with a big stainless-steel countertop and a place for fridge, freezer and stove.

He couldn't recall what had been in here before it closed, so obviously it hadn't been memorable.

Violet probably knew.

He brought out his phone and took a quick snapshot of the real estate agent's phone number and information. He wasn't quite sure what his plan was yet, but the cogs had officially started turning in his head.

The sound of a chime jingling down the way drew his attention from the empty spaces. The dance class had ended, and students were leaving.

He picked up the pace and headed toward the studio. He reached for the door just as a flurry of dark curls knocked him in the chest.

She hadn't been looking where she was going. Her head was down, and her phone was out.

"Oh, sorry," she murmured, not looking up.

"Paige?" He already knew it was her. She had that same sweet, vanilla-like scent from Saturday.

Slowly, she lifted her head, her brown eyes going wide when she realized it was him. "Oh ... hello."

She hadn't smiled yet, but that didn't matter. His smile was wide enough for the both of them. He knew she'd be drop-dead fucking stunning with her hair down. He hadn't been wrong. "Hey!"

She made to move past him, but he blocked her path. Not in a creepy predator way, though. More in an awkward, he thinks she's going left so he goes right, she thinks he's going left so she also goes right kind of deal.

A chuckle bubbled up at the back of his throat, but she seemed to almost growl and sigh in frustration.

"Sorry." He laughed.

She exhaled. "It's fine." She took a wide step around him and headed off in the direction of her car.

Mitch chased after her. "Paige, can we talk for a second?"

He wanted to reach out and grab her arm, but when she stopped in her tracks and glared at him, he shoved his hands in his pockets and took a step back.

"No," she bit out, turning away from him again and continuing on into the parking lot.

He followed her. "Why not?"

"Because."

"That's not a good enough answer."

"Well, it'll have to do, because that's all you're getting from me."

He snorted. "Spoken like a true parent."

She reached a cute little red sporty Mazda 3. She hit the fob and it unlocked, then she spun around to face him. "You're coming off a little pushy here, buddy. Back off. How would you feel if a guy was behaving this way with your daughter?"

Mitch's face fell, and he took several steps back. Fuck, she was right.

He was behaving like one of those entitled jackasses who couldn't take no for an answer. The kind of jackass that kept him awake at night in fear for Jayda, the kind of jackass he vowed to protect her from.

Mitch ran his hand over his face, then threaded his fingers up into his hair. "Shit, you're right. Sorry."

Her lips flattened. "I'm not interested, okay? If you're trying to ask me out, I'm not interested. Please accept my decline as enough."

He held up his hands. "Okay. I do. No dates. No wooing."

Her eyes softened slightly, and she gave him one curt nod. "Thank you."

"I came here to talk to you about something else though ... too."

Her head cocked slightly to the side, and her eyes squinted in curiosity. "Which is?"

He grabbed the big manila envelope out from under his arm and thrust it toward her. He didn't step forward, though. He didn't want to invade her space. If she wanted it, she would have to close the gap between them. "I know you said you didn't want to see any photographs of yourself, but, well ... I think you need to see this one."

More curiosity flooded her face. Hesitantly, she took a few steps toward him and reached for the envelope, making sure not to let their hands touch. With careful movements, but not retreating back toward her car, she opened the envelope. She pulled out the single photo, which Mitch had color-corrected to black and white, and her hand flew to her mouth, covering her gasp.

"You might not think you're talented, but you are. I've never photographed anyone like you before, with so much expression and raw emotion on your face. You poured your entire soul into your performance on Saturday, and it showed. I don't know what you were dancing about, what feelings and memories you were channeling, but I know they were painful ones."

Tears brimmed her eyes, and a sudden sob choked behind the hand that still covered her mouth. She still hadn't looked up at him. The hand holding the photo began to shake.

Mitch wanted desperately to go to her, not because he was attracted to her and wanted to get to know her, but because he could see she was hurting. He wanted to take away the pain.

"Please don't take this as anything more than the compliment it's meant to be, but you are the model I have been searching for my entire career. I have photographed hundreds, if not thousands of people, and I've never met anyone like you. If you'd be willing, I would love to photograph you again."

Finally, she lifted her head. Her eyes, although full of tears, were fierce.

He took a step back and held his hands up again in surrender. "Nothing sexual, I swear. You can wear whatever you want. Overalls, mechanic's coveralls, a parka."

Her glare faded.

"Just think about it, okay? I can pay you, if you're wanting to make it more professional and keep it like a business transaction."

Her eyes left his and flitted back down to the photo. "How much did you have to Photoshop this?"

He shook his head. "I blurred the background, lifted the glare from the sun off your cheek and brightened up the hue around your head a bit, but that was it. I didn't touch you. I didn't have to. You were perfect."

A sigh slipped past Paige's lips, and her shoulders slumped. "Thank you for this and for the offer. It's flattering, but I'm going to have to pass. I'm no model."

Curiosity got the better of him. "What do you do for work, if I may ask?"

It was as if she'd stuck a giant pin out and popped the protective bubble that surrounded her. She dropped her shield. It was nothing tangible, but Mitch noticed her change in demeanor instantly. She was no longer afraid of him.

"I'm the head pastry chef at Narcissus."

As if it had ears, his stomach rumbled.

Mitch had a sweet tooth that was virtually insatiable. He probably had three bags of Jujubes in his car, all of them open so that they got good and stale and practically ripped out his teeth as he gave his jaw a good workout.

He wasn't sure how to respond, so all he did was nod and say, "Very cool."

"Cakes and confections are where I'm most comfortable. With a piping bag in my hand and flour on my cheeks. I don't belong in front of the camera."

He could just imagine watching her in action. In her element, the images would be amazing with her hair tucked up in a chef's hat, sweat on her brow and happiness in her eyes. He'd love to photograph her in her natural environment.

But instead he simply nodded again. "Message received. But if you ever change your mind, please let me know. I could even take some family photos of you and Mira."

Something akin to intrigue crossed her face but then vanished just as quickly. "I'll let you know."

Her eyes flicked up and focused on something behind him. Mitch spun around just as Violet stepped off the curb into the parking lot. She was next to him in seconds.

Ah, reinforcements.

"I hope my brother isn't harassing you too much," Vi said with a snicker.

Mitch cringed from her choice of words.

Thanks a lot, sis.

Thankfully, Paige shook her head and smiled shyly. "Not

at all. He just brought me this photo he took of me dancing on Saturday."

Violet smiled. "I saw that one. It's incredible, isn't it? You should be a model."

Paige snorted and averted her eyes. "Uh, not for me, thanks."

Violet shrugged and tucked her purse tighter under her arm. "Well, then just enjoy this photo. You should definitely frame it."

Paige's eyes drifted back down to the photo. "Yeah, I might."

"I'm going to swing into the liquor store and grab a bottle of wine," Violet announced, turning to Mitch. "You want me to pick you up some beer?"

He nodded. "Yeah, San Camanez mixed summer pack, please."

His sister gave him a thumbs-up before heading off in the direction of her car, offering a friendly goodbye and wave to Paige.

Paige slid the photograph back into the envelope, and Mitch took that as his cue to leave. "I should get going," he said, drawing Paige's attention away from the envelope. "Jayda went out for ice cream with a friend, but I'm sure she's home by now, and it's well past her bedtime."

Paige's head bobbed in an absentminded nod, but she didn't say anything.

Fuck, this was awkward.

Mitch exhaled and turned to go. "See you around."

"Thank you," she called back, though it was more like a strained whisper. A whisper that prompted him to turn back around. "And I'm sorry, I'm just not a fan of being in front of a camera."

Mitch's mouth dipped into a frown. "I'm sorry too."

4

THURSDAY AFTERNOON, Paige knocked gently on the office door. Her entire body had been one giant ball of nerves since the moment she woke up. A pit the size of a bowling ball rattled around in her stomach, and a tension headache that was slowly morphing into a migraine pulsed in her forehead.

She waited for the "okay" from the person on the other side of the door.

She knew Marcelle or Marcy or whatever the hell her name was was in. She'd pranced her Louis Vuitton *everything* (shoes, bag, scarf, dress, coat) through the kitchen not twenty minutes ago and ordered Paige to join her upstairs for a meeting when Paige was finished rolling out the pastry dough for her pie.

Paige even heard the fluttering of papers beyond the door. Marcy was in there. She was deliberately keeping Paige waiting.

The BITCH.

Paige knocked again, this time harder, longer and louder. "Marcelle?" she called out.

Still nothing.

She knocked again. "Marcelle? It's Paige. I'm here for our meeting."

Goddamn it, she hated what this woman was making her do. Tristan had an open-door policy. The staff could come to him with whatever they needed whenever they needed it. He told them that family didn't knock and family didn't shut each other out, so he always left his office door open.

She was going to knock one more time, then if the bitch didn't respond, she was heading back downstairs. She had a fucking job to do. She had things to bake.

She lifted her fist and was about to go all Muhammed Ali on the door when it swung open.

"Paige." Marcelle's smile was as fake as her hair color. Nobody was that white-blonde without the help of a colorist and a whole hell of a lot of bleach. "You're late."

Paige bit back the fury that frothed inside of her and reluctantly brought her fist down to her side. Oh, what she would have given to be able to go all Muhammed Ali on Marcy's stupid face.

But instead, she apologized.

What the actual fuck?

"Sorry, Marcelle. I had to finish up the pie before the dough warmed up. The dough was all rolled out, and you know what it's like trying to work with warm dough."

Marcelle *clickety-clacked* her heels back to behind her desk and stared down her hella-plastic-surgeried nose at Paige. "No, actually, I don't."

Paige walked into the office and took a seat in the chair that faced Marcelle. "You need the dough to be cold, to keep the butter from melting. You want the lumps of fat in the dough because that's what creates the—"

Marcelle held up a hand that still had on those shiny, pointy black fake nails. "Nor do I care."

Paige's gaze fell to her lap. "Sorry."

"Moving on. I'd like to discuss your schedule."

Paige lifted her head. "What about it?"

The other woman lifted a shoulder and looked at Paige as if she'd just asked the dumbest question in the world. "It's only three days a week and seven hours a day."

"Yes, that's what works."

"For whom?"

"For me. For the kitchen."

Marcy's eyes grew hard, so much so Paige felt herself move back in her seat. "Well it doesn't work for me. Effective immediately, you will be working forty hours a week. Three mornings, two evenings. Your schedule is set by me and it is non-negotiable or flexible. These are the days and hours we need you here."

Paige went to open her mouth, but Marcelle apparently wasn't finished.

"I see here you had a *significant* amount of time off last year. Why?"

"Personal reasons. Medical." Tristan and the rest of the kitchen staff knew why, but they were family. They supported her. They understood. Marcelle was not family. She was the enemy and had zero right to know anything about Paige. None.

She could tell Marcy was itching to demand Paige disclose more, but she also knew better than to pry.

"I also see here you have requested *more* time off, though it says the dates are not concrete. What the hell am I supposed to do with that?"

Paige's mouth dropped open. "I, uh ... I have an upcoming surgery, but I'm still working with the insurance company, so we don't have a set date yet."

Intrigue glimmered in Marcy's icy-blue eyes. She leaned over her desk. "Getting some work done, are we?" She tapped her nose. "Probably for the best."

Paige's eyes went wide, and she reared back. "Uh, no."

Marcy sat back again. "Well, I can't just *fill* your position if you decide to spring your surgery on me. That's not very professional. Get a concrete date, and then I'll see what I can do. But I'm not making any promises. If I start making concessions for you, everyone will want special treatment."

How was she supposed to do that? How was she supposed to get *concrete dates* from the hospital? She was pretty sure Seattle Memorial was not at all concerned with how their operating room schedule affected the schedule at Narcissus. Marcy was out of her goddamn mind.

Paige had been to see the surgeon, after her doctor had sent off the referral, but her doctor wanted to see her one more time before they gave the okay for her to get her tubal ligation. Since it was the summer, everyone was taking vacations, so Paige wasn't going in to see her doctor for another couple of months. It would be ages before she had a *concrete date.* She'd just wanted to be nice and let Tristan know she might need to take more time off later in the year. He'd been totally cool with it and must have made a note in his binder so he wouldn't forget and book her for any big catering gigs while she was in recovery.

However, it wasn't like she was having a ton of sex either, so the risk of getting pregnant again was pretty nil. Still, she wanted to get a jump on things. Nip the potential for pregnancy in the bud so it was one less thing she had to worry about.

Marcy tapped her nails on the schedule book in front of her. "Now, I'll need you to work Tuesday through Saturday. You can work Tuesday and Wednesday nights." She lifted her head, waiting for Paige to accept.

Paige shook her head. "I can't do Wednesday nights. I'm sorry. I could do Wednesday day, but I have a class on Wednesday nights."

"Class?"

Paige shook her head. "It's just a thing. I've registered for it, paid for it, so I can't miss it."

Marcy made a face that said she wasn't used to being challenged, wasn't used to being told no. It was the same face she walked around high school with for four fucking years. "What is it?" she snapped. "I won't give you the night off unless you tell me what it is. I already told you this schedule wasn't negotiable."

Paige exhaled. "It's a dance class. My daughter started dancing at the studio, raved about how great the instructor was. I saw that they offered an adult class on Wednesday evenings, so I joined. Just something for me, you know?"

Marcy's lip twitched. "Why are *you* dancing? It's not like you did it in high school." A smug look fell across her overly tanned face.

That's right. Paige had tried out for not only the dance team but also the cheerleading squad and had been told by Marcy that she wasn't good enough. And all her lackeys and minions followed in her taunting. Marcy was the boss of everyone, apparently, including the seniors. Marcy was God.

Paige wasn't sure how she'd earned her deity status, but the girl ruled the school. Even the teachers seemed to bow to her. Could've been because her father was a wealthy politician in the city, carried a lot of clout and was a major contributor to the school. Either way, Marcy Thibodeaux had ruled both Villa Academy and Lakeside with her manicured, spray-tanned fist.

And God help anyone who challenged her.

"Hmmm, little Paigey McFatson. Why are *you* dancing? *Paigey McFatson.*

Paige's gut twisted. Her heart clenched, and frustration shot heated tears to her eyes. She blinked them back, determined not to let Marcy see how much her words still affected Paige.

How was one person able to make her feel so small and so insecure all over again? She was thirty years old. She was a professional chef. She'd been through enough heartache in her life to make anyone go stir-crazy. She was past all the high school drama. Past the insecurities and shyness. Past the feelings of not being good enough. Wasn't she? Compared with the shit she'd been through in the last few years, the garbage that Marcy put her through in school was small potatoes. Small potatoes she was incapable of forgetting, apparently.

"I'm dancing because I want to," she said quietly. "Because it makes me feel good. It's something just for me."

"Hmmm."

Hmmm?

She didn't owe Marcy an explanation, so why did she give her one? Now it was just more ammo the woman had against her. More slings and arrows in her quiver of complete and utter bitchiness.

A diabolical smile spread across her mouth. Her teeth, obvious veneers, were too straight, too big and too white to be real. "All right then. You can work Wednesday day. Tuesday and Thursday nights then. Does that work for you?"

"I ... I don't know if I'm ready to work forty hours again."

Marcy huffed impatiently. "Wow, it's just take, take, take with you, isn't it? What the fuck's your problem now?"

Paige clenched her molars together until a dull but satisfying ache pulsed in her jaw. "Nothing," she finally said, releasing a long breath. "Thank you for letting me have Wednesday evenings off. I will start working forty hours if that's what you need."

A lazy, triumphant smile coasted across Marcy's lips. She

knew she'd won. She'd browbeaten Paige, belittled her, name-called her until she caved.

Mean girl Marcy, the bully of Lakeview, was back, and she was apparently out for blood.

———

MITCH PULLED open the heavy wooden door of the restaurant. It was almost four o'clock, so not quite the dinner hour yet. He hoped things would be quiet and he would get a chance to speak with Paige before all hell broke loose for dinner.

"Table for one?" the perky little blonde hostess asked, grabbing a menu from the box behind her.

"Sure. And while you're at it, might I speak with the head pastry chef, please? Is Paige in today?"

Her lips twisted in thought. "I believe so. But I'll double check. Right this way, sir."

He followed her deeper into the restaurant, which probably only hosted a dozen or so patrons, most of them well over sixty years old, enjoying the early-bird dinner when it was quiet and peaceful.

There was certainly something to be said for dining like a senior. Less noise.

"Here we are." She placed the menu down on the table built for two. "I'll run to the back and see if Paige is available."

He thanked her, then opened the menu, flipping to the back that listed the desserts. His mouth immediately began to salivate.

Roughly two minutes later, he heard the *thump thump* of double kitchen doors swinging open, followed by the soft footsteps of who he hoped was Paige. He was anticipating anger on her face when she saw him, but instead he got something else. Something much worse.

Mitch was up and out of his seat before he knew what was going on, his arm around her. "What's wrong?

She shook her head and murmured, "Not here."

"My car is out front," he offered.

She nodded, allowing him to usher her out of the restaurant. Both of them ignored the questioning looks from both patrons and staff.

It wasn't until they were safely inside his car that he spoke again. "Paige, what happened?"

Her whole body shook, and more tears fell. She was trying to speak, but every time she opened her mouth, she choked or hiccupped and just ended up crying more. He did the only thing he could think of. He reached across the center console and pulled her into his lap. Then, because it was a tight squeeze, he pushed the seat all the way back to accommodate both their frames. He held her tight against him and absorbed her sobs. Absorbed whatever pain was inside her, whatever was making her cry like he'd never seen anyone cry before.

And she let him.

In fact, she clung to him.

Her fingers bunched in his shirt, and her hot tears trickled down his neck, but he didn't care. All he cared about was that Paige wasn't going through whatever this was alone. He was able to comfort her, care for her.

He wasn't sure how much time had passed before she lifted her head, her face a mottled shade of red and her cheeks and lips damp. He wiped the tears away with his thumbs and pushed the stray tendrils of dark curls off her forehead. "Ready to talk?" he asked.

She took a hard swallow and shut her eyes for a moment, breathing deep. "My new boss. The new owner."

"What about him?" Had he made a pass at her? Been inappropriate?

"Her," she corrected. "Marcy Thibodeaux. The bully, the mean girl, the absolute worst person I have ever met in my entire life. She made every day at school hell. From kindergarten until my junior year, she tormented me. Teased me. She put ketchup on my seat so when I sat down it looked like I'd leaked through from my period. She nicknamed me Paigey McFatson. She cut my hair with scissors when I sat in front of her in English class. Burned it in the chem lab. She put snakes from the biology department in my locker. It took me going to France for a yearlong exchange my senior year to finally be rid of her. To finally be rid of the harassment and the fear of being the butt of one of her jokes, the victim of one of her horrible pranks."

"Holy shit." Rage replaced all other emotions inside Mitch. How could anyone do such things to another person, let alone someone as sweet as Paige?

Paige nodded. "But that wasn't the worst of it."

There was worse?

"I was taking AP calculus in my junior year. Her jock boyfriend needed a tutor, otherwise he'd lose his football scholarship, so the math teacher asked me if I'd tutor Garth. I refused. I didn't want to be anywhere near him or his girlfriend. I knew better. Not after the hell she'd put me through for so many years. But apparently my math teacher was hard of hearing or simply just a man who refused to take no for an answer, and suddenly there was Garth, on my doorstep."

"And Marcy didn't like that very much, did she?"

"Nope. Garth was actually a really nice guy. I couldn't understand why he was with her. I helped him bring his math grade up from a D to a B minus. He was able to keep his scholarship, and his parents were really happy, so they took us out to dinner to celebrate."

"Oh fuck."

This was like the plot for a fucking angsty teen rom-com. Mitch could almost see the writing on the wall.

"Marcy found out. She spread a rumor that I carried a gun to school. That I was plotting and planning a shooting spree. She typed up fake plans and a *hit* list with her name at the top. Stashed it all in my locker."

"Holy. Fuck. Was there a gun?"

She nodded. "It was fake. But she'd managed to get her hands on one and put it in my locker as well. I was arrested and detained."

"Your parents didn't get you a lawyer?"

"Of course they did. But until the lawyer showed up, and then even after, I was terrified."

"What happened?"

"Garth. He found out what Marcy did and turned everything over to the cops."

"And what about Marcy?"

"Her father is a politician. He greased the right palms, and it was like it never happened."

"Did Garth dump her?"

She nodded. "He did. He actually asked me out shortly after, but I said it would be like signing my own death warrant if I dated him. Marcy was already gunning for me. I didn't want to throw kerosene on the bonfire by dating her ex-boyfriend. That was the final straw. My parents and I spent every waking moment after that looking into new schools and exchanges. I needed to get away from her; I needed to get away from Seattle. Leave the gossip and gun rumors behind. I stayed in France for several years. I wasn't ready to come back. I wanted the city to forget about me. I went to culinary school there, worked in a few kitchens for a couple of years before I came home. By the time I returned, no one knew who I was anymore. The stories had died down. I was a nobody, and I liked it that way."

"And now this bitch is your boss?"

She let out a long, slow sigh before nodding. "And now this bitch is my boss."

He hadn't even been aware of it, but he'd been drawing circles on her back. She hadn't moved away or asked him to stop. So he didn't. "I'm assuming she's done something new to upset you, or are these tears just from the memories flooding back of all that she did to you?"

Paige sniffled. "A bit of both. She called me up to her office to talk about my schedule, and from the very first second, she was just terrible to me. Called me my old nickname, belittled me, demanded I tell her why I needed Wednesday night off."

"Did you tell her?"

She rolled her eyes. "She said she wouldn't give me it off unless I did."

"Fucking bitch."

"You got that right."

"Are you going to be able to go back in there and work for her? Is this going to work? Do you love this place *that* much to put up with someone who treats you like that? Who framed you for domestic terrorism?"

Paige used the collar of her black chef's coat to wipe up a few remaining tears. "I don't know. I mean, I love my job, but I just can't see myself working for her for much longer. Not if she continues to torment me like this."

She blinked a few times, then looked down. Realization of where she was dawned on her face, and she quickly scrambled back across the center console into her own seat. "What are you doing here?"

Ah, crap. Their nice moment was gone.

"I thought I told you I didn't want to date. I thought you understood and accepted that?"

Mitch rolled down the windows of his car. It was stifling

hot. "I don't understand why, but I accept it. I came here to ask you if you do catering. Or if Narcissus does catering. I swear to God, my intentions were nothing but platonic."

"Oh." She blinked those big brown eyes of hers, and her mouth made a delicate little *O* shape. "For what?"

"I'm opening up my own photography studio. Just signed the lease this afternoon. I want to do a grand opening. Have it catered, hire a bartender, maybe a guy to play the guitar. What do you say?"

"You want *me* to cater it? Or you want Narcissus to cater it?"

He shrugged. "Either-or. If you do catering on your own, I'd rather just pay you. You do more than pastry, right?"

"I'm a classically trained chef. I just prefer pastry." He enjoyed the slightly snooty tone to her voice. She was getting the fire back in her belly. Thank God.

"That's what I thought."

"When?"

"I'm not sure yet. I get the keys on Monday, and then I'll have a look at the place and see how much work needs to be done. I'm hoping to open by late August. Sooner if I can. I'm just tired of working in the kitchen at home. I miss having a proper studio and a collection of my work on the walls for customers to come in and see."

She pouted, and her nose scrunched in such a cute way, all he could think about was kissing the tip of it. "I'll give it some thought. I might be off work then, so ... "

"Off work for what?"

Her brows narrowed, and her lips flattened.

Oh shit.

"It's personal," she snapped.

Mitch held up his hands. He seemed to do a lot of that with her. "Sorry. I didn't mean to pry."

She blinked a few times, her look of irritation seeming to

fade each time she batted her damp lashes. "I'm just tense. I shouldn't have snapped at you like that. I'm sorry. Just this whole Marcy Thibodeaux thing has me losing my mind." She smacked her forehead with the heel of her palm. "Oh, sorry, *Marcelle* Thibodeaux."

He wished he could take her hand and reassure her someway. But he was not getting any of those vibes from her. Instead he just offered her a small smile. "Don't let her win. You're strong. This isn't high school anymore. There's no more Garth. Yes, she's your boss, but that restaurant will also be lost without you."

The face she made said she didn't quite believe him but appreciated his attempt. Her hand landed on the door handle. "I should get going. Might wind up with demerits if I'm late. Have to drop and give her twenty or swab the deck or some dumb shit like that."

Mitch snorted. "Can you bake a laxative into a pastry you give especially to her?"

She opened the door, but when she turned back to face him, she was smiling. "If only. I don't think the woman has touched a carb in twenty years. I'd have to drop the laxative on her iceberg lettuce and pray she ate the whole damn thing."

Mitch rolled his eyes. "Ugh. I hate women like that. I love food. So should my woman. We get so few joys in life."

She stepped out of the car chuckling. "I couldn't agree more." Paige shut the car door but then leaned into the window, leveling her soulful eyes on him. "Thanks, Mitch. You were here when I really needed someone. I was starting to spiral, but you saved me from going down into the well, so thank you."

Mitch's heart constricted inside his chest. "You don't need saving, Paige. You're incredibly strong."

Her lips pursed, and she fixed him with a look that said she didn't quite believe him. "Well, thank you all the same."

He flashed her a big smile. "Any time, Paige. And I mean that."

He watched her walk away, contemplating going back in and ordering a dessert to go and whether or not that would be in poor taste. Much to his regret, he put the car in reverse and headed down the street to the Dairy Queen.

5

SATURDAY NIGHT WAS POKER NIGHT.

Mitch had been looking forward to it all week.

He always looked forward to poker. He looked forward to his weekly meeting of the minds with other single dads. He'd only been a member of The Single Dads of Seattle for a few months, but in that short span of time, they'd come to feel like family. He could gripe and moan about the struggles of being a single parent—a single father—and not worry about anyone judging him. There was also another widower in the group, Atlas, and although the two of them hadn't chatted much, because Atlas didn't really talk much to anyone, he felt a sort of kinship with the man.

They were both raising daughters alone after their wives had passed and doing the best they could given the circumstances. He wanted to reach out more to Atlas, but the vibes the man was throwing off said he wasn't ready to talk yet. Things were still too raw, too fresh.

Having decided to take an Uber so that he could drink more than just a single beer, Mitch and his mixed summer six-pack of San Camanez walked up to the front door of Liam's house hand-in-hand shortly after seven o'clock.

Liam, the founder of The Single Dads of Seattle, was a divorce attorney and apparently a damn good one. He lived on the shore of Lake Washington in a house worth well over seven figures.

Dare to dream.

Not bothering to knock, because as Liam said, *family doesn't knock*, he turned the doorknob and walked inside. The sound of several men's voices floated around the corner into the foyer, drawing him toward the dining room, where the card table would be set up.

The sky outside was still an ugly yellowish-brown from all the wildfire smoke. So with nowhere to escape, the summer heat was trapped in the city, making everyone not only overheated but also struggling to breathe from all the smoke.

He'd kept Jayda indoors most of the day because the air quality warning had been disconcerting. The app on his phone said breathing the air outside for an hour was equivalent to smoking six cigarettes.

Yeah, no way was he subjecting his child's precious little lungs to that.

Thankfully, though, Adam had brought Mira over, and the two girls played for hours. Mitch had managed to get a fair bit of work done, all the while flipping back to photos of Paige and letting those light brown eyes of hers bore directly into his soul.

How on earth she could work for a woman like Marcy was beyond him. That woman needed to be put in her place. She needed to be put away.

"Yo!" A slap on his back brought Mitch out of his thoughts of Paige. He craned his neck around to find Zak, Adam's brother, grinning from ear to ear behind him. "How goes it?" Zak had a lowball of some amber liquid with a cube of ice in his hand. He tipped it up and drained it, crunching on the ice.

"Pretty good." Mitch continued into the kitchen and put five of his six beers away. He popped the cap on the one in his hand and took a long swig, letting the cool brew slide down his throat and into his stomach, instantly cooling his whole body. Liam had the air-conditioning running, but even that was no match for the sauna that was Seattle.

"This heat, huh?" Zak said, shaking his head as he wandered toward the leather-top bar in the corner of the dining room to pour himself another drink. "I can't imagine what they're dealing with in California if it's this bad up here. Kept the kiddos indoors today."

Mitch nodded. "Me too. Adam brought Mira over, and she and Jayda just played in her room all day. I feel bad keeping them inside during the summer, given how fucking rainy Seattle is the rest of the year, but I just can't send them out with the air like that."

"I hear ya. The gyms have been packed. Nobody is running or walking outside, so they're all heading indoors to get their sweat on. Been good for business. Loads of new members, but it's also been a bit nutty. We don't usually see these kinds of numbers or new signups until the rainy season hits. Had to call in more staff."

"I know!" came the voice of Liam. He swirled what was of course scotch around in his crystal glass. "I was there last night, and it took forever to get on the fucking treadmill. You need more of them."

Zak rolled his eyes. "I'll get right on that, oh wise one who gets a free membership."

Liam snickered as he moved into the kitchen, grabbed a few bowls of potato chips and pretzels, brought them back out to the dining room and set them on the table.

Adam was already there. He, Mark and Emmett were sitting at the table, watching Atlas shuffle the cards like he was some blackjack dealer at the Mirage in Vegas.

"Where's Scott?" Mitch asked, wandering over to the table and taking a seat next to Emmett.

Liam joined them all around the table after refilling his glass. "He took Freddie down to San Diego for the week." Scott was Liam's younger brother, but unlike Liam, who was a high-powered attorney at one of the busiest law firms in the city, Scott was in advertising. Both had smart mouths, though, which often landed them in hot water with their exes.

"We playing cards?" Atlas asked with a grunt, shuffling the cards once more. His dark gray eyes held frustration. His light blond brows furrowed, creating a deep crease between them as the men around the table continued to banter, ignoring the cards in front of them. Mitch would put Atlas in his early forties, older than the rest of them. His daughter Aria was four and a sweet little thing.

Jayda and Mira had taken to her right away the first time they met her, and the girls played together beautifully. Come to think of it, all the children played well together: Emmett's daughter, JoJo; Scott's son, Freddie; Liam's son, Jordie; Mark's son Gabe; Zak's kids Tia and Aiden. Not that they got all the kids together that often, but when they did, Mitch hadn't heard a squabble among them.

He gave himself and all the other dads at the table a mental pat on the back. They were all raising good kids. They were all good at raising kids. Fuck this shit that dads could only have the kids on the weekends. Mitch had no choice but to be a full-time father, and in his opinion, he wasn't fucking up too badly at all.

Atlas impatiently drummed his fingers on the green felt card table. "I got shit to do at home."

Liam shot Atlas a look. "Cool the fuck down."

Atlas grunted and began to deal out the cards. Liam and Atlas worked together at the law firm, so unlike the rest of the guys, who were still a bit unsure of Atlas and how to act around him, Liam was no-holds-barred and couldn't give two shits about how he spoke to the man. Thankfully, though, Atlas was used to Liam's sharp tongue and rarely reacted with more than a grunt or shoulder lift.

"How're things going with Mitch's sister?" Liam asked, turning his attention to Adam not thirty seconds later. The glimmer in his brown eyes said he was hoping his comment would stir the pot.

Adam lifted his shoulder, though it would be hard for anyone to miss the smile he was trying to hide. "All is well. Violet's amazing."

Liam snorted. "Not that you could say anything different with her brother sitting right there."

Adam didn't speak, but his eyes held all kinds of amusement.

Liam tossed his head back and laughed. "Another one bites the dust." He elbowed Mitch. "I know she's your sister, but if Adam asks me for representation for his next divorce, it's bros before hoes."

Mitch shot him a look. "Watch it."

Liam chuckled. "I'm just saying, you guys and your women. I keep telling you that love is a fallacy ... " He faced Zak. "But do you think they'll listen?"

Zak scrubbed a big palm over his rust-colored beard and made a face like he didn't completely agree. "It's called hope, you jackass. And unlike you ... and me, who are jaded as fuck from women who ripped out our hearts and tried to take our children, these dumb fuckers still have a bit of hope left inside them. Don't you think the world needs more of that?"

Liam scoffed before taking a sip of his scotch. "I don't

need love. All my love goes to Jordie. Richelle gets the *D* when she wants it, but that's *all* she gets, and she's completely content with that. So am I."

Emmett lifted his head from where he'd been scrutinizing his cards, his amber eyes narrowed on Liam. "We ever going to get to meet this elusive *Richelle*? She seems to good to be true. A woman who wants nothing from you but sex. No strings, no love, no money, no commitment. You sure she's not just a blowup doll you bring out every Wednesday night?"

Liam snorted. "My blowup doll's name is Tabitha, and she comes out of hiding on Saturdays once you fuckers go home."

A few of the guys around the table snickered.

Mark, who'd been quiet until now, cleared his throat. "I get it, man, I do. I was super jaded when Cheyenne left. Jaded and angry. I mean, she left her son. She couldn't handle Gabe's autism diagnosis or his outbursts, so she just left. Ended our marriage, signed over her rights and custody. I was angry for a long time." His gaze settled on Adam, the only other man at the table who'd also found love again. "But anger takes *way* more energy than love. Love is easier."

Adam nodded.

Liam rolled his eyes. "I'll take my filthy Wednesday night sex with no strings over love any day, thank you. No muss, no fuss."

There were grumbles of frustration around the table. Some of the men who had been burned by women seemed to not entirely disagree with Liam, though they weren't so jaded as to spout off the way he was, while others, like Mitch and Atlas, remained quiet. Mitch missed Melissa every minute of every day, and he bet Atlas missed his wife too. He couldn't imagine ever divorcing his wife, ever falling out of love with her or becoming so cynical about love he'd swear off it for good.

As Jayda liked to say, love was what made the world go round.

Melissa taught her that.

"On that note of positivity," Mark said with a long sigh, his blue eyes weary from probably a long day at the hospital, and now Liam's anti-love rant, "let's play." He placed a stack of chips in the center.

"Thank fuck," Atlas murmured, matching Mark's bet. "You fuckers talk too much."

There were grumbles from Liam about the fact that talking and griping were part of the reason why he started poker night, but his irritation with Atlas quickly ebbed once the bets had been placed.

Atlas, who had become the designated dealer most nights, turned over the next card. There were a few agitated grunts. Emmett and Zak both folded, getting up to grab themselves new drinks. Liam increased his bet, as did Adam, Mitch and Mark.

"You dating my ex-wife?" Adam asked completely out of the blue, interrupting the concentrated silence at the table as the stakes and pot began to grow. His blue eyes were lasered in on Mitch across the table.

If the table hadn't already been dead silent, it was now. You could hear a fucking pin drop down the hall.

Were people holding their breath?

Oh fuck. Mitch was.

He swallowed and exhaled. "No."

Adam's eyebrow lifted just a fraction.

"But I'm trying to." His mouth split into a big grin. He and Adam had had almost the exact same conversation just a few months ago when he asked Adam if he was trying to date Mitch's sister. Adam had responded the same way.

Everyone at the table was still quite tense.

Including Mitch.

He'd tried to take the edge off by being funny, but now he wasn't so sure that was such a good idea.

Adam's eyes softened just a touch. "Okay." He scratched his beard. "I think you might actually be good for her. You know her story already, *our* story."

Mitch nodded. "I do."

Acceptance fell across Adam's face. "You don't need my blessing, but just know I support this. I think it could be really good."

Phew.

He caught Zak's smirk out of the corner of his eye. Had he said something to Adam? Or had it been Violet who had mentioned his impromptu visit to the studio on Wednesday night?

Mitch took a sip of his beer to coat his dry throat. "Thanks. She's not making it easy though." His chuckle felt forced, so he took another drink of beer.

Adam's grin widened. "The good ones never do."

Liam let out a whoop. "What a twist. I did not see that coming." He cupped his hand to his ear. "Do I hear banjos playing? What does that make your kids? Sister cousins?" He snickered at Mitch. "Does that make you stepdad and uncle to Mira?"

Both Adam and Mitch rolled their eyes, telling Liam to shut the fuck up at the same time.

6

It was Tuesday afternoon. Mitch was just finishing packing up from his on-site photo shoot, cursing the horrible weather and the shitty lighting it lent to the photos. If only the winds changed and blew all that smoke out to sea, then they would have their clear blue skies again ... until the rains came.

Adam was off work for the remainder of the summer, having decided to take six weeks off to be with Mira rather than teach a summer semester, so he'd offered to take the girls to the splash park in the morning and then keep them in the house once the city turned into a sauna.

Mitch was done with work for the day, but he also had picked up the keys to his new photography studio the day before and was itching to take a peek inside. The possibilities and ideas on how to lay things out, what colors to paint the walls and new props to add to his cache had swamped him all weekend, so much so he'd hardly slept a wink. Well, and the fact that he couldn't stop thinking about Paige sitting on his lap Thursday afternoon in his car. That had ignited all kinds of fantasies and dirty dreams. Most of them involved her, straddling him in the front seat of his car wearing nothing but that adorable chef's hat.

How was she doing?

She was probably at work. Slaving away icing a chocolate gateau with ganache or caramel or something.

His stomach rumbled, and his mouth watered.

Even if she didn't want anything to do with him romantically, he needed to make nice with her in order to get a taste of her confections. She still hadn't given him a yes or no as to whether she'd cater for him.

He needed it to be a yes.

Rolling down the window of his car, he started the ignition at the same time his phone started to ring in his back pocket.

Keeping the vehicle in park, he answered it. It was Violet.

"Hey, sis, just leaving the ranch now." He'd been hired to do a photo shoot for a dude ranch just outside the city that specialized in therapeutic horseback riding for children and people with special needs. It'd been a great day with great people and majestic creatures. Even though the sky looked like something out of a dystopian movie, the subjects had been so cooperative, he knew he'd be able to make something beautiful for the ranch's website and billboards.

"Mitch!" Violet's voice was panicky.

"What? What's wrong?" Was it Jayda?

"Mira. She ... she ate a bunch of berries ... poisonous berries. She's been rushed to the hospital." His sister's words were a mix of fear and crying. "I'm with Jayda, but Adam had to run with Mira to the hospital. I'm trying to get ahold of Paige, but she's not answering her phone. I didn't think she worked Tuesdays."

Mitch let out a shaky breath. "She does now. New boss. Big bitch. Making her work more hours."

"I ... I know she'd want to be there too."

"I'm on my way back into town. I'll swing by her restaurant and grab her. She shouldn't be driving once she's been given the news."

Violet breathed out. "Thanks. Let me know when you guys get to the hospital."

"Will do." He hung up.

———

"Is it supposed to look like that?" Marcy asked in a snide tone, glaring down at the soft, thawed bananas in the big mixing bowl.

Paige bit back the snarky response and instead just answered a curt, "Yes."

"That looks disgusting."

"I assure you, Marcelle, it's fine. When you freeze bananas, they turn black. When you thaw them, they turn into disgusting, slippery slug-looking things. But trust me, they're totally safe to eat. Packed full of sweet, fruity deliciousness. It's the best way to add the bananas to my banana-bread bread pudding."

Marcy turned her nose up. "Well, I think it looks gross."

Paige squished two more bananas out of their skins into the big stainless-steel mixing bowl. "I agree. But it won't for long, and then it will taste amazing. I'll bring you up some when I'm done."

Scoffing, Marcy circled around behind Paige. "Don't bother. I haven't eaten sugar in years."

And I thought I wouldn't ever have to see you again, but surprise surprise.

The double wooden doors from the restaurant side swung open, and a flush-faced hostess appeared.

Marcy and Paige's heads both popped up from where they'd been staring into the mixing bowl of mushy bananas.

"What?" Marcy asked snottily. It wasn't just Paige she treated like gum on the bottom of her shoe; it was the entire staff. Only it seemed she thought Paige was dog shit on the bottom of her shoe, not just gum, and treated her with extra disdain.

The hostess's eyes darted to Paige. "There's a man here to see you, Paige. He says it's urgent. It's about your daughter."

"Adam?" Paige didn't wait for the hostess to respond and was already wiping her hands on a dish towel and making her way toward the double doors.

Mitch was standing just on the other side. His eyes held a worry that made Paige's stomach drop to her feet with a hard *thud*.

"Mira's in the hospital," he said quietly, taking her arm and pulling her out of earshot from curious staff.

"What happened?"

"She ate some poisonous berries. That's all I know. Adam is with her. Violet called me. She said she couldn't get in touch with you."

Paige pulled her phone out of the pocket at the front of her apron. She opened the screen only to see a slew of missed calls, texts and voicemails. She must have forgotten to turn her ringer back on this morning.

"I can drive you," Mitch offered. "I wouldn't want to drive if this was Jayda in the hospital."

Paige nodded. "Just let me grab my purse."

"Where the hell are you going?"

Paige froze. She hadn't even turned around to head back into the kitchen, but Marcy's cold voice stopped her in her tracks. The nosy woman must have followed her out. How long had she been standing there? Or had she been listening at the door? Mitch would have reacted if they weren't alone when he told her about Mira.

Paige refused to turn around. The look on Mitch's face

said he knew exactly who was behind her and he wanted to give the woman a piece of his mind. His hatred for Marcy bolstered her own, and her spine straightened. "I'm going to see my daughter. She's in the hospital."

Marcy made a noise in her throat. "Not right now you're not. You're in the middle of a shift. You're in the middle of a dessert."

Mitch's eyes pinned on Paige, and his nod was barely discernible, but she caught it. He had her back no matter what.

Slowly, Paige turned around. She took a step toward the harpy that was her boss, got right up in her face. It didn't matter that Marcy had a good couple of inches on her. Paige was in mama bear mode and would take down the threat with her bare hands if she had to. "I am leaving. Now, please move."

Marcy's cool blue eyes widened, but not out of fear—out of surprise. Then they narrowed, and a wicked smiled curled her lips. "Leave and you're fired."

Everything inside Paige wanted to protest. Wanted to cry and scream and throw whatever was within arms' reach at this horrible human being. But she shoved it all down and didn't react. She didn't even blink. The only thing that might have given away her nerves was the heat in her cheeks and whether or not it was painted across her face in a splash of pink. Her pulse also thundered in her ears. Could Marcy hear it too?

"So be it," she said calmly. Then she pushed past Marcy, making sure to throw her elbow into the woman's side just a touch, and made her way into the kitchen. Even though she was scared out of her skin for her daughter, she moved around the kitchen calmly. Mira was with Adam. She wasn't alone. Paige needed to take care of everything here first, then she could leave and never have to worry about coming back.

She grabbed her purse, her bag, her recipe books, her distributor list and the cornbread molds she'd inherited from her grandmother. All eyes in the kitchen were on her as she coolly released the buttons on her chef's coat and laid it on the table next to her unfinished banana-bread bread pudding.

Marcy had stepped inside and was watching her, a smirk of satisfaction on her face. Meanwhile everyone else in the kitchen looked like they were ready to cry.

Jane sidled up next to Paige. "I'll follow you," she whispered, pulling Paige into a big hug, her body shaking in sobs. "Just let me know where you end up, and I'll follow you. I know a lot of us will. You're the heart of this kitchen. The heart of this restaurant. It's going to tank with you gone. Your bread pudding is what put this place on the map."

Paige squeezed her tight. "I'll text you later. Right now, I have to go." She pulled out of the young woman's embrace and steeled herself before she turned around to face Marcy again. She blew out a breath, then spun around.

"Big mistake," Marcy said snidely as Paige came up next to her. "I'm sure your kid is fine."

Paige dug down deep, and instead of hauling off and smacking the grin off the woman's overly tanned face, she smiled. She lifted her shoulders in a shrug she hoped conveyed nonchalance, even though inside she was so tightly wound, blood wasn't reaching her extremities. "I hope you're right, *Marcy*. I hope my daughter is fine." Then she pushed open the doors and let Mitch escort her through the restaurant and out to his car.

Only once she stepped out of the restaurant and heard the double wooden doors behind her swing closed did she release the breath she'd been holding. She opened Mitch's car door after she heard it unlock and climbed in. Narcissus.

Her home for the last eight years. Her family. All gone in the blink of an eye.

Mitch turned on the ignition and put the car into drive.

Paige leaned back in her seat and shut her eyes.

She'd just been fired.

She was jobless.

And in some ways, homeless.

Yes, she had a *home*. But it was her parents' home. It was their pool house. Narcissus had been her home away from home. It was where she could just be Paige the pastry chef. Nobody in the kitchen judged her for what she'd been through or the choices she'd made. Most of them came from turbulent backgrounds and had all been through a transformation or redemption, finding food as their solace, as their savior. A creative outlet, an art form that earned their restaurant rave reviews from food critics and reviewers alike.

And now it was all gone. All because she'd chosen to put her child above her job, just like any good parent, any understanding person would.

Marcy Thibodeaux was not an understanding person.

Paige questioned whether the woman was even human.

She certainly didn't have a decent, *humane* bone in her body.

"You know," Mitch started, drawing Paige out of her thoughts, "when Jayda was two, she broke her arm. I was on a photo shoot for a really big tourism company, but when Melissa called me, I left immediately."

She didn't bother looking at him but instead took in the dreary yellow-brown sky and the way it seemed to cast the entire city into a disgusting smoky hue. "Yeah. Did you lose the contract?"

"No. I gave them a discount of twenty percent and an extra day of shooting for being so understanding. They said it wasn't necessary, as they all had kids and knew what it was like, but I did it to show my appreciation. The lighting was better on the days I went back anyway."

She turned her head and studied his profile. "Why are you telling me this?"

"Because you need to find people in your life like that. People who understand what it's like to have kids. That kids come first. Whether they have children or not, you need people in your life that understand that family is priority number one. We work to live, not live to work. Or"—he lifted one shoulder—"do what I do and be your own boss. Make your own hours."

Paige pursed her lips in thought.

Be your own boss.

She continued to study his profile. It was a nice profile, with a strong chin, nicely shaped nose, just a touch long but not unsightly. His brows were thick, but he didn't have that protruding Neanderthal brow that some men had. Even his ears were nicely shaped. Well, at least the one she could see.

No doubt about it, Mitch Benson was a decent-looking man. A handsome man. A sexy man.

They came to a red light, and he turned to face her. He reached out and rested a hand on her shoulder. "Mira's going to be okay. Kids eat weird shit all the time. And don't we all eat something like eight spiders a year in our sleep?" He shuddered and made a grossed-out face before turning back to the road and hitting the gas when the light turned green. "I remember when Violet was like five, she ate half of one of those little mushrooms that grow in the front yard. She brought the other half to our mother to *share*. My mom lost her shit, tossed Vi into the car and raced her to the hospital."

Paige's eyes grew wide, and she could feel her heart rate pick up the pace. "What happened?"

Mitch's shoulder lifted just a touch. "Well, Vi is still alive, obviously, so she didn't die. I think they gave her something to make her barf, and then they held a bowl under her mouth until they found the mushroom."

Paige made a face. "I hope that's all they need to do for Mira." She brought her index finger to her mouth and began to chew on her nail. "My poor baby, if she has to get her stomach pumped, she's going to be so scared."

Mitch took a hard right. Traffic was chaotic for a Tuesday afternoon in the summer. It was going to take them ages to get to the hospital.

"Do you mind if I ask you something?"

She couldn't decide if she appreciated his attempt to keep her distracted with conversation or irritated. Her mind was on her baby, sitting in that hospital probably terrified and with doctors and nurses bustling around her. There wasn't much she could do from her seat in the car, though, so maybe the distraction was welcomed.

She blew out a breath. "What?"

"Why does Adam have custody of Mira?"

Her mouth opened, but he cut her off.

"I mean, not that I think he shouldn't, because the dude is a great father, but you seem like you have all your shit together too. You're a great mom."

Oh, if only he knew how little shit she truly had together. It was rather laughable really.

They came to another red light. He glanced her way, worry in his emerald eyes. "You don't have to answer if you don't want to. I realize now I may have stepped out of line."

Paige pressed her tongue into the side of her cheek, and she met his stare. "How much has Adam told you about us?" She'd be a fool to think Adam hadn't disclosed even the CliffsNotes version of their relationship and the dissolution of it to Mitch. People say women gossiped and hashed things out to get over them, but so did men. They just did it differently.

Color seeped into Mitch's cheeks beneath his scruff. "Enough."

"Then you know I wasn't in the right place ... *mentally* to be a good mother."

His lips flattened out in thought before he spoke again. "But you are now, right?"

"I'm better, but I'm not back to *normal.*"

He made a noise in this throat like he disagreed. "Define *normal.* I'll never get back to *normal.* My wife died. When you lose a piece of your heart, you never get back to *normal.* That piece doesn't grow back. You don't replace that piece. The hole remains, but slowly, over time, the hole might get smaller, or new pieces to the heart might get added, making the void not seem so big and all-consuming. But the hole is always there. The heart will never grow back to being *normal.*"

Her bottom lip dropped open, and she simply stared at him.

Did her heart have too many holes though?

And then, as if he read her mind, he continued. "And no, your heart does not have too many holes. It's still capable of so much love. Love for yourself, love for others, others to love you. You have a few holes." He paused. "Four?" She nodded once. "You have four holes, but you have a big heart, so over time, you will be okay."

Holy crap.

They sat there at the stoplight, their gazes locked. Mitch's eyes said everything. They held so much. Sorrow, pain, loss, fear. But also hope. He still carried hope with him.

Paige needed more hope.

The sign for the hospital was up on the left. The light turned green, and he hit the accelerator.

He pulled his eyes from her and put them back on the road.

She was equal parts relieved and disappointed.

She looked straight ahead. "Thank you for that."

"My pleasure." His voice was soft, but there was a light-heartedness to his tone that made warmth spool through her like tiny threads caught on a summer breeze.

"I'll do the catering for your grand opening."

They turned into the parking lot. "Thank you."

"I don't know where I'll do it or how I'll do it, but I'll do it."

His grin was all the encouragement to achieve the impossible that she needed.

She unbuckled her seat belt and had to stop herself from opening the door and doing the ol' tuck and roll. "Don't thank me yet. You haven't received my invoice yet."

His warm chuckle wrapped around her like a cashmere throw. "I think we can come to some kind of arrangement."

7

ONCE THEY KNEW that Mira was okay, Mitch left the hospital. Paige and Adam needed some alone time with their daughter, who was hooked up to an IV and drinking her weight in apple juice, and Mitch needed to go see his own child. After gathering Violet and Jayda back at the house, Mitch drove them all to Paige's restaurant—correction, *former* restaurant, and Violet drove Paige's car to the hospital. Mitch left Violet there, and he and Jayda continued on to his mother's house.

The Benson family had been hit with quite a blow over the last year and a half. First, Violet lost her partner, Jean-Phillipe, to a nasty tumor in his spine, then Mitch lost Melissa in the car accident, and not nine months ago, they lost their father to pneumonia.

They say things happen in threes. And Mitch hoped to God that *they* were right, because he wasn't sure his family could handle any more loss, any more death.

From the outside looking in, it might appear that he had his shit together, that he was getting over Melissa and the massive hole her death had created in his world, but appearances can be deceiving.

He had a daughter to raise. Jayda needed her father present and accounted for. She didn't deserve a shell of a man who was so grief-stricken he couldn't get his ass out of bed, couldn't eat, couldn't sleep, couldn't work. She needed him now more than ever.

So he grieved in silence.

He grieved alone.

When the house was quiet, the sky dark, and he knew his child was safe and warm in her bed, he grieved. He missed his wife. He cursed the world, the semitruck driver who fell asleep at the wheel and rolled his big rig on the highway, crashing into his wife and pinning her in her car for hours before she died en route to the hospital. He cursed and cried, screamed into his pillow until he let sleep take him.

Then in the morning, when the house was up and the birds were chirping, he plastered on a happy face, made his daughter breakfast, brushed her long, blonde hair, helped her get dressed, and started a new day.

And as the seasons changed and the days continued, things did get easier. He didn't cry every night. He didn't let the grief consume him the way he used to. Because Melissa wouldn't want him to. She would want him to be happy, to find the joy in life and each and every moment, just the way she did.

Violet was doing better too. She'd found love again with Adam, and although Mitch knew she could never replace Jean-Phillipe, she didn't have to. Adam added something new to her life; he didn't take anything away, didn't diminish the memory of Jean-Phillipe or all that he'd given Violet over the years. He simply made her life richer. Mitch saw that firsthand.

Their mother, however, wasn't there yet. And she condemned Violet quite violently when she'd first started seeing Adam, accusing her of treating Jean-Phillipe like no more than the family dog, easily replaceable—all you had to do was wash the dog bed before you brought the new one home or something heavily offensive like that.

They got it. She was grieving. Their father had been her first and only love. They'd been together for nearly forty years, and she couldn't imagine moving on at her age. Understood. Mitch was the last person to tell someone how to grieve or for how long, but the way his mother was handling the loss of their father worried Violet and Mitch. Mitch more so because he had moved Jayda back to Seattle from Arizona to be close to her grandmother, close to her family, and at the moment, Mitch wouldn't leave Jayda with his mother if she were the last breathing person on earth. At least he wouldn't leave her with his mother at his mother's home.

He didn't bother knocking before he opened the front door of his childhood home. Though once it was open, he rapped his knuckles lightly on the door just to be courteous.

"Mom," he called out, making his way through the dark house, weaving around the stacks of boxes and bins.

"Nana!" Jayda stumbled, but Mitch caught her before she ate linoleum. He paused their voyage to check to see what she'd tripped over.

Son of a bitch.

It was a goddamn mousetrap.

Fuck.

"What's that?" Jayda asked, wrinkling her cute little nose as Mitch picked up the sprung and empty mousetrap— scratch that, *rat* trap, off the floor.

Mitch shook his head. "Nothing, sweetheart." He took her hand. "Stay close to me."

He hated that he had to protect his kid from his child-hood home as if they were making their way through an enchanted forest and feared a beast might jump out at them at any moment. But after what he just found on the floor, a beast just might.

"Would it kill her to open the blinds once in a while?" he muttered, watching the dust particles float in the air in the sliver of light that snuck through a crack in the brocade curtains. "It's stifling in here."

"What does stifling mean?" Jayda asked.

"Hot. Stuffy," he replied. They continued on through the house. He knew they'd probably find his mother in the living room in front of the television. That's where she spent most of her time.

The delightful warble and cheep of Rhodo, his mother's new parakeet, a rescue, echoed throughout the house. He hoped that bird kept her swearing to a minimum while Jayda was here. He'd yet to hear her curse words, but his mother had certainly been privy to them and was none too pleased to find out she'd been gifted a recycled foul-mouthed feathered companion.

They rounded the corner into the kitchen-slash-living room, and Mitch nearly fell flat on his ass.

This was not the kitchen he remembered being in last week. Or the week before. The living room was a million times different as well.

For starters, they were both clean.

The drapes were drawn open, letting in the summer sun. The windows were open too, and the big oscillating fan in the corner swept the breeze clear across the room, ruffling the hair that tumbled over Mitch's forehead.

"Nana!" Jayda said, finding Mitch's mother sitting on the floor in a pile of papers. "Thank goodness you opened the windows. The house is *stifling*."

Mitch snorted as he walked toward his mother, running a hand over the back of Jayda's head when he came up behind her.

"Mom, what's gotten into you?"

His mother still hadn't lifted her head. She was busy studying a piece of paper in her hands. "Hmm?" she asked, not really paying attention. "What now?"

"The house ... it's ... clean-*ish* ... -*er*. It's cleanish-er than it has been in ... well, a long time. What's come over you? Did you hire a cleaner?"

Finally, his mother lifted her head, tipping her glasses up into her hair. "Your sister has been coming over when she can to help me sort through boxes and chunk out. Marie-Claude also stayed in Seattle for a week and helped."

"Marie-Claude? As in *the* Marie-Claude, Violet's former dance instructor?" He scratched his head, then dragged his hand over his face, finally pinching his chin in confusion.

His mother nodded as she pushed herself up to standing with the aid of the couch behind her. "The very same. When she came out for Violet's performance at that Art in the Park thing, she came by to see me. After the show, she came back here, and we had a very long conversation. She helped me see that although I am certainly allowed to grieve however I choose, that what I'm doing is not fair to you children either. If something were to suddenly happen to me, I would be leaving you with quite the mess. And you both already had your own"—she paused before blowing out a breath—"for lack of a better term, your own messes to clean up. Your own lives to turn right side up again after losing Jean-Phillipe and Melissa."

Mitch's head slowly shook in disbelief. He could kiss Marie-Claude. "Wow, Mom, that's ... that's incredible. And then she stuck around for a bit and helped you clean?"

"She did, yes. We started in your father's study, then

worked our way into the kitchen and living room. I'll tackle the front room, hallways and bedrooms last. Violet's been coming over too." Even though she was a good foot shorter than her son, she still managed to stare down her nose at Mitch. "And don't think I didn't know that you've been secretly taking things to the Goodwill and the recycling depot for months now. I'm not stupid."

Mitch's cheeks grew warm. "I just keep having these nightmares that there's going to be this huge earthquake and you're going to get buried alive in an avalanche of boxes."

She pursed her lips, not seeming to find the cause for concern or humor in any of it. "Yes, your sister told me. She also told me you've been calling me a hoarder and watching a show with the same name."

He'd have words with his sister later.

"We're just worried about you, Mom, that's all."

Jayda was sticking her fingers in the bird cage, and Rhodo was playfully pecking at the tips. He wandered over and opened up the cage, allowing the bird to hop out onto his finger. Once she'd found her perch, he brought her out, then transferred her to Jayda's finger. The little girl giggled, then carefully sat down in the nearest chair and watched as Rhodo bobbed along her short digit, murmuring in her deep and raspy bird voice.

"I understand you're worried about me, son, but I am doing better."

He took in the somewhat clear and tidy living room, save for the pile of scattered papers on the floor beneath their feet. "It looks like it. I couldn't be happier."

"Marie-Claude said something similar happened to her mother and father. Her mother died first, and her father didn't do a thing with their property in France. Let the house fall into complete disrepair and let his grief consume him. So when he finally passed, Marie-Claude, who was living in

America by that time and who was also an only child, had a big pile of work on her hands. She said it took her months to sort through all her parents' belongings and get the house in a state to sell. I never want to saddle you children with such a task."

"Well, thank you." Relief didn't begin to describe how Mitch felt. Thoughts of the mess he and Vi would be stuck with if his mother was buried alive in a pile of boxes had become a recurring nightmare. He nodded at the piece of paper in her hand. "What's that?"

A slow smile crept across her mouth. "An old love letter from your father."

"I didn't know Dad wrote you love letters." He'd never really considered his father a romantic at heart. Yes, he knew he'd loved his mother deeply, but showing affection was never his dad's strong suit.

She nodded, studying the letter again. "Not very many of them, but he did, back when we were courting and he would go out on the fishing boat for weeks. He'd write me a letter, then leave it and a bouquet of flowers on my doorstep."

Stories like this warmed Mitch's heart. Particularly because his mother was able to talk about his father without becoming wracked with grief and shutting down completely.

This was real progress.

She took one more look at the letter, then carefully folded it up and tucked it in her pocket, lifting her head back up to Mitch's face. "What have you guys been up to today?"

Once again, his mother nearly knocked him flat on his ass. She hadn't asked him how his day was or what he'd been up to in ages. She really was getting better. She looked better too: better coloring, her hair was done, her face washed, her clothing clean.

He let out a sigh of relief before filling her in on the terrifying news about Mira.

"And why did you think it was your job to go and get this *Paige?*" she asked, lifting an eyebrow at him after he'd finished his story.

Mitch could tell Rhodo had had enough of Jayda, so without saying a word, he took the bird back and placed her inside her cage. Jayda, being the agreeable child she always was, didn't even make a peep in protest and just grabbed a puzzle from the bottom of the bookshelf and opened up the box.

Mitch turned back to face his mother, ready for whatever opinions she was going to throw at him. "Because we've become friends. She's Mira's mother, Adam's ex-wife, Violet's dance student. Our paths cross—a lot."

"And you're interested in her."

Mitch's eyes flicked down to Jayda, who had stopped what she was doing and instead stared up at him with big blue eyes. The same eyes as her mother's.

Mitch swallowed hard. "It's new. That's all I'm going to say. She's dealing with some of her own losses right now, so I'm going her speed."

His mother blinked a few times. Was she preparing her barbs for him, the way she had for Violet? Or had she accepted that unlike her, who swore she'd never love again, her children were different? They were younger, and they wanted to find love and happiness again. They deserved to find happiness again.

Finally, after he was nearly ready to pass out from holding his breath, she spoke. "Good idea taking it slow. Nowadays, everybody rushes relationships. There's something to be said for the slow burn. The wooing. The courting. The dating. Nowadays people jump into"—she brought her voice down low and just mouthed the word *bed*—"so quickly that it's no wonder the divorce rate is so high. Sure, you're compatible that way, but it's all the other ways that fill up the rest of the day. You need to be compatible there too."

Mitch's lip twitched. "Spoken like a true romantic, Mom. Solid advice. I'll be sure to send Jayda over and you can give her the same talk when she has her first boyfriend. Which will be when she's thirty-five."

His mother rolled her eyes. "I'm sorry to hear about little Mira. I hope she's okay."

"She's okay," Jayda piped up, having gone back to her puzzle. "She ate the wrong berries. I told her not to, but that girl is stubborn."

Both Mitch and his mother struggled not to laugh.

They knew another girl who was also quite *stubborn* and sassy. And far too mature for her age.

"So, I'm opening up a new studio," he said, wandering into the kitchen and grabbing a glass of water. He brought Jayda and his mother one too. Even though the fan was creating a bit of breeze in the house, it was still really warm. Every night he hoped they'd wake up to clear skies. That the winds would shift overnight and blow the smoke out to sea. So far, no such luck.

His mother thanked him for the water. "A new studio. That's wonderful. Where?"

"In the same strip mall as Violet's dance studio."

"Oh, perfect."

"I hope to open it by the end of August. I just got the keys yesterday, so I'm going to head there tomorrow and see what has to be done, maybe start painting."

"Well, if you want any furniture, you're welcome to whatever is in your father's study. Couch, chair, desk, whatever. Marie-Claude suggested I turn that room into my room."

He wrinkled his nose. "As in your bedroom?"

She shook her head. "No, *my* room. A room just for me. For my hobbies, crafts or whatever else I might want to do."

Mitch's eyes went wide. "Wow, go, Marie-Claude. We should have brought her over sooner."

She made an irritated face that said he needed to stop talking before she took her slipper off and smacked him upside the head. Mitch snickered at the memory of her doing just that on occasion. Never truly painful, but it got her point across that she was none too pleased with his behavior.

"The room gets such great lighting, I might set up a canvas and easel and start painting again."

Mitch nearly spat out the water in his mouth. "You paint?"

A small smile curled her mouth, then she pointed to the floral painting over the fireplace. "Who do you think painted that?"

It was stunning, in deep burgundies and browns, mixed with vibrant turquoise and emerald greens. He'd never really bothered to get up close to the painting to see the signature of the artist. He'd always just assumed it was something his parents had bought or been given as a wedding gift. But his mother had painted it. His mother was an artist.

"After I gave up on dancing, I tried my hand at painting. I'd always had a knack for doodles and drawing, but I'd never really pursued it. So one day, I bought some paints and a canvas and started. I did it for years."

"Why'd you stop?"

"Yeah, Nana, why'd you stop?" Jayda had finished her puzzle and wandered over to where Mitch and his mother sat on the couch. Jayda climbed up into his mother's lap.

"Kids, sweetheart. I didn't have time to paint and take care of my children. And then I just forgot about it. Didn't have a good space for it. My life became a flurry of dance recitals and PTA meetings. I didn't have time for painting. I didn't have time for me."

Mitch's mouth dipped into a frown. His heart hurt for his

mother and all that she'd lost. Not only had she lost her husband but, so many years before that, she'd also lost her passion to paint.

"Oh, don't look at me like that. I'd do it all over again for the amazing life I had with your father and you kids. That's just the way it is with mothers. We make sacrifices." Her eyes turned gentle. "And fathers too. Though it makes me so happy that you were able to turn your passion, your artistic talent into a career."

Never without his camera bag around his shoulder, Mitch didn't say anything, but instead pulled out his camera and quickly fixed on the lens. He adjusted the settings to account for all the light in the room. "Just hold that pose, you two."

Jayda and his mother both smiled. It was the same smile.

"Perfect."

Jayda looked into his mother's eyes and gently cupped her face, pressing her forehead to her grandmother's, so they were now nose to nose. His daughter definitely knew the poses, knew how to work it for the camera.

She had to. She'd had one in her face since birth.

His mother closed her eyes and pressed a kiss to the top of Jayda's head.

Click.

Click.

Click.

When the moment had passed, he tucked the camera away. "Ah, lady muse, you never know when's she's going to pop her head up," he said with a chuckle. His phone chirped in his pocket, and he pulled it out. Violet had texted to say that Mira was being discharged and they were all heading back to Adam's to have dinner. Mira had asked to see Jayda and asked for pizza. She also said that Mitch should invite their mother.

Mitch lifted his head from his phone to find his mother

and Jayda in a deep and private whisper. Then Jayda threw her head back and laughed as his mother tickled her in the ribs.

Mitch's heart hadn't felt this light in a long time.

"Who wants pizza?"

8

THE NEXT NIGHT was Wednesday night. Paige was done with dance class for the evening and feeling like a million bucks.

Mira was okay. The berries, although not edible, were not fatally poisonous, and her daughter seemed to have recovered back to her old self in record time.

Dance class had been invigorating and energizing, but most importantly, she no longer had the boss from hell.

Once again, Marcy Thibodeaux no longer had any power over her, and it felt good.

The sky was the limit for Paige, and she felt really good about it.

Sure, she loved everyone at Narcissus and had come to know some of the regular patrons, but she hoped that once word got out she was on her own and starting something new, people would follow her.

Now she just had to figure out what that something new was.

She said goodnight to Violet and the other dancers, not ready to head home for the night but not sure where to go either. She was walking past the rows of empty and closed stores in the strip mall when she stopped in front of one with its lights on.

Mitch was inside, and he was painting up a storm. Music played, and a box of barely touched pizza sat on the floor next to a water bottle.

She could hear him singing to the Rolling Stones from the other side of the glass and fought to hide her smile.

Before she knew what she was doing, her feet had taken her three doors down to the liquor store, where she bought a bottle of sparkling white wine and a sleeve of plastic cups. Then the next thing she knew, she was knocking on the door, shaking the bottle and smiling like she hadn't smiled in ages as his paint-splotched face grinned back at her, his green eyes softening when he made his way to the door.

"Good evening," he said like Dracula, holding open the door for her. He used his phone to turn the music down. "To what do I owe the pleasure?"

She rolled her eyes. "You can't celebrate getting a new studio space without a little bubbly." She eyed up his pizza. "Plus, I'm starving."

Mitch chuckled. "Help yourself."

She handed him the bottle of wine and sank down to her butt on the floor. "You'd think a person would grow tired of pizza. But I could eat this shit every day."

She heard the cork pop, and within seconds he was settling down on the floor with her and handing her one of the red plastic cups.

His chuckle was warm and carefree. "I'm inclined to agree. Pizza is just so damn awesome. All the food groups."

"Exactly." They were about to drink when a thought crossed her mind. She lifted her cup into the air. "A toast."

His eyes twinkled as he lifted his cup to touch hers. "A toast. To what?"

"To new beginnings. To new spaces. New people. New faces."

"You getting plastic surgery or something? New faces?"

She rolled her eyes. "No. I mean you. You're a new person in my life, a new face I'm seeing practically every day it seems. You've got a new space, a new place of business and hopefully that means you're going to be meeting lots of new people and new faces all the time. I thought it made sense. And the fact that it rhymes is just a bonus."

His very full, very kissable lips twisted as he fought back a laugh. "All right then. To new beginnings. New spaces, new people, new faces."

They tapped cups, then both took a sip. Their eyes remained glued to each other as they continued to drink the cool, bubbly wine.

Pleasure splintered through her, stealing her breath.

Finally, Mitch set his cup down and dove into the pizza. "What's got you so happy? Not that I'm complaining. I like this side of Paige."

She lifted a shoulder before digging back into her own slice of pizza. "Just realized that getting fired yesterday was a blessing and not a curse. It was nice hanging out with everyone last night after Mira's scare. Seeing the girls play together. And then dance class was great tonight. I slept well. I'm just in a really good head space right now. I'm feeling positive about things."

His hand came out, and he rested it on her shoulder. His eyes held the kind of genuine happiness for someone you rarely saw these days, at least from someone who wasn't directly related to you. "That's amazing, Paige. I'm really happy for you."

"Thanks."

"And let me guess, the first person you thought of, who you wanted to share your good mood with, was me, right?"

His grin sent a shiver of something not altogether unpleasant coursing through her.

She tossed her head back and laughed, only to hear the soft *click* of a camera. Paige opened her eyes and tilted her head back down to find Mitch holding his camera.

"Sorry," he said sheepishly. "It's a curse, really. I always have it with me. Almost always have it on. You never know when the moment is going to be there. The right shot. And you have one of the best smiles I've ever seen."

Paige wasn't quite sure what was coming over her, but she knew that she wanted to get to know Mitch more. She wanted to explore this friendship, this whatever it was. She also knew he was one hell of a photographer. She had his shot of her dancing professionally framed and it sat on her nightstand. She said good night and good morning to it every day. He'd captured her in such a raw and vulnerable state, and yet the beauty of it, of her, was right there.

"I'll make you a deal," she said, finishing the last bite of her pizza. "You get this studio up and running, and I'll be your first model." His eyes went as wide as dinner plates, and she had to keep herself from laughing. "That is, if you still want me to?"

"Want you to?" He stood up, grabbed a drop sheet, a folding chair and one of his big studio photography lights. "I'll do it right now. We don't need a portrait studio. We don't need props."

She chuckled, enjoying his glee. "Let's just wait."

He shook his head. "No, I'm serious. You look incredible right now with your hair up but coming out in wild tendrils all around your face. All in black. It's stunning. Perfection. Just go sit on that chair right there against that white wall."

Rolling her eyes, she did what she was told. Within seconds, he had a makeshift background set up with a drop sheet and the photography light on and pointed at her.

"Just do your thing," he said, hunkering down into the crouch position and pointing the camera at her. It began to click. "Smile; don't smile. Look at me; don't look at me. Just be you. Just be Paige. Glorious, sexy Paige."

He moved from one side of her to the other, the snap of the camera echoing like a gong around the empty space.

She had no idea what to do. How to act or move. What to do with her face, her hands. This wasn't what she'd been expecting when she finally agreed to model for him. She thought he'd have props for her. Like a Schwinn bike and a summer dress with a bouquet of daffodils or something. Props. A theme.

But instead he just wanted her to be Paige.

How was that interesting?

How was that photo-worthy?

Slowly, she felt her happiness meter begin to dip.

Her great mood from earlier that day was tanking, and fast.

She wasn't a model.

This wasn't her.

He must have sensed her change, because he pulled the camera away from his face. "What's wrong? What changed?"

She shook her head and stood up, moving away from the chair and out from under the bright lamp. "This was a bad idea," she said softly, standing next to a door that must have led to the adjacent business space next door. "I'm not a model. I don't know how to pose."

She felt the heat from his body at her back. His hands landed on her shoulders, and she fought the urge to lean into his warmth, his strength, his protection. "I didn't want you to pose. I wanted you to just be you."

She turned around to face him. "I don't know how to do that anymore. I don't know who I am anymore."

Every day she struggled to pull herself from that darkness

caused by losing Anthony. By losing all her babies. Some days it was so crippling, she wasn't sure she would be able to get out of bed. Knowing that she'd failed. Knowing that she'd lost her children. Adam's children. It had damn near destroyed her. Now, she didn't know who she was anymore. With each miscarriage, with each death, a piece of her had died too.

Some days were better than others, and since starting dance with Violet, more days were good than bad. But that still didn't mean Paige recognized the woman who stared back at her in the mirror each morning. That she didn't question every decision she made, every minute of every day.

He took her hands in his. "You're Paige. You're one of the strongest, most courageous women I've ever met, and that's saying a lot because I hardly know you. But I noticed your strength from the moment you stepped on to that dance stage and poured your heart out in front of hundreds of people, let them know your story, your heartache and all the things you've overcome to be who you are today."

"And who is that? Because I don't feel strong at all. I feel weak. I feel like a failure."

How on earth did he know who she was when she didn't even know?

He shook his head. "Oh no, honey. You are a warrior. You're still here. You're still alive. You're still fighting. You're picking up the pieces of your life and charging forward."

She pushed down the urge to snort. How did he make her sound like this incredible warrior princess when inside, she felt like no more than an endless loser? A woman who failed to do what women were designed to do, and that was carry a baby. Keep a baby safe inside her body until it was ready to join the world. Time and time again, her body had proved to her she was flawed, she was a failure.

"There are too many pieces to pick up now," she whispered. "Too many pieces of me missing. I'll never find them all again. Never get them back."

"You have a hell of a lot more pieces in your basket now than you did a month ago. Hell, I'm guessing than you did a week ago. Because a week ago you didn't have the possibility of being your own boss and running your own restaurant at your fingertips. Now you do."

She shook her head. "One minute I think it's a great idea. The next minute I think I made a colossal mistake."

He pulled her hand closer to the door linking the two storefronts. "Look in there." She peered through the small window. "What do you see?"

Paige's eyes went wide as she took in the empty restaurant space. It had a full kitchen with a stainless-steel counter, a place for a fridge and stove. She couldn't see everything, but from the layout, the place had probably enough seating for twenty people. Not a huge restaurant, but it was a start. The kitchen was big. Catering big.

She turned back to face Mitch.

"These two spaces used to be a yoga studio and smoothie and snack bar, hence the door between the two. It's for rent just like this place was," he said with a big grin. "We could be neighbors."

She blew out a breath. "Neighbors."

He was still all smiles. "That's right. Though don't bother popping over for a cup of sugar, because I won't have any." He bobbed his eyebrows up and down playfully. "Unless that's not the kind of sugar you're looking for."

Paige couldn't stop the laugh that bubbled up inside her, and she swatted him on the chest.

Click went the camera.

She rolled her eyes as she shrugged innocently. He just had this way of pulling her out of the darkness and making her see the good, making her smile. She needed more of that.

She needed more of Mitch.

"ARE YOU ALWAYS THIS HAPPY? This positive?" she asked, peering back into the empty restaurant space for half a second.

He shook his head, his smile still wide. "No. At least I wasn't before I met Melissa."

He left the mention of Melissa hang. Would Paige retreat? Would she shutter her eyes and pull away? She was in a vulnerable state right now, down on herself, down on life. He needed to pull her back to where she was just moments ago, when she'd knocked on the door all smiles, waving a bottle of bubbly in front of him. That Paige was in there. He just needed to sift through the self-doubt, take her hand and pull her back out to the top of the rubble pile. She needed to stand on top of her mountain of flaws and failures—though he didn't think she had nearly as many as she thought she did —and instead embrace all that life had to offer her, all that was at her fingertips.

She didn't seem to be put off or upset by his mention of Melissa, thankfully. Instead, she simply nodded in encouragement before moving away from the door and wandering back into the middle of the studio. She picked up a paint roller, so Mitch followed suit, and before he knew it, they were painting.

He went on. "She had what her mother called 'Pollyanna Syndrome.' She was just always happy, always positive and upbeat. I mean the woman could find the silver lining in just about anything. The plague? She'd probably say, 'Well, it could be worse. At least it's not raining.'"

Paige chuckled. "I know a few people like that too. My mother is one. Always looks on the bright side."

"It's refreshing as much as it is annoying," he confirmed.

She bobbed her head and snickered. "That it is."

"I see so much of Melissa in Jayda though. Her love of life, of nature. Both loved animals, made friends easily and wouldn't hurt a fly if you offered them a million dollars to pull off his wings. She also looks just like her mother."

Paige smiled. "Jayda's beautiful. And Mira absolutely adores her. She's all I hear about when we're together."

"Thank you. You've done a pretty remarkable job with Mira as well."

Paige's face fell, and she turned away. "That was Adam's doing."

Mitch put the paint roller down, moved into Paige's space, grabbed her roller and set it down too before making her look him square in the eyes. The sadness that lingered behind those soft brown orbs made his heart clench inside his chest. "Listen to me. No, it wasn't *just* Adam. It was you too. She's half you. You were the best mom you could possibly be, and then"—he cupped her face, his pinky resting against the pulsing vein in her slender neck—"you did what you thought was best for her again. You stepped back. You knew you weren't well. You knew you couldn't be who she needed to be, so you sought help. How can the child be well, be happy, feel loved, if the mother or father isn't those things as well?"

A tear slipped down her cheek, and he wiped it away with the pad of his thumb.

"I wish you could see yourself the way others see you. The way *I* see you. How beautiful you are, inside and out. Your strength, your heart. Those are more powerful than you realize."

She blinked spiked lashes and watery eyes at him.

He never broke her gaze.

He needed her to know that what he said he meant with

every fiber of his being, with every cell in his body. She was so much stronger than she believed. She needed to learn to believe in herself again. She needed to learn to love herself again.

Their faces were just inches apart, and a warm shot of her breath hit his lips.

He took her mouth.

She didn't push him away, didn't balk or protest.

Instead she welcomed him. He released her face and wrapped his hands around her waist, pulling her body against his, cradling her delicate frame in his arms. She melted into him, letting her arms float up and wrap around his neck, pulling him down to her almost in desperation.

Her lips were soft, and she tasted like sparkling wine as he swept his tongue inside. A moan rose up from the back of her throat. He deepened the kiss, his hands roaming up her back and into the wild curls on the top of her head. He pulled the hair elastic free and threaded his fingers into the dark, tight waves. His blood began to race south and pool between his legs. Undoubtedly, she could probably feel it against her lower belly.

She pushed her hips against his.

Oh yeah, she felt it.

He also knew he wasn't ready to take it any further than a kiss.

For one, he didn't have any condoms on him.

Two, just last week, Paige had wanted nothing to do with him. If he wanted things between them to be real, which he did, they needed to take things slow.

He'd promised himself that they would go at Paige's speed, and he intended to keep that promise, no matter how much his balls protested otherwise.

And three, he knew he was ready to pursue something with Paige, but he also hadn't *dated* in years. How did people do it anymore? How did thirty-somethings date? Did people date? Or was it like his mother said, people just jumped into bed with one another and figured out the rest later? There was no wooing, no courting, no getting to know the person before you stripped down in front of them and showed them all your freckles.

He wanted to woo Paige. He wanted to court her and date her and find out exactly what made her tick. They'd both been through a hell of a lot in the last couple of years, and she deserved respect for all that she'd overcome.

He broke the kiss but held her against him. Both of their chests heaved, and warm puffs of air from her mouth hit his face.

"We're taking this slow, baby," he said, pressing his lips to her forehead. "I really like you, and I don't want to push. Don't want to rush things."

He heard her swallow and felt her nod. His fingers were still threaded in her hair, his palm against the back of her head.

"I like you too," she whispered.

Mitch's heart skipped a beat, and his smile hurt his face. He pulled her away just enough so he could look into her eyes. "Well, that's just about the best news I've heard all day. Possibly all year."

She worried her plump bottom lip between her teeth. "I'm okay taking it slow ... but ... "

He lifted his eyebrows. "Hmm?"

"Can we do that again? I forgot how much I love just kissing."

Mitch groaned, and his cock lurched against her thigh in protest. "Baby, we can kiss all night if you want to." Then he dipped his head and took her mouth again, reveling in her little moans and whimpers as she fit perfectly into his arms.

As if she were meant to be there all along.

9

THURSDAY MORNING, Paige practically floated into her parents' kitchen. "Good morning!" she sang, sidling up to the counter next to her father and pouring herself a cup of coffee. She hugged the mug against her chest with both hands and let the steam drift up her nostrils.

Both her parents stopped what they were doing and stared at her.

"Good morning to you too, sweetheart," her mother said, standing over a compost bucket, shelling peas from their garden. "What's got you in such a wonderful mood?"

Her father, who was nearly a foot taller than her, wrapped his arm around her shoulder. "We love seeing you like this, angel. We really do. It's like we have our old Paige back." He planted a kiss to the side of her head. "I take it you're over being fired from Narcissus then?"

Paige grinned before taking a cautious sip of her coffee. "I am *so* over it. I have big plans. Hardly slept a wink last night thinking about it all."

Her dad took a seat at the kitchen table, then pushed out another seat for her. She sat down. Her mother joined them, bringing over the big bowl of peas and the compost. Soon they were all sitting around the table, like they had so many times before, shelling peas and solving all the world's problems.

The Three Musketeers.

"So, spill," her mother said, wiping a loose lock of salt-and-pepper hair off her forehead.

Paige leaned forward and tucked the stray curl behind her mother's ear so she wasn't constantly battling with it. "I've decided to open up my own restaurant. I've always wanted to, you guys know that. I have all these recipes that I've been dreaming about just stored in my head, or in my notebook, and I was never really able to try them at Narcissus."

"You're always welcome to try them here at home, honey," her mother offered. "We love when you cook for us."

"Especially your experiments," her father offered, his copper-brown eyes twinkling. "I still dream about that duck in the raspberry sauce you made. Brag about it to all my golf buddies."

"Thanks, Dad. But I want to be my own boss. I was only given so much freedom at Narcissus, and only with desserts. I want complete control over the menu. I want every recipe to be mine and to be able to change it whenever I see fit. Daily, weekly, seasonally. Whenever I want. I also want to move out. Get my own place. A place for Mira and I, where she has her own room and I have my independence."

Her parents stopped shelling peas and looked at her.

"Not that I don't appreciate everything you've both done for me these past couple of years, but I'm in a better place now. It's time to move forward. It's time to be a grown-up again."

"You think you're ready?" her mother asked with concern in her blue eyes.

Paige nodded. "I think so. I want to talk to Adam about

getting more time with Mira. Changing the custody agreement. I'm in a good place. The dancing has helped, and now that I'm going to be my own boss, set my own hours, I think that's going to help too. I'm taking back control."

Her parents nodded slowly but exchanged wary looks with each other across the table.

"I'm not moving out tomorrow," she said impatiently. "I'll have to find a place first. But I'd like to be on my own by the end of the year."

Relief passed across both their faces.

"That's a good goal, honey," her father said, resuming his task with the peas. "Let us know if we can do anything to help."

Paige sucked on her bottom lip for a second before answering. "Actually, there is."

Without missing a beat, both her parents said, "Anything."

"I need a loan."

"How much?" her father asked, still remaining unfazed.

"I'm not sure yet."

He shrugged as if she'd asked him to spot her a fiver and not write her a check for tens of thousands of dollars. "Okay, well, let me know."

Paige hid her smile behind her coffee mug as she took another sip. "Thanks, Dad."

Her parents simply smiled.

Despite her rough go at school with Marcy Thibodeaux, Paige had had a wonderful childhood. An only child, she and her parents were more like best friends than anything else. They treated her like an adult from very early on, encouraging independence, honesty and including her in the big family discussions. In most ways, they treated her like an equal.

They were her rocks. The people she knew she could always count on, no matter what.

Both her mother and father had been very successful in their fields, although they had retired shortly after Mira was born to focus on their grandchild. Her father had been a very successful property developer and her mother a cardiac surgeon.

They'd had Paige in their mid- to late thirties, both being established in their careers and living in the home they were in now, in the very upscale Laurelhurst suburb of Seattle.

As a family, they traveled a lot, which had sparked Paige's interest to study abroad for her final year of high school. That and the fact that Marcy was a psychopath and Paige had finally had enough of her torment.

Even though they missed their daughter, Frank and Nancy encouraged her to spread her wings and head to France on the yearlong exchange. They visited her every few months while she was there, becoming quite close with her host family. They even tagged along when Paige and her host family went skiing in Switzerland for Christmas break, all of them sharing a chalet together and laughing around the table at dinner.

Her parents still remained close with the Marchands and went on annual vacations with them.

It was also the Marchands, particularly Madame Marchand, who had fostered and nurtured Paige's love of cooking and baking. A professional baker herself, with over twenty years of experience, Genevieve Marchand was the mentor Paige never knew she needed. She taught Paige everything she knew about pastry and encouraged her to apply to Le Cordon Bleu in France. Paige did and she was accepted, working under such greats as Lucien LaCroix and Francesca Olivier.

She stayed with the Marchands—who had no children of

their own and pretty much adopted Paige as their own surrogate child—for several years, going to school and then working in various restaurants in France.

The whole time she was gone, living abroad and mastering her craft, Paige's parents had her back. She knew she always had a home in Seattle to come back to, parents who loved and supported her, but she also had a home and parents in France. She had the best of both worlds and was all the richer for it.

They'd been sitting in silence for a while, quietly shucking peas and enjoying the pleasant gurgle of the small pond just outside the back door, when Paige's father spoke up, causing her mother to jump in surprise.

Paige chuckled. "So jumpy, Mom."

Her mother rolled her eyes. "Your father always does this to me."

Frank chuckled before continued on. "Do you have a space for your new restaurant? Or would you like me to get in touch with my Realtor? I'm sure Anton has some great locations he could show you."

Paige smiled at her father. "Thanks, Dad, but I found just the place. I called about it this morning, and it's available. The rent is reasonable, and I'm going to go look at it this afternoon."

Her mother's crystal-blue eyes went wide. "Wow, look at you. Very productive."

"I want to set a good example for Mira, make her proud of her mom," she said, feeling the emotions claw at the back of her throat. She struggled to keep her face calm, even though her body rioted with a tension that made her neck ache with knots.

A big warm hand landed on hers, pausing her efforts in shelling peas. Her father pressed his hand against hers until her palm landed on the table. "She is proud of you, honey. We all are."

Tears stung the backs of her eyes. "I know, Dad, but I'm not. And I want to be. I want to be proud of myself. I want to do all the things I set out to accomplish, achieve all the goals I made before—" She choked on a sob, unable to go on.

Her mother's hand landed on Paige's other wrist. "And you will. We'll do whatever we can to help you, sweetheart."

A lone, hot tear slipped down her cheek, and she smiled through the emotions that made the muscles in her mouth want to dip into a frown. "Thank you. I know I can always count on you guys."

They squeezed her hands at the same time.

"Always, honey," her mother said, leaning over to kiss the side of Paige's head. "Always."

HAVING SECURED the new restaurant space with the Realtor on Friday that week, handing over checks for first and last month's rent, Paige was feeling good about life once again. The last few days had been a roller coaster of emotions, but at the moment, she was on the crescendo, making her way back to the top. She needed to keep this good mood going.

She needed to cook.

She needed to cook for people.

Sending a mass text to everyone important in her life, she grabbed a pen and pad of paper from her nightstand and began compiling her grocery list and menu.

Adam had been at his weekly poker night the night before, so she and Mira had a sleepover. The two of them stayed up late, eating popcorn and watching a movie, enjoying some real mother-daughter time. It was a night

Paige would never forget, and she hoped Mira wouldn't either.

Her little girl was still fast asleep in the bed next to Paige, her dark curls falling over her face and her long lashes feathered over her cheeks as she snored lightly.

Paige tucked the pen behind her ear and brushed the hair off Mira's face, marveling at the perfection of the little person beside her.

Her cheeks held a rosy glow, and her lips were a rich pink and pouty. She really was the most gorgeous thing Paige had ever seen.

Mira was her masterpiece.

As Adam had said, they may have botched their marriage, but at least they did one thing right. They'd done one thing perfectly. Mira was perfection.

Her daughter stirred in her sleep, her face scrunching up tight before relaxing again.

Paige stifled a chuckle, then turned back to her list.

She wanted to wow everyone at the table. Make things she'd never made before but had been dreaming about for months.

Almond-crusted halibut.

Lemongrass-ginger ceviche.

Polenta with basil and heirloom tomatoes.

Her mouth watered and her mind raced as the ideas and recipes flooded her thoughts like a dam breaking.

"What you doing, Mama?" came a tiny, groggy voice next to her. "You coloring?" Mira sat up and scooched in next to her mother, resting a hand on her thigh, rubbing her eyes with her other hand. "You making a shopping list?"

"I am, baby. Would you like to come grocery shopping with me?"

Mira yawned as she nodded. "Yeah, but I need breakfast

first. And my vitamins. And I need to get dressed. And I need to do my hair and have a pee. Can we go in like five hours?"

Paige snorted, running her hand over the back of Mira's wild bedhead hair. "How about one hour?"

Her little girl nodded, blinking back the fatigue that still glimmered in her striking blue eyes. "Okay, one hour. Are Grandma and Grandpa awake yet?"

Paige nodded, jotting down another ingredient for the most ultimate dessert ever. "They're early risers. Grandpa's probably been for his run already, and I bet you Grandma has a fresh batch of cinnamon buns on the counter, still warm from the oven."

Mira shook her head as she slid out of bed. "Those two are nuts. They're just going to be falling asleep in front of the TV tonight by like eight thirty or something."

Paige tossed her head back and laughed. What a little mynah bird. She'd obviously heard Paige mutter something similar to her parents at one point. It was true though, her parents were early birds, only to be nodding off before eight thirty in the evening as they watched the news.

Mira slipped into her Crocs next to the sliding glass door of the pool house and reached for the handle. "You coming, Mama?"

Paige scribbled down a few notes, then slid off the bed, pulled her robe on and stuffed her feet into her slippers. "Right behind you, baby."

"I'LL GET IT!" Mira hollered, her little feet thundering down the hall toward the front door. The bell had chimed, and Paige was up to her elbows in flour and pastry dough, so she couldn't very well leave the kitchen.

"Mom," Paige called, "can you go with her, please?"

Even though Paige was almost one hundred percent certain it was their guests on the other side of the door, one can never be too careful. Adam had mentioned that Mira opened the front door the other day while he was in the bathroom, and it had been a man going around neighborhoods offering to pressure-wash people's driveways.

Needless to say, Adam had given their daughter quite the in-depth lecture about the dangers of opening the door to strangers, and then he'd also reiterated the scenario to Paige with terror in his eyes.

Mira seemed to understand the severity of her actions, but she was also four, so that didn't mean she wouldn't do them again without so much as a second thought. Her impulse control left much to be desired.

She heard the front door creak open, and the house was suddenly flooded with the sound of voices. More thundering feet, this time belonging to two little girls, echoed down the hall. Seconds later, Mira and Jayda appeared.

"Hi, Mrs. Mira's Mom," Jayda said, blinking big blue eyes at Paige. Her long blonde hair was braided in two plaits down either side of her head, reminding Paige of Heidi.

"Hi, Jayda. How are you, sweetheart?"

Jayda made a face that one would expect to see an adult make when they were weighing the productivity of their day. "I'm doing okay, thank you. Spent most of the day outside in the sprinkler. I'm glad the winds finally changed and I can go outside again. That smoke was gross."

"So gross," Mira echoed. "It hurt my *froat* and my lungs. Made it hard to *breave*."

"*Th*-roat," Jayda corrected, making the correct mouth and tongue shape to create the *th* sound. "Bree-*th*."

Mira mimicked her. "*Thhhh*-roat. Bree-*vth*."

Jayda shrugged. "Close enough."

Paige held back a laugh.

Click.

She glanced up from where she'd been half working the pastry dough into layers and half paying attention to the girls to find Mitch standing there with his camera out.

She rolled her eyes. "That's like another appendage for you, isn't it?"

"Almost as important as *other* appendages." His grin made her tingly all over.

She had the pasta roller attachment hooked up to the stand mixer and was getting ready to feed the dough through. With the back of her wrist, Paige pushed a stray lock of hair off her forehead, then went back to work working the dough.

"Here." Mitch skirted around the little girls. "Allow me." He tucked the lock behind Paige's ear, the touch of his finger against the shell of her ear making everything inside her turn to jelly. Not to mention the heat of his big, hard body mere inches from hers.

Memories of Wednesday night in his new studio flitted back into her mind, and she felt her cheeks grow warm. Mitch Benson was one hell of a kisser.

"What are you making, Mrs. Mira's Mommy?" Jayda asked, bringing Paige back to the now.

She hadn't realized she'd shut her eyes, and when she opened them, Mitch was staring back at her, the smile on his face far too cocky for her liking. She batted him playfully on the chest, getting flour on his nice navy polo.

Served him right.

Paige turned her attention back to Jayda. "I'm making a sfogliatelle," she said, chuckling when Jayda's eyes went wide in confusion.

Jayda rolled the word around on her tongue, then wrinkled her nose before asking, "What's sfo-ee-ya-tell-y?" Her pronunciation was slow and clear, and for six years old, she did a pretty good job.

Paige fed the dough through the roller. "It's an Italian dessert with layers of fluffy puff pastry and a creamy ricotta filling inside. You might know it better as a lobster tail."

Jayda nodded. "I know bear claws and apple fritters, but I've never had a lobster tail."

Paige loved how precocious and curious this little girl was. No wonder Mira had taken to her right away.

"Well, then, tonight's your lucky night. But I'm also doing a twist on a classic. I'm adding white chocolate and fresh raspberries to the filling. Then we'll sprinkle it with icing sugar once they've cooled and top them with melted white chocolate and more raspberries."

Jayda and Mira both looked at each other and went *ooohhh*.

"Would you girls like to help me sprinkle the icing sugar when it's time?"

Mira and Jayda nodded.

"Great. I'll call you when they're ready."

Thankfully, the girls took their cue and headed outside to the backyard, where it seemed Adam, Violet and Paige's parents had brought out the bocce ball set and were starting up a game.

Paige turned back to the pasta roller and slid the pastry through for a second time. Once it came out the other side, she folded it in half, then fourths, only to feed it through the roller once more. She needed to repeat this process several times before moving on to the next step.

Click.

"Do you ever just live in the moment?" she asked, flicking her eyes up to Mitch's for just a second before turning back to her dough.

Warm hands encircled her waist, and she immediately felt herself relax in his embrace. He planted a kiss to the side of her head. "I've missed you." The low rumble of his voice turned to a gritty hoarseness that made her nipples pearl instantly.

Her eyes fluttered shut, and she leaned her head to the side. He took her invitation and kissed her neck.

"I've missed you too."

His teeth scraped up the length of her neck before nipping that extra-sensitive spot just below her ear.

"How's this for living in the moment?" he whispered, his breath warm against her ear. A hunger echoed in his tone that mirrored her own.

She opened her eyes, set her dough on the counter and spun around in his arms to face him, looping her arms over his shoulders. "I'd say it's pretty good, but we could do better." Her fingers threaded their way into the soft hair at the nape of his neck, and she tugged his head toward her, pressing her lips against his. "I'm probably getting flour in your hair," she murmured.

"Fuck if I care," he whispered back, capturing her mouth once again and taking over the kiss, tightening his grip on her waist and wedging his tongue between her lips, exploring the recesses of her mouth with long, lascivious sweeps and twirls.

Fire swept down her spine, landing deep down in her belly and continuing to travel south. She moaned into his mouth and pulled harder on his hair.

A throat cleared.

As if made of opposing magnets, Mitch and Paige flew apart.

"Don't mind me," her mother sang sweetly. "Just came to grab the pitcher of lemonade for everyone."

Paige blew out a breath and averted her eyes from both her chuckling mother and a sheepish but also very triumphant-looking Mitch. How could some men look like the cat that ate the canary at the same time they resembled a proud male lion who'd just won the right to mate with the lioness?

Paige's mother was there and gone as fast as Mitch and Paige had separated their lips.

They waited until the door to the backyard was firmly shut before finally lifting their eyes to each other.

Click.

Click.

Click.

"I can't help myself," Mitch said, his grin making Paige's panties get wetter by the second. "Your lips are all puffy, your cheeks are rosy, and your eyes are bright. The gold really comes out and sparkles when you're excited." She wasn't sure how, but his smile grew even cockier. "Or in this case turned on. You really are the most expressive and incredible person I've ever photographed."

Paige pursed her lips and looked away. She wasn't used to such compliments.

A knuckle landed under her chin, and she was forced to meet his gaze.

"Take the compliment. Own it. You are stunning, and that's nothing to be shy about." It wasn't a request. It was an order, and the way his eyes narrowed and his stare intensified, it made her want to obey him without hesitation.

His head dipped, and he brushed his lips against hers once again, only this time he kept it light, kept it soft. But that didn't mean it wasn't just as hot as when he'd thrust his tongue into her mouth and breathed her in, swallowed her gasps and coaxed moans from deep in her throat. This time the kiss spoke of all the things he could do with his mouth, with his body, with his hands but was holding back, teasing her, tempting her. Making her want all the things he wasn't giving her.

And boy, oh boy, did she want them.

His tongue traced along her bottom lip, drawing a whimper from her before she could stop it. She was putty. Putty in his hands. As moldable and malleable as the pastry dough.

She was about to pull his head back down to her, take his lips in the need-driven kiss she knew they both craved, when voices big and small drew nearer and the doorknob to the backyard jiggled.

Mitch pulled away, and she went back to rolling out her pastry dough just as the kitchen filled with people.

Paige hid her face and focused intently on the dough, her bottom lip firmly between her teeth as she struggled not to smile.

Click.

10

THEY DINED ALFRESCO.

From the outside looking in, one might think it weird for Adam and Paige, exes, and their new partners, children and Paige's parents to all be dining together.

But it wasn't.

It was wonderful.

Paige was surrounded by all those she loved dearly.

And all those she was coming to feel deeply for—Mitch, Jayda and Violet.

In just the span of a few weeks, they had become her extended family—people who cared about Mira and Adam just as much as she did, and for some reason, cared a lot about her as well.

She was dancing on air by the time she brought out her sfogliatelle. Everyone had raved and swooned over her dinner.

And if she allowed herself a moment to brag and puff up her chest, she had done an amazing job.

Almond-crusted halibut in a fresh mango and chili chutney; prawn and scallop ceviche with lemongrass and ginger; a cold asparagus salad with almonds, turkey bacon and crispy onions; creamy polenta with truffles and brown butter; and, of course, the dessert. Her magnum opus. The dish that had been haunting her dreams for weeks. White chocolate-, raspberry- and ricotta-stuffed sfogliatelle with powdered sugar, more white chocolate and fresh raspberries.

"Ah," Paige's dad sighed, making a dramatic show of releasing the buckle on the belt of his khaki shorts. "Going to have to add a mile or two to my run tomorrow morning after a meal like that." He leaned over and pecked Paige on the cheek. "You've outdone yourself, sweetheart. Everything was superb."

Paige grinned.

Click.

She rolled her eyes.

Mitch and that damn camera.

She turned to Mira and Jayda, who both had subtler versions of the meal. She believed in introducing all kinds of flavors and foods to children early, but certain flavor profiles can be overwhelming for developing palates, so she gave them the same dishes as the adults but with less spice and a few less truffles.

You don't waste truffles on children. You just don't.

"What did you think of it, honey?" She ran her hand down the back of Mira's soft, dark curly hair, twirling one of the perfect Shirley Temple ringlets around her index finger.

Click.

Mira looked up at her mother, her face covered in powdered sugar and raspberry filling. "I love the sfoggy, Mom. Can I have another?"

Everyone around the table chuckled.

"I think one is enough for today, honey. But I made plenty, so you can always have one tomorrow."

Mira pouted but consigned herself to her fate and eventually nodded, licking her finger and wiping up all traces of the dessert off her plate, then popping her finger into her mouth with a big smile.

"Are you going to serve these dishes at the restaurant?" Violet asked, leaning back in her chair and making a slight face of discomfort before she rested her hand on her stomach. "Whoa, I am full."

Paige nodded. "Something like these. But more lunch-friendly. So I'll put the halibut into a wrap, the ceviche into a to-go cup. I plan to make the restaurant open for breakfast and lunch, with a big emphasis on fast and fresh service to go. It only seats about twenty people, so we need to make our focus the mid-week lunch rush. We'll be available for daytime, evening and weekend catering. I don't feel like accommodating the dinner crowd. Given the location, we'll do well enough with the brunch and lunch rushes that we shouldn't need to be open for dinner. I really want to focus on the catering side as well. Keep our menu tight but variable. Rotate the menu and the dishes every month to six weeks to stick with what's in season. I've already reached out to a bunch of my supplier contacts and set up new accounts."

Adam's eyes went wide at the same time he casually draped an arm around the back of Violet's chair. "Wow, you got organized fast."

"Passion breeds motivation," Mitch chimed in. "She's even hired staff."

"You have?" her mother asked.

Paige stood up to start clearing plates, but Violet and Adam stood up as well and stopped her, saying they would do it.

"Jane from Narcissus is coming on board. She told me she'd follow me wherever I went. And she's brought along three others. I already have a competent staff of four who I know are hard workers. They know my style, how I like to work, and I know that I'll be able to give them a lot of responsibility right off the bat."

Her father welcomed Mira into his lap, sneakily giving her a piece of his sfogliatelle. "That's wonderful. I always liked Jane. A bit of a wild child at heart, but her work ethic is there."

"Exactly."

Mira jumped off her grandfather's lap and beelined it over to the patio railing where the hummingbird feeder hung, swarmed by the little long-beaked speed demons as they ate their supper on the fly.

Smiling, Paige wandered over to stand next to her daughter.

Since Mira was very small, she'd always had a way with the hummingbirds. Normally a very loud and busy child, Mira settled right down into an almost catatonic calm when the birds were around. And the birds loved her. Paige had countless pictures of Mira covered in hummingbirds since before she could even walk.

"The Anna's hummingbirds are here year-round," Paige's father said with delight in his voice, "but the Calliopes and Rufous are summer visitors."

"The Rufous are my favorites," Paige's mother chimed in, "with their beautiful colorings and sweet faces. It's why I plant so many fuchsias and geraniums, to bring the little darlings."

Mira stuck out her finger, and within seconds, one landed on her. Then another on her hand, followed by another on her shoulder.

"That's incredible," Violet said, having returned from the kitchen.

Paige stuck out her finger, and one landed on her.

"Paige was the hummingbird whisperer as a kid," her mother said softly, "and it looks like she passed on that trait to Mira."

Click.

Click.

Click.

Paige lost count of how many times she heard Mitch's camera. She also stopped paying attention.

"You should name the new restaurant the Hummingbird Café," Adam offered. "Seeing as you're such a whisperer."

Paige didn't move but spoke softly. "I thought about that, but there is already a bar by that name, the Hummingbird Saloon, so I don't want people to get us mixed up." Another hummingbird landed on her shoulder. "Plus, lilacs and lavender have always been my favorite flowers, and I've wanted to have them in my restaurant name for years."

A small tug on her shirt had her moving her eyes from the bird on her hand to the little blonde girl next to her. "Can I try?" Jayda asked with hope in her wide, blue eyes.

Paige nodded, slowly moving her hand down and next to Jayda's outstretched arm. "Gentle now. Very quiet. Very still. They startle easily."

Jayda's head bobbed.

The hummingbird's wings began to beat, and his feet lifted up from Paige's hand. Her heart sank at the thought that the little bird was going to leave, but then it zipped over a couple of inches, hovered above Jayda's hand, then put its feet back down.

Her smile made Paige's heart double in size. "It tickles," Jayda whispered.

Paige nodded with a big grin.

Click.

Paige took a step back and marveled at the scene. Two

little angels, illuminated with the low-hanging evening sun behind them, whispering to the birds.

Click.

Click.

She lifted her head to catch Mitch's eyes, but he was focused on his camera, only it wasn't pointed at the children. It was pointed at her.

Click.

One eyebrow slowly slid up her forehead, and she shook her head with a lopsided smile. "Take pictures of the children, please," she said softly, knowing only he could hear her.

She didn't have to see his mouth or even both of his eyes to know that he was smiling. He said she was expressive, but so was he. His face held laugh lines she loved to watch crinkle around his eyes and on his forehead whenever he smiled or laughed, which with Mitch was an awful lot.

Her heart did a little *thump thump* in her chest, and she withdrew her gaze from his and focused back on their daughters.

Just like earlier in the kitchen, she didn't have to see him to know he was now behind her.

"Violet and Adam are going to watch Jayda tonight," he said, his mouth close to her ear. "I'd love to come back so we can talk."

"Talk?" She was glad they weren't looking at each other, because she was sure the man held all kinds of wicked intentions in his eyes.

"Yes, talk. I want to talk with you. Get to know you. I said before that I was going to take it slow with you, and I mean every word of that."

Heat raced up her neck and into her cheeks.

But what if she didn't want to take it slow?

Tonight's meal had gone better than she ever would have

expected. Her life was on the upswing. She wanted to ride the high, ride the wave as long as she could. And that meant taking it to the next level with Mitch. She hadn't felt this way about a man since Adam, and for the first time in much too long, she wanted to feel a connection with someone, explore the connection she already felt growing with Mitch. She needed to feel his pulse pound beneath her lips, his hands roam over every inch of her body.

Mitch made her feel like she was the most beautiful woman in the room, like she was worthy of love, and she liked that feeling. She liked it a lot.

Like a drug, she needed more of it.

"I have Mira tonight," she whispered.

"Does she stay with you in the pool house?"

"Yes."

His low, masculine growl caused her nipples to pebble.

"But once she's asleep, we could wander to the other side of the yard where there's a big hammock and have a glass of wine and *talk*," she said, continuing to keep her voice low.

Another growl, but this time it was more like a purr. "Don't say talk like that. My intentions are pure."

Paige's lip twitched. "But what if mine aren't?"

His pinky finger grazed her hip. "You're making it very hard for me to be a gentleman, Paige."

"Your compliments make it very hard for me to want to take it slow."

"That's not my intention with them. I just believe that beauty in all forms should be celebrated, shared and given credit where it's due. And you are a true beauty."

Paige shifted on her feet. They were in the shade of the big patio umbrella, and the evening wasn't overly hot, but her body was an inferno. This man had a keen ability to turn her body to lava with just a few words. Hell, with just a look.

"Nine o'clock. Side gate. And bring a condom." Then she walked away and began to help Violet gather the plates and take them inside, unable to control the giant smile that seemed to have become permanently plastered to her face.

Click.

11

MITCH PULLED INTO THE MCPHERSONS' driveway. The clock on the dash of his car said eight fifty-eight.

Thankfully, Jayda had been exhausted and fell asleep with no problem. She'd been dead on her feet by the time they arrived home from dinner, asking to skip her bath and instead just head straight to bed.

Mitch hadn't argued.

She was asleep before he even left her room, and during the hour he spent doing photo edits on his laptop downstairs, he didn't hear so much as a peep from upstairs.

Violet and Adam were watching a movie in the living room, with Adam planning to spend the night, so Mitch was free and clear to head over to see Paige.

He thought it would be weird, letting Adam know that Mitch was heading over to see his ex-wife at nine o'clock at night, but Adam didn't seem the least bit fazed or put out by it. If anything, he seemed relieved that Paige was moving on.

Mitch pushed the sound of dueling banjos out of his head as he shut the door of his car and made his way up the driveway toward the side gate that led to the pool house.

Even though it hardly made a sound, the scrape of the metal gate lock echoed around the quiet backyard like a gong in a cave.

Slowly, he made his way up the path.

All the lights in the house were off, but the backyard remained illuminated by small solar garden lights staked into the ground three feet apart all around the flower beds. It made the whole garden look like a fairy haven.

The door behind him opened, and he spun around, expecting to find one of Paige's parents with a baseball bat, ready to take out the intruder.

He threw his hands in the air to claim innocence, that he wasn't there to defile their daughter in a hammock.

Paige's chuckle made him put his arms down.

"What are you doing?" She closed the door behind her, a couple of blankets, a bottle of wine and two wineglasses in her arms. It also looked like she had a baby monitor clipped to her hip.

He shook his head. "I thought you were your parents."

"And so you tossed your hands in the air to let them know you were unarmed?"

He rolled his eyes and took the wine and glasses from her. "Something like that."

"They know you're coming over." She stepped ahead of him and led him through the garden and around the side of the house, where fruit trees lined up like leafy sentries, protecting the yard from the prying eyes of both the neighbors and the sun.

"They do?"

She glanced at him over her shoulder. "I don't keep secrets from my parents. Our relationship is open, honest and adult. They also really like you."

It still felt weird to know that her parents were aware of

him coming over in the middle of the night to *talk* with their daughter.

Maybe it was because Mitch had the completely opposite relationship with his parents that he just couldn't understand it.

She stopped in front of a wide, blue-and-white-striped hammock, kicked off her sandals, placed the blankets and baby monitor on the grass and then gingerly slipped onto the hammock. Once she was on, he handed her the wine bottle and glasses, then kicked off his own shoes and joined her.

"They were devastated at first," she started, twisting off the top of the wine bottle and pouring the first glass, "with the divorce between Adam and I. My parents love Adam, and they thought we'd be able to work it out."

Mitch accepted the glass from her. "And why didn't you?"

She let out a shaky breath before leaning over the side of the hammock and putting the wine bottle down on the ground. Then she leaned back in the hammock to stare up at the stars. Mitch followed her.

"After we lost Anthony, I went into a bit of a tailspin," she started. "I'd lost three other babies after Mira, all at various stages of pregnancy. But they'd all been miscarriages. They were hard. Almost impossible to bear, particularly the last one, because the baby had been sixteen weeks, and I'd already started to feel it moving inside me."

Mitch reached for her hand and linked their fingers together. She squeezed, and he squeezed back.

"So when we got pregnant with Anthony and the pregnancy went past sixteen weeks, I became a nervous wreck. I was paranoid that something was going to happen to him. That I would eventually lose this one too. Compared to Mira's pregnancy, it was a walk in the park. No morning sickness, no gestational diabetes, no hypothyroidism, nothing. But that didn't help. I didn't want to talk about the pregnancy, didn't want anyone to touch my belly out of fear something might happen to the baby. I made myself sick."

He glanced over at her and could see her chest rising and falling rapidly. This had to be hard for her to talk about. But he also knew that she wanted to. She was a strong enough woman that if she wanted to change the subject she would, and he would just have to deal with it. But this was part of them getting to know each other. She was showing him another side of herself, the vulnerable side, the injured side. So he just remained quiet and held her hand.

"On Anthony's due date, I knew something was wrong. His movements had slowed right down, and I could just feel it in my gut that he was in distress. We called the doctor, and they downplayed my nervousness. Probably because I'd been a train wreck the entire pregnancy, so they were tired of my theatrics."

Mitch growled. He hoped to fucking God that hadn't been the case.

"But Adam insisted they see us, so we went in, and they checked on the baby. Sure enough, he was in distress. His heart rate had dropped alarmingly low. They ran us to the hospital and performed an emergency C-section, but it was too late. The cord had wrapped tight around his neck, and he was stillborn."

Mitch's breath rattled in his chest as he struggled to keep it together. He could not even imagine the pain Paige had been through. To lose so many babies, particularly one at birth who had been healthy and viable just hours before—it was a miracle she was still as vibrant and full of life as she was.

"I went off the rails after that. I wanted nothing to do with Adam or Mira. I tried to harm myself in the hospital room bathroom. They had to sedate me and strap me to my bed. I didn't want to live anymore. I wanted to be with my babies.

The nurses pressured me to pump and donate my milk to other infants who needed it, but I couldn't. I knew I should have, but I just couldn't. Their guilt tripping was strong, though. They even sent a mother and her new baby into my room to try to convince me to pump. She'd had breast cancer and a double mastectomy, so she couldn't breastfeed. Turns out the nurses hadn't told her why I was in there, and when she found out that I'd lost my baby, she broke down, apologized and left."

"Holy fuck. I hope you sued those fucking nurses."

She made a noise in her throat that he took to mean she hadn't, but she wished she had. "Anyway, once they discharged me, Adam and my parents agreed that it would be a good idea if I went to a facility for a while." She glanced over at him, and even in the darkness he could tell she held fear in her eyes. "Not a mental hospital."

He squeezed her hand again to reassure her that even if it was, he didn't judge her; he didn't care. "I didn't think that."

"It was a therapy retreat center in Colorado. They had meditation and counseling, yoga and mindfulness. I was there for eight weeks."

"And did it help?"

She nodded, turning her face away from his again to stare straight up through the branches of the trees once more. "It did. My therapist there helped me realize that I had fallen out of love with myself. I hated myself for what I had done. For what had happened. I blamed myself for losing all those babies. I considered myself a failure and unworthy of love. Anybody's love. She didn't tell me to leave Adam, but she helped me come to the realization that in order to heal, I needed to feel guilt-free, and that I would never feel guilt-free if I stayed with Adam. I would always believe deep down that he blamed me for losing the babies. That I lost *his* children. I failed him."

"Did Adam say those things?" Anger bubbled in Mitch's veins. Adam didn't strike him as that kind of a rat bastard.

She shook her head. "Not at all. He was so supportive through all of it. Gave me whatever I needed. But in the end, I think that made it worse, that he didn't blame me." She exhaled. "You probably think I'm crazy."

"I think no such thing."

She squeezed his hand again, and her chest rose and fell on a big exhale. "Thank you."

They both stopped to take long, quenching sips of their wine. Mitch could tell she wasn't finished yet. She wanted to get it all off her chest, all out in the open.

"It didn't matter what kind of reassurance Adam gave me. I felt like I had failed him. Like I had failed us. Particularly with Anthony because he had been perfect. I'd carried him to term no problem. But I'd also been so nervous that I began to think all my anxieties became toxic for him, that I transferred all of my stress to him, and that's what caused him to be stillborn."

"No, that wasn't it at all." Mitch's heart ached for the woman beside him. He wanted to take her in his arms and not let her go until she understood that none of it was her fault, that she wasn't a failure. That she was worthy of love, worthy of a fulfilling and meaningful life.

"Deep down I know that, but I can't help how I feel. So I ended the marriage. I needed to love myself again before I could even fathom the idea of someone else loving me. And I didn't want to put Adam and Mira through that. She needed stability and a parent present and always there for her, and he needed a partner who wasn't a depressed flight risk. I gave him custody. But I think I'm ready to ask for us to renegotiate our agreement. I think I'm ready for shared custody."

"That's great. You're an amazing mother, and Mira just

adores you. If you feel ready, I'm sure Adam will have no problem sitting down to sort something out with you."

She mhmmed and sighed. "I also want to get a place of my own. Move out of here and get a place for Mira and me. But I won't do that until after my surgery."

"Surgery?"

"I'm getting my tubes tied. I'm done having children—or should I say, I'm done losing them."

"You don't know if that would—"

She cut him off. "I'm not willing to risk it. I have Mira, and that's all I was obviously meant to have. I couldn't handle another loss." She turned to face him. "It would destroy me."

He nodded. Her eyes' piercing golden-brown shards speared him. Even with the muted light from all the solar lights, he could still see the intensity, still see the conviction and expression written all over her face.

"I support you," he finally said. "Whatever you need from me, I support your choice. Your body, your choice. Always."

"Thank you. I know Adam resented me for a long time for ending our marriage. He said he'd do anything if I would just try again. But I couldn't. I had failed him. He kept saying that it was *our* loss. That *we* lost the babies. And I would get mad at him and say that *I* lost them. The pain on his face was more than I could bear. I felt that if I called them my losses, then it was just my failure for me. But when he called them *our* losses, I felt like I had failed him too. That I had somehow killed his children and that no matter what he said, he held some resentment toward me for it. Like something I was doing or not doing was the reason we kept losing the babies."

"That's not it at all. Please tell me you know that now."

"I do … in some ways. It's still hard. I think I'll always feel like I failed him. Like I failed us. Failed Mira. Failed our family."

"Is that what your solo dance performance was about?"

"Yes. My therapist suggested I find something to channel my feelings into. A sort of creative outlet where I can be in my own head, let my thoughts run free and have my body do the explaining. It was a constructive sort of therapy that I've come to almost rely on each week to release all the negative thoughts inside my head. I don't know what I would do without that class ... without Violet."

Mitch finished his wine, then carefully placed his glass on the ground beside them. Paige did the same.

He shifted so that he was lying on his side, facing her. "Look at me."

She rolled to her side as well. Spiked lashes and watery eyes blinked up at him. "I'm sorry," she whispered. "I didn't mean to bring the mood down so much. It's just when I get talking about it, I can't really stop. I need to get it all out, otherwise it just festers inside of me." She averted her eyes and stared at their still intertwined hands. "I understand if you're overwhelmed and want to head home. It's a lot to process."

He released her hand and grabbed her by the side of the head so she could focus on him and only him. "Look at me, Paige. Look. At. Me."

Once more, she lifted her gaze to his.

"You are not blame. You hear me?"

Her bottom lip trembled, and her whole body shook. She didn't believe him. After all this time, after everything she'd been through—therapy, divorce, all of it—she still didn't believe that she wasn't at fault.

"It was not your fault. Sometimes super fucking shitty things happen in life, and it is *not* fair. I will never tell you that those babies weren't meant to be, or everything happens for a reason, because that's simply not true. Those babies should have been welcomed into this world, happy and healthy, by two loving parents. But they weren't, and that's fucked up. Big time. But it is not your fault that they weren't. You didn't kill them. You're not a bad mother because you couldn't carry them to term. You are one of the strongest, most courageous women I've ever met, and you are an amazing mother to Mira. You have to stop blaming yourself."

A tear sprinted down her cheek. Without letting go of her head, he wiped the tear away with the pad of his thumb.

"You need to believe that you are not the monster you think you are, because if you keep letting the demons on your shoulder convince you that you are, you'll never get better. You'll never enjoy the life you have ahead of you."

"But what about my babies' lives? What about Anthony?" she stammered, more tears trickling down the crease of her nose. "How can I move on? How can I live my life when they didn't even get a chance at theirs? Should I just pretend that they never existed? Ignore their due dates as they come and go each year? Ignore the *what ifs* and *if onlys* in my head?"

He shook his head. "No. You mourn them like you would any other person in your life. Like I mourn Melissa and my father. But you don't let the grief cripple you. Melissa wouldn't have wanted it to cripple me, and neither would my father. And those babies, if they'd come to term and grown into children and adults, would never want you to give up because of them."

"I just feel like this ultimate failure."

He wiped more of her tears away before pressing a kiss to her forehead. She needed the comfort, the connection, and truth be told, so did he.

"I understand how you feel like a failure," he started.

Her head shot up from where she'd been staring at their knotted hands. Surprise made her eyes go wide.

"I felt like a failure when I lost Melissa. That I should have been able to do something to save her."

Now it was her turn to cup his cheek. "There wasn't anything you could do to save her."

"I know. But I still feel like had I been ... "

"But then Jayda could be without either of her parents."

He nodded, taking her hand from his cheek and kissing the inside of her palm. "I've never told anybody this, but Melissa was twelve weeks pregnant with twins when she was killed. We'd also lost one baby after Jayda was born before Melissa died in the accident."

Paige's breath hitched. "No," she whispered, more tears sliding down her cheek. "She lost so much."

"*We* lost so much," he gently corrected. "Those were my babies too. My wife. I lost children; I lost a partner. Jayda lost a mother. She lost siblings."

She nodded. "Right. I'm sorry."

"It's okay. Just know, I'm not going anywhere. I'm not overwhelmed. I don't need to process. What I need is for you to trust me and continue to open up like you have here tonight. I want the real deal with you, Paige and I'm willing to put in the work to get it."

She brushed her lips against his before saying, "I'm going to be a lot of work. There's a lot of self-doubt going on upstairs." She pointed at her head.

Her breath was warm against his mouth, the sweet smell of the wine and the fragrant flowers in the garden a heady combination. "Yeah, but I already know you're worth it." Then he sealed his lips over hers and did his best to ease her pain, easing his own heartache in the process.

12

PAIGE LOVED the way she felt when she was with Mitch.

Desired.

Sexy.

Whole.

Mitch was a clean slate. A fresh start.

And yet at the same time, he knew all of her secrets, all of her flaws, and he still wanted her. He still pursued her despite the fact that she wasn't perfect, that she was scarred and broken.

He slid his tongue into her mouth, possession in every stroke.

Paige dissolved against him, welcoming his arms around her, his body over hers as they set the hammock to a gentle rocking. He settled in between her legs, never breaking their kiss. Even through his khaki shorts, she could tell his length was impressive as his thick erection pressed against her thigh, causing a rush of heat to shoot through her.

The summer night air was dense with the scent of flowers and fresh-cut grass. The stars overhead twinkled, and the breeze that swept across her bare arms and legs was a welcome reprieve from the inferno raging inside her.

She broke the kiss long enough to mutter, "Condom."

If he hadn't come with provisions, this couldn't go any further.

She couldn't risk it.

He grunted a yes but then angled himself up onto his elbow and peered down at her. "That's not why I came over here. We don't have to if you're not ready."

Paige fought the urge to laugh. She was no virgin. Instead she cupped the back of his head and brought his head down until their lips just touched. "I want this. I want you." She shifted beneath him. The hammock wasn't going to work. They didn't have enough room to move. "Not here, though."

He pushed himself off her and waited for her to sit up, watching as she climbed off the hammock and laid out the blankets she had on the grass.

"Much better," he said, the rough and gravelly tenor of his voice making her shiver. He was such a gentleman. She knew he wanted this just as much as she did, but he was willing to hold back, taking his cues from her and willing to go slow if she needed to.

But she didn't need to.

She needed this more than she'd needed anything in a very long time.

She needed Mitch.

Mitch didn't judge her.

Mitch didn't demand anything of her.

Mitch just wanted to make her feel good, make her feel beautiful and special and like she could take on the world.

Right now, she didn't want the world, though. She just wanted the man standing in front of her.

She knelt down on the blanket and held a hand out to him. He joined her, the two of them kneeling there in the dark backyard, holding hands, bodies pressed against each other, mouths open, breathing each other in.

She'd showered and changed after everyone left that night. Sweat from working in the kitchen all day, combined with flour from the sfogliatelle, had her standing under the cool spray of the shower for nearly half an hour to rinse away the grime. She emerged refreshed and invigorated and ready for Mitch. Choosing to go braless—because what woman wasn't tired of wearing a bra by nine o'clock at night?—she tossed on a dark blue tank top and a flowy black skirt, letting her hair dry naturally after applying a liberal amount of curl cream. She was all for the natural look, but if she didn't tame the mane with some product, she would look like she'd stuck a fork in an electrical socket.

That was the curse of having curls.

His hands fell to the hem of her tank top, and he lifted it up. She raised her arms, helping him guide it over her head. It fell to the ground beside them.

"I would love to photograph you naked," he murmured, leaning forward and pressing a warm, wet kiss to her collarbone. His hands came up, and he gently cupped her breasts as his lips began to roam across her skin, chasing the goosebumps. "Your skin is so perfect." He kissed the slight swell of the top of her breast. "So pale." His tongue swirled around her areola, and she let her eyes flutter shut. "I can see every vein beneath the surface." He drew her nipple into his mouth and sucked.

Heat raced through her, landing firmly between her legs. Her lips parted, and a whimper escaped before she could stop it.

"One day, I hope you'll let me. Just for my eyes and only my eyes. You really are the perfect model." His mouth moved over to her other nipple, and he gave that tight and needy bud the same exquisite attention he had the first.

Paige arched her back slightly, pushing her breast against his mouth, wanting him to suck harder, pull and nip, make her feel alive.

A snap of pain had her eyes flashing open.

He sawed his teeth back and forth over her nub, giving her exactly what she needed, exactly what she craved.

Paige's fingers made their way into his hair, and she gripped it by the roots, holding him right where she wanted him, savoring her, teasing her, tormenting her to within an inch of her sanity.

He released one of her breasts and pushed his hand down beneath the waistband of her skirt. "Are you wet?" he murmured against her breast, taking the nipple back into his mouth and sucking hard.

She tilted her head back up toward the stars. "Yes."

"How wet?"

Paige swallowed. "I don't know."

"Hmmm," he hummed, the vibration of his mouth on her racing at hyper speed right down to her clit. "Perhaps I should investigate."

She licked her lips in anticipation at the thought of Mitch's head between her legs, his lips, his tongue, his fingers pleasuring her.

She nodded, giving his head just the slightest push.

His warm chuckle against her heated flesh made her melt. "I love a woman who knows exactly what she wants," he said, pushing her down to the blanket and pulling her skirt off in the process. When he realized she'd also gone without panties, his eyelids dropped to half-mast. "And boy, do you know what you want."

Paige snagged her bottom lip between her teeth and smiled. "I want you."

Mitch's smile was pure triumph, pure adoration.

He sank down to his belly on the blanket and pushed her

legs open, running a finger up between her slick, plump folds. "You're so wet," he purred. His thumb rested on her clit. Her pulse began to thunder in her ears. His thumb jiggled, and her hips leapt off the blanket. Mitch's eyes gleamed with victory, and the diabolical smile that slid across his lips made her want to push him to the blanket and sit on his face. Smother the smile and put him to work.

But instead she watched him. Watched him slowly explore her body. He picked up her leg, and beginning with her ankle and working his way north, he planted featherlight kisses on each and every one of her erogenous zones: her ankles, behind her knees, her inner thighs, her hip bones, her belly button, the swells of her breasts, the hollow of her throat, the side of her neck and, finally, once again, her mouth.

His kiss, like all the rest on her body, was light and gentle. But she didn't want light and gentle. He'd worked her up into a frenzy. She wanted hard. She wanted passionate. She wanted powerful.

With her hands in his hair again, she pulled him against her, prying his mouth open with her tongue and sweeping inside. He pushed back with his tongue, realizing her desperation for more, and took over, deepening the kiss, pulling whimpers and soft mewls from the back of her throat.

Her hips lurched off the blanket, desperate for friction, but he hovered too high above her. She needed to feel his weight on her, needed to feel his warmth, his strength against her body. Protecting her.

She released his hair and moved her hands lower, grappling at the buckle on his belt, frantic to feel him in her palm.

His hand fell on top of hers and he stilled her efforts, breaking their kiss at the same time. "Not yet," he murmured against her mouth before trailing kisses back down the same path he took before until his face hovered just over the apex of her thighs.

He nuzzled her mound and spread her cleft wide with his fingers. When he finally drew her clit into his mouth and sucked, she cried out and her body bowed on the blanket, her heels digging into the cool earth. He flicked her tender nub with the tip of his tongue, swirling it around the hood before sucking hard on one of her folds, tasting it, then switching to do the same to the other.

Two long, strong fingers slid inside her channel and pumped, curling right where they needed to and pressing up hard on that magical little spot.

Paige's eyes shut once again, and her lips parted. No words came out.

He kept her spread wide with the fingers on his other hand, letting the cool evening breeze sweep across her damp core until she shivered. Only then did he drag the flat of his tongue up from her perineum to the shaft of her clit, following it with his rough, stubbly chin.

She'd been white-knuckling the blanket for dear life but let go and brought her hands up to her breasts, caressing the weight of them and tweaking her nipples, bringing herself more pleasure.

She pulled hard on one until a small but delightful throb swirled through her chest and down to her clit, pulsing and joining with the pleasure Mitch gave her.

She was close, so damn close.

She tapped on his head to let him know he could stop, but he simply grabbed her hand and put it back on her breast, continuing to swirl that magnificent tongue around her clit and rub the sensitive spot inside her.

She pushed up into his mouth, feeling his nose knock her mound. She wasn't even sure he could breathe.

She didn't care.

"You're going to come hard for me, baby," he purred against her swelling clit. "So hard. I can't wait to taste you."

Those dirty words did it.

He pressed up even harder on that sweet spot inside her, sucked like a Hoover on her clit and she detonated. A barrel of gunpower and Mitch held the match. She exploded around him, pouring her juices into his mouth as her pelvis pushed up off the blanket and hard against his face.

He took it all, and he demanded even more.

At the peak of her orgasm, when the bright lights were flashing behind her closed eyelids and her pulse beat like a gong inside her ears, he added a third finger inside her and pressed up more on her G-spot. He sucked even harder on her clit. The man did not quit.

He wanted more.

She gave him more.

Just as the first orgasm was crossing the finish line, its arms raised and a smile on its face, another one took off, crashing through her unexpectedly and causing her whole body to shake. She was in the throes of a new climax at the same time she was in recovery from the first one. Her body didn't know what to do. It didn't know how to respond, how to react.

She simply lay there and trembled, a cyclone of pleasure swirling through her, about to pick her up, thrash her around and then drop her unexpectedly from the sky.

How would she ever recover?

Mitch would protect her. He would take care of her.

As she was finally coming down from the second orgasm, her body like a rag doll, she felt him pull his fingers from her, and his mouth released her clit. She hadn't bothered to open her eyes yet, but she knew he was taking off his shorts from the sounds that competed with her still-hammering pulse and the crickets and frogs in the backyard.

Seconds later, she felt his hard, warm chest brush against hers. "Open your eyes, Paige," he ordered.

With the laziness of a satisfied feline basking in the window on a sunny day, Paige pried her eyes open. He hovered above her, the muscles in his biceps, shoulders and pectorals flexing as he held up his own weight. She felt his cock, thick and encased in latex, poised at her center.

She lifted her hips, eager to have him inside her.

He stared down into her eyes, the green of his irises glowing like hanging moss in the solar lights that lined the garden. His arms bracketed her head, and he brushed the hair off her face with his hands. "You're incredible," he whispered, his lips brushing lightly against hers. She tasted her own arousal on his tongue, which only turned her on even more. Sour and slightly sweet.

"Mitch," she murmured against his lips. "Please."

She felt him smile, his mouth widening against hers. He did a little hip swivel, pushing in just the tip only to pull it back out again.

She growled and grappled at his back, lifting her legs up to push his butt cheeks with her heels.

She. Needed. Him. Inside. Her.

"Please!" she pleaded.

Once again, their eyes locked. His pupils were huge, and his nostrils flared. But it was his smile and the way his eyes focused on hers that made her heart swell, that made her want Mitch more than anything she'd wanted in a very long time.

Finally, with a speed that frustrated her to no end, he eased himself inside her.

She was tight. She knew she was. It'd been over two years since she'd had sex, and that had been with Adam.

He went slow, probably because he thought he might hurt her.

She didn't want slow.

Her body stretched to accommodate his length and girth, welcoming him in, squeezing him, rippling around him as pleasure speared through her, radiating outward from her core.

With a grunt from him and a sigh from her, he hit the hilt. They both paused.

Finally.

Thank God.

Paige swallowed and wrapped her arms around his shoulders, loving the feel of his strong, corded muscles and the way they bunched and flexed beneath her fingertips as he held himself over her.

Then they began to move.

They fit together perfectly. Moved together flawlessly. He rocked into her. She bucked up against him, clenching her internal muscles around him, drawing him deeper inside her, welcoming him home.

He dipped his head and sucked on one of her nipples, drawing the tight bud into his mouth once again and scissoring his teeth over it like he had before. She bowed her back to give him greater access, tilting her head to the sky. That also changed the angle, and his lower belly grazed her clit just right.

She'd already had two orgasms, but another one was right around the corner.

She was close. So close. Quivering, rippling, clutching, on her way to reaching the summit. When she finally did, she arched her back even more, pressing her breasts up toward the stars and deeper into his mouth. Every muscle in her body went rigid as Mitch pumped harder and faster, searching for his own sweet release.

His teeth found her neck. He grunted, and air fled his lungs just as she felt him begin to pulse inside her. She peppered kisses along his sweat-misted shoulders and neck, loving the manly, musky scent and taste of him. Salty, but also uniquely Mitch.

He lifted his head and then gently rolled to the side, tying off the condom and putting it to the side in the grass. He drew her against him so her back was to his chest, then he grabbed the second blanket she'd brought out and fanned it out over their bodies. Once she was nestled in tight to him, he laced their fingers together and kissed her shoulder.

She sighed and melted deeper into his embrace. "How many condoms did you bring?"

His chuckle made her insides turn to jelly once more. "A few. But you need to give me a few minutes." He kissed her shoulder again. "You're incredible."

She spun in his arms to face him, her heart feeling lighter than it had in far too long. She kissed him lightly on the lips, then the nose and finally the cheek before she said, "You make me feel incredible. And I never want it to end."

13

MITCH HAD no idea what time it was, but he didn't really care either. In his mind, all that mattered was that it was sexy time.

Paige was an insatiable woman. Once she'd opened up to him and realized he wasn't going to run for the hills, that he wanted her, flaws and all, she'd become this incredible, powerful, slightly demanding sexual goddess, and he was reaping all the benefits.

After having sex the first time, they'd lain on the blanket in the backyard for a while, talking again, but this time about lighter things. About her time in France, working as a chef and her plans for the restaurant. Then she'd pushed him onto his back, sheathed him in another condom and ridden him like a wild woman of the west. He'd never seen anything quite so glorious in all his life—her pale skin, near-translucent in the darkness; her hair a wild mass of curls, falling over her face like a veil as she leaned forward over him, pushed a nipple into his mouth and finally let go.

They were once again cuddled up on the blanket, but she was playing with his cock and he had his fingers between her legs, when his phone in the pocket of his shorts began to ring.

Who the fuck was calling him this late at night?

"Do you need to get that?" she murmured, her hand stilling but also squeezing.

He nodded and reluctantly removed his hands from the sweet heat between her legs and sat up. She let go of his shaft and sat up with him. He grabbed his phone. It was Adam.

Fuck.

"What's up?" he asked, hoping to God it wasn't anything serious and that Jayda was okay.

"I have to take Violet to the hospital," Adam replied, panic thick in his voice. "She's bleeding and having really bad cramping."

Mitch's eyes darted to Paige. Her own eyes had gone really wide.

"I'm on my way."

"We need someone to stay with Jayda."

"I'm coming with you. She's my sister."

"Okay, I'll call your mom, see if she can come over and stay with Jayda."

Paige's hand landed on Mitch's shoulder. "I'll go stay with Jayda. My parents can watch Mira."

Mitch nodded. "Paige says she will come over and stay with Jayda."

Adam seemed distracted on the phone. "Okay, hurry." Then he hung up.

Paige was already up off the blanket and getting dressed. Mitch did the same, and in within seconds they were high-tailing it around the side of the yard to the pool house.

"I'll be right behind you," Paige said, heading into the main house. "You go home."

Mitch nodded, already making his way down the path toward the side gate. Moments later, he was in his car, desperate not to break any speed laws but knowing he needed to get to his sister as fast as he could.

Should he call his mother?

Would Violet want her to know what was going on?

Eventually, because he needed something to keep his mind from going off the deep end, he decided he would not call their mother just yet. They didn't know what was wrong with Violet, and there was no sense sending their mother into a tailspin if he didn't need to.

Adam was with Violet right now. She wasn't alone, and Mitch would be there shortly. Violet was in good hands. She was going to be okay.

He just had to keep telling himself that.

MITCH PACED the waiting room of the hospital. Even though he was family, Violet had asked him to wait outside. Adam was in the exam room with her, and Mitch couldn't decide how he felt about that.

"It's my vagina, Mitchel," she'd said through gritted teeth and pain on her face. "Get out!"

Adam escorted Mitch to the door. "She's just scared. Once the exam is over, I'll come out and let you know how she is. I'm sure she'll want to see you once they're done."

There wasn't anything Mitch could do, and that's probably what bothered him the most. Once again, just like with Melissa and his father, he was helpless.

He raked his fingers through his hair and brought his hands down over his face. She just had to be all right. Their family couldn't take any more loss. Violet was the glue that held them all together. She was their rock.

It felt like hours, but it was probably no more than fifteen minutes or so before the exam room door opened and a bewildered-looking Adam stepped out.

Mitch raced to him. "She okay?"

Adam nodded. Fatigue, worry and shock all paraded across his face. His blue eyes were wide and red-rimmed. "Violet's pregnant."

Mitch took a step back. "She's what?"

Adam nodded, staring at the floor, his complexion getting paler by the second. "She's pregnant. But she had an IUD, which was why there was so much cramping and bleeding."

"Did she ..." Mitch's hand flew to his mouth before he could utter it.

Adam shook his head. "The baby is fine. They took out the IUD, did an ultrasound. Baby is about eight weeks. They're sending her for blood work."

Mitch blew out a long, slow breath.

His sister was pregnant.

Violet was pregnant.

Now that they knew that she and the baby were okay, his mind immediately went to Paige. How was she going to take this news? Who should be the one to tell her?

Adam must have picked up on his brainwave. "I think you should be the one to tell Paige," he said, stifling a yawn. "I know I'm her ex and that it should come from me, but you two have a connection. She'll respond better if you tell her."

Mitch nodded, catching Adam's yawn and doing one himself. The clock on the wall in the waiting room said it was nearly three o'clock in the morning. "How do you suggest I do it?" He scratched the back of his neck, worried that any way he told Paige could send her off the deep end. They also couldn't keep it from her. She'd want to know if Violet was okay and what happened at the hospital.

Adam's cheeks puffed out before he exhaled dramatically, wandering over to one off the worn tweed hospital chairs and taking a seat with a loud sigh. "I dunno, man. The fact that my new girlfriend of only a few months is pregnant with my baby, after Paige lost so many of ours—I honestly have no idea how she's going to respond. She could be fine, or she could spiral."

"I know. That's my fear. I also worry that she'll say she's fine, but inside she's a mess."

Adam parted his legs and placed his elbows on his knees, hanging his head low. "Anthony's death damn near killed her. I love her, but she's unpredictable."

"I love her too."

Adam's head snapped up, his blue eyes squinting as he studied Mitch's face.

Mitch stood up straighter. "I know it's early, and we haven't said it to each other yet, but deep down I know. I feel it. I love her, and I'll take care of it. I won't let her spiral. I won't let her go off the deep end."

Slowly, Adam nodded. "Sometimes you just know." Mitch couldn't tell if the man was just too tired to smile or if he was unsure of Mitch and his intentions with Paige. Mitch hoped it was the former but didn't really give a shit if it was the latter. Adam wasn't Paige's keeper, and Mitch didn't need Adam's permission for jack shit. He simply told him how he felt about Paige out of courtesy because they were friends.

Adam leaned back in the chair and pulled on the ends of his hair. "Good luck, man. I'm glad she has someone who understands her, someone she's willing to let in. After Anthony died, she shut me out for good. She needs somebody like you who gets her."

Phew.

Mitch stepped forward and thrust out his hand, Adam took it, and the two shook hands.

"Violet should be back from getting her blood work if you want to go in and see her," Adam said, leaning back in the chair and shutting his eyes. "I don't think they'll keep her much longer. Once they know she and the baby are okay, they'll send us home."

Mitch nodded. "Okay, I'll head in and see her, then go back and see Paige and Jayda" He slapped Adam's knee and smiled. "Congratulations, man. Even though it's a bit of a surprise, a baby is a blessing. We need more life, more people in the family. There's been far too much death in the last few years."

Adam didn't bother to open his eyes but smiled and said thanks, then he yawned again. "I guess I better get used to this exhaustion again."

Mitch chuckled as he made to take his leave and go find Violet before he headed home. "You're not going to be sleeping through the night for a very long time, my friend. Best prepare yourself now."

MITCH UNLOCKED the door to his home, careful not to make too much noise in case everyone inside was asleep. He assumed Jayda was asleep, but he wasn't sure where Paige had decided to sleep. He'd offered her his bed, but she said she'd be just as comfortable on the couch.

He tossed his key into the key bowl in the entryway and wandered down the hall toward the living room. Sure enough, there was Paige looking as breathtaking as ever, asleep under a thin knitted blanket.

He knew he shouldn't, that this was neither the time nor the place, but he couldn't stop himself. He grabbed his camera from the bag over his shoulder and quickly took a few pictures of her looking as peaceful as he'd ever seen her. Her thick, dark hair splayed out over the throw pillow behind her like chocolate curls, her cheeks held a healthy pink flush, and her long lashes fanned out over her high cheekbones. She was spectacular.

But he was trigger-happy and hit the button one too many times.

She stirred, opening her eyes and stretching her lithe frame. "Violet's pregnant," she said, blinking a few times before she sat up.

Mitch's mouth dropped open, and he made his way around the couch to face her. He sat on the coffee table and positioned her knees between his, taking her hands in his.

Paige's eyebrows rose up in question. "She is, isn't she?"

"How did you know?"

She lifted a shoulder. "Lucky guess. I've also been around the pregnancy block a few times. Is she okay?"

He blew out a breath, stood up and made his way into the kitchen. He grabbed a beer out of the fridge. "You want one?"

She shook her head.

"Wine?"

"Sure."

Moments later, he returned with a glass of white wine for Paige and a beer for him. "Violet and the baby are okay. She had an IUD, which is why she had cramps and bleeding."

Paige nodded. "I've heard IUD pregnancies are rare. I've also heard that when they do happen, they don't usually go to term. I'm glad they're okay." She took a sip of her wine.

Mitch's head spun. This was not at all how he anticipated her reaction to the news. Was she really as okay as she seemed?

He tipped back his beer, letting the cool brew slide down his throat as he contemplated what to say next. It didn't matter that it was nearly four o'clock in the morning and he probably wasn't going to see more than an hour or so of sleep. Coffee was not what the moment called for.

He pulled on his chin before speaking. "You sure you're okay? I know it can't be easy hearing that Adam and his new girlfriend are having a baby." He wanted to rest his hand on her thigh, ground her, reassure her.

She sipped her wine. "It's hard, I'll admit it. But I kind of figured he'd find somebody someday and they'd have a child together. It happened sooner than I thought, but I'm also better than I thought I would be." She reached for his hand. "And I have you to thank for that. I think it'd be a lot harder if I didn't have someone in my life the way Adam has Violet."

He snorted, squeezing her fingers and lifting the back of her hand to his lips. "You're saying I'm a distraction?"

She kissed his cheek before yawning. "A wonderful distraction. And hey, thank you for being concerned about me, but I'll be okay. I would never in a million years wish anybody to lose a baby, no matter how many I've lost. I wouldn't wish that kind of pain and loss on my worst enemy. Not even Marcy Thibodeaux." She rested her head on his shoulder.

He tilted his head and kissed her forehead.

"I never thought you would, baby. You're not like that. But you are allowed to feel weird. You are allowed to feel hurt and sad."

She nodded, not taking her head off his shoulder. It felt good to have her close again. He wrapped his arm around her waist, and they leaned back against the couch.

"Thank you. I do feel those things, but I'm also happy for them. Babies are wonderful, and Adam is an incredible father. That baby is so lucky."

He kissed her head again. "Your strength never ceases to amaze me."

She hummed a small dismissive thanks before changing the subject. "Hey, who painted that floral in your hallway?"

He grunted. "The pink flowers?"

"Yes, the peonies. They're stunning."

"My mother."

She sat up, her brown eyes going wide, though the dark circles beneath them betrayed her fatigue. "Really? She painted that?"

"Yeah. Apparently, she used to paint a bunch before she had kids. Now she's picking it up again, which Vi and I are really happy about. She was going a little loopy and hoardery after our dad passed. Rarely left the house, wasn't bathing or eating. Stacks of boxes and crap everywhere. I was having dreams that she was going to get buried alive in a tower of boxes and we wouldn't find her for days."

Paige chuckled. "Oh my."

"Yeah, it was bad for a while. I was sneaking boxes and garbage out when she wasn't looking. Taking stuff to the thrift stores and recycling. She caught on, though."

"And was she mad?"

"No. She seems to have turned a corner and is now starting to go through things herself. Vi is helping when she can. So am I. And the painting is a great sign. Seems like she's finally regaining some of her spark and independence. That pink one was one of her first off the easel since she started again."

Paige's mouth twisted, and she looked off into the distance in thought, humming.

"What's going on in that head of yours?"

"I've been looking for an artist to paint a mural on the one main wall in the restaurant. Nothing too over the top or gaudy. But it is called The Lilac and Lavender Bistro, so I should have some lilacs and sprigs of lavender scattered around. Do you think she'd be open to a commission?"

Would his mother be up for it? Would she be willing to step out of her comfort zone to follow her passion? She was cleaning the house up a bit, sorting through the junk and all the boxes. She seemed to be in a better headspace. Perhaps this would give her another nudge toward embracing her new life rather than mourning her old one and wallowing in grief.

He stroked his chin and took another drink of his beer. "I could certainly ask her."

Paige's smile was brighter than the sun. "Thank you. I would love to have a piece of your mother's art featured in the restaurant." She rested her head back on his shoulder and melted back into his body. "Her work is amazing."

He rested his cheek on the top of her head. "You're amazing."

She yawned, which made him yawn for the umpteenth time. "I'm also exhausted." She set her wine down on the side table, then put her head back on his shoulder and shut her eyes. "Wake me up when it's time for school, okay?"

He chuckled as he put his beer down next to her wine and drew the knit blanket over both of them. "You got it." He closed his heavy eyelids.

"Oh, and Mitch?"

He pried one eye open to find her looking at him with one open eye as well. "Hmm?"

"You're amazing too."

14

PAIGE OPENED the door to Mitch's studio. It was two weeks before the opening of his new studio, and he'd asked her to come help him pick out which photos to blow up and frame for the walls.

She'd just finished dance class and was feeling incredible.

Violet had them working on some new dance numbers, and Paige absolutely loved the way the new music and tempo fit with how she was feeling at the moment. It was as if the dance routine had been made for her.

"There she is," Mitch said, all smiles as he greeted her with a glass of wine and a kiss on the cheek. "How was dance class?"

She thanked him for the wine and wished he'd kissed her hard on the lips instead. "Dance was wonderful. Violet has us working on a new routine, and I'm so excited. She really has the best taste in music. Knows exactly how to pair it with the right kind of dance moves."

Mitch chuckled and wrapped a warm arm around her waist, leading her deeper into the studio and around the corner. He had every light on and a big long table set out where eventually he would put his backdrops for portraits. "My sister lives to dance. I'm certain that baby is going to come out dancing."

Paige took a sip of her wine and nodded, every muscle in her body relaxing into his embrace. She leaned back against his chest. "Probably."

He stopped them in front of the table, but before Paige could look down at all the photos he had laid out, he spun her around to face him.

Her brows furrowed, and she gave him a quizzical look.

Mitch placed his hands on her shoulders, his lips set in a thin line.

Something was up.

"I asked you to come tonight to help me pick out some photos to put up on the wall for the opening of the studio."

She nodded. "Yeah, I know."

"I'd also like these photos to stay on the walls for customers and admirers to see when they come in. In my opinion, these are the best of my work. These photos are why I fell in love with photography to begin with and why I continue to love what I do every day."

Paige's eyes searched his face for a clue. He was being cryptic, and it was beginning to freak her out.

"You're the most talented photographer I've ever met," she said. "I'm sure what you've picked is going to wow everyone. You'll be booked for months, possibly years once this place opens and the public can see what you can do. The greater Seattle area isn't going to know what hit it when Mitchel Benson Photography opens for business."

His green eyes flared, and his lips hit hers hard, startling her and making her lose her footing.

But Mitch saved her.

He caught her and righted her before she stumbled into

the table, his hands firmly on her shoulders, keeping her in place, keeping her safe.

"What's going on, Mitch?" she asked. "Why are you being so weird?"

His eyes closed for a moment, and then he spun her around to face the table.

Paige gasped.

Over half of the photos were of her.

Dancing.

Smiling.

Laughing.

Sleeping.

Sitting with Mira.

Standing with Mira, each of them with a hummingbird on their finger.

There were several of her in the kitchen baking. Flour dusted her cheeks, and her hair was tucked up in a bun at the back of her head with only a few tendrils creeping out at her temples.

Then there were the shots of her posing on the chair during their little impromptu photo shoot that first night they'd kissed.

There were other photos of other people as well.

Jayda and a woman who Paige assumed was Melissa. A few others with an older woman who looked a lot like Violet, so that was probably Mitch's mother. One of an older gentleman with a similar nose and smile to Mitch—his father. There were some scenery and wedding shots as well, a few wildlife images and other various pictures of children dancing. There were stunning images of Violet and her former dance partner, Jean-Phillipe, dancing on stage, as well as a new one of her and Adam dancing at Art in the Park.

But there were more of her than all the others combined.

He wrapped his arms around her waist, and his chin fell

to her shoulder. "I won't put any of them up if you don't want me to, but these are the best of my work."

She reached out and made to touch one photo of her. Her eyes were closed, her mouth open mid-laugh. She looked beautiful and carefree. Happy and comfortable in her own skin. The woman in the photo looked flawless.

Was that really how the rest of the world saw her?

Was that how Mitch saw her?

Or was it all lighting tricks and catching her at the right moment?

Smoke and mirrors.

She pulled her hand back before it landed on the photo.

"It's okay," he whispered, his breath warm against her ear. "You can pick it up if you'd like."

She did, bringing the black and white shot closer to her face for further inspection.

"That's one of my favorites," he said, kissing her shoulder. "Your smile is electric. The laugh lines around your eyes and mouth aren't too deep, but they are there and they are genuine. Your head is tossed back showing off that long, sexy neck of yours." He kissed said neck, and a shiver sprinted down her spine. "This is how I see you. This is who you are."

She shook her head and put the photo back down on the table with the rest of them. "That's not who I am." She spun around in his arms to face him. "I don't recognize that person."

Mitch searched her eyes, worry in his own deep-green orbs. His hands on her arms fell to his sides, and he stepped away. She mourned his touch, mourned his warmth and the security and comfort she got from his closeness. He moved around to the other side of the table and picked up another photo. This one was of Melissa and Jayda. Jayda was sitting on her mother's lap, and the two were quietly reading.

"This woman had a wicked temper," he started. "Not five

minutes before I took this photo, she and I had been bicker-
ing. She also held a grudge and could give me the silent treatment for days. I'm pretty sure she *was* giving me the silent
treatment when I took this."

Paige's eyes narrowed on him as he scrutinized the photo
of his late wife and their daughter. His Adam's apple bobbed
in his throat before he spoke again.

"Melissa wasn't perfect. She had flaws. One of those flaws
was how goddamn stubborn she was. Her second pregnancy
was really hard. She had morning sickness all day long. We'd
been trying for a baby for a while and miscarried once
between Jayda and the twins. She'd been asked to teach an
additional class; one of her colleagues was going on sabbati-
cal, and the department asked Melissa to fill in. I asked her
not to. She was having a hard time with the first trimester and
already working full time. But she wanted tenure and figured
teaching the extra class would get her there quicker. Make up
for the semester she planned to take off after the babies were
born.

"It was a late evening class they'd roped her into teaching,
and she got stuck in traffic on the way home. I'm sure she was
exhausted. I'm sure her hips and back ached. She was probably nauseous and tired. Maybe she could have swerved and
avoided the semi-truck that flipped just ahead of her if she'd
been alert and not thinking about all the things going on in
her body. Maybe she'd still be alive. But my wife was stubborn. She never asked for help. Never showed weakness or let
me take care of her. I often wonder—maybe if I'd pushed her
harder to not take on that extra class, she'd still be alive.
Maybe I should have put my foot down rather than given into
her stubborn streak." He laughed tightly. "Melissa used to say
that the pants in our relationship were so stretched out they
were virtually unwearable because we constantly battled to
both wear them. Perhaps if I'd battled just a little bit harder,

made her see my side of things, she wouldn't have been in the car that night on the road." He clenched his jaw and gritted his teeth. "But she was just so *fucking* stubborn."

A tear slipped down Paige's cheek, and she wiped it away.

Why was he telling her this?

He put the photo of Melissa and Jayda back down on the table and walked back around to stand next to Paige. He turned her to face him, his hands back on her shoulders. His touch grounded her. His warmth reassured her. His closeness calmed her.

"When I look at that photo, I don't see the fight we'd just had. I don't see her stubbornness. I don't see her temper. I know it's all in there, because she was a multifaceted woman, and that came across in everything she did. What I do see is a wonderful mother, a spectacular wife, a generous friend. I see a woman with flaws but that those flaws are what made her who she was. And who she was was spectacular. Our flaws, our imperfections, our scars and war wounds are what shape us. They are what make us unique and *not* Photoshopped, they are what make us real. They are what make us who we are."

He picked up a different photo of Paige. It was one of the ones of her dancing on stage at Art in the Park. Pain showed on her face as she danced to the music, let her emotions unfold with each movement and beat.

"I see the pain you hold close to your chest in this one. I see your struggles and your self-doubt. But I also see your strength. I see your openness and willingness to change and improve yourself. Melissa didn't like change. She was not an overly flexible person. She liked things her way, and that was that. But you are. You're flexible, you're adaptable, and much of your strength comes from your willingness to bend, to go with the ebb and flow of life. The swells and squalls, the calms and storms."

Her bottom lip quivered. She didn't see half of that. All she saw were her imperfections. How her leg should have been higher and her arm straighter.

"What do you see?" he asked.

Paige worried her bottom lip between her teeth for a moment before she spoke, her voice coming out in a croaked whisper. "I see a woman in pain. I see a woman who is nervous and unsure of herself. I see a woman who is very aware of her flaws and failures and focuses on them more than anything else, to the point where they nearly consume her. I see a woman who is trying to be a dancer, but she can't quite get her leg up high enough or her arm straight enough. The crowd probably sees that too, and they're judging her for it. I see a woman who no longer knows where she fits into the world." She choked out the last sentence before swallowing down the hard lump in her throat and turning her head away from his intense stare.

He wouldn't let her body turn away though. He held her steady, kept her standing when she wanted to crumble.

"I don't see any of those things," he said softly. "Yes, I see your pain, but I also see your strength." He pointed to her face. "Look at the determination in your eyes, the focus, the intensity. You went out and performed in front of hundreds of people all on your own. Your classmates were sick with food poisoning, so instead of fading away into the shadows and letting Violet go on for a second time to save the show, *you* saved the show. You went onto the stage alone and danced your heart and soul out." He shook the photo in his hand, a touch of frustration lacing his tone. "You are so strong. You need to see how strong you are, how beautiful you are both inside and out. Stop blaming yourself for what happened. Stop letting the bad things influence all the good. Stop criticizing everything you do or can't do and instead celebrate yourself and all of your successes. Celebrate all that you've overcome, all that you've achieved. You are a warrior, Paige. I don't know how you can't see that."

He stepped into her space. The heat from his body made her sway a bit where she stood, but she welcomed it. He bent his knees just a touch so they were eye to eye.

Hot tears burned the back of her eyes, and her throat ached from holding back the emotions. She struggled to swallow and began to tremble. How could he see her like that? How did he see such strength inside her when she didn't even know where to find it?

His eyes pinned on hers, and his fingers tightened just a touch on her upper arms. "Love yourself. Love yourself the way you love others, which is fully and without quarter. Love yourself the way you love your child, your parents, your friends and family. Love yourself the way others love you. You deserve to be loved. Open up your heart to yourself, and love yourself."

His knuckle fell under her chin, and he lifted her head up just a touch. "The way *I* love you."

Paige's eyes grew wide.

He must have noticed the shock because one corner of his mouth lifted up in a shy smile. "Yeah, I love you. Kind of surprised the crap out of me too." His eyes darted back and forth across her face in sudden panic. "That's not what I mean. Shit." He stepped back and ran his hands through his hair. "I'm not surprised that I could love you. That's not what I meant. I mean, I'm surprised that it happened this fast. That I fell for someone so quick. I hadn't even been looking to start dating when you danced across the stage and into my life. And then I couldn't get you out. Not that I wanted to."

Paige's lips parted.

"I love you, Paige. I'm not sure when I knew. I don't know if I had some defining moment like they do in the movies, but I know that I do. With all my heart."

His eyes searched her face again, worry settling in.

"Mitch ... I ... " She took a deep breath. "I ... "

He shook his head. "I don't expect you to say it back. That's okay if you're not there yet. If you're not ready. But just know, I'm not going anywhere. I love you, and I want to be with you." He picked up another photo. This time it was one he'd taken of just her with a hummingbird on her finger. "I mean, how can I not love someone who even the humming-birds love?" His smile was lopsided and boyish. "Kind of a no-brainer."

Paige half-laughed, half-sobbed.

"Let's get back to the great mood you were in before I ruined it all," he said with a regretful tone. "I'm not sure how I always do it, but I manage to take a great moment between us and make it all dark and depressing."

With another laugh, this one far lighter and carefree because her heart was feeling lighter and looser by the second, she looped her arms around his neck. "You do no such thing. You want to talk and dig deep."

He stared into her eyes. "I want to know you. I want to know everything."

Her eyes fluttered shut for a moment before she opened them again, opening up her soul to Mitch. "I want to know you too. And I ... I have strong feelings for you too, it's just ... "

"You need to love yourself again first before you can love anybody new."

She nodded.

He got it.

"Yeah."

"Then let's get you loving yourself again." He pulled away from her embrace, and they faced the table once again. "Now, help me pick some pictures. I measured it out, and I figure I have space for about eighteen to twenty-four, depending on how I group them. I have thirty-six on the table here."

"Of which twenty are of me," she said with a bit of sarcasm in her voice, enjoying the fact that the air in the room was no longer tense and filled with heavy emotions and the thick, overwhelming fog of her self-doubt and flaws.

Before she knew what was happening, Mitch had pushed all the photos to one side of the table, grabbed her around the waist and plunked her on top of the heavy wood. He wedged himself between her legs. "I could add another twenty right now if you'd finally let me photograph you naked." His teeth scraped up her neck, and he nipped that soft, extra-sensitive spot just below her ear.

She chuckled as her hands went to work on the button and zipper of his shorts. "Yeah? Maybe you should give me the camera and I can photograph you naked."

His growl, low and primal, made the embers of arousal inside her ignite to long, licking flames. Heat chased across her skin and liquefied her insides. "Maybe another time. I'll need to do some push-ups and crunches before I sit down for a nude shoot."

She tossed her head back and laughed, loving how both open and full her heart felt when she was with him. He made her laugh like she hadn't laughed in far too long, and it was a feeling she didn't want to let go of.

He took the exposure of her neck as an invitation and raked his teeth up her throat. She gasped from the small snap of pain as he nipped her chin before wedging his tongue between her lips and capturing any further gasps.

The moment turned frantic and need-driven in seconds. They were peeling off layers and kissing in between the disrobing until her dance gear was off and she was in nothing but her thong, sitting on the cool wood of the table. Mitch stood before her, shirtless and sexy with his shorts pooling around his ankles and his impressive length standing up straight in his dark gray boxer briefs.

A small damp patch of precum showed on his boxers, which made her salivate with the need to taste him.

He must have caught her wavelength, because the enormous smile on his face made her once again toss her head back and laugh.

Like a vampire starved for sustenance, he was on her. His teeth scored her neck as his hands made their way around her hips, and he cupped her butt, bringing her center closer to him.

"Condom," she breathed, pushing his boxer briefs down slightly and running the pad of her thumb over the damp crown of his cock, swirling the precum around the shiny purple head.

"Always packing now." His voice was a deep rumble in his throat.

His eyes flared as she brought her thumb to her mouth and sucked.

He released her butt and crouched down to retrieve the small square foil packet from his shorts pocket. Within seconds, he was sheathed and ready.

"This isn't why I called you here," he said, cupping her butt once again and rocking her clit against the long line of his cock.

"Liar." She laughed, locking her ankles behind his back. "We both know what I was coming in here for. It's why I have condoms in my bag as well."

With a grunt and a sigh, he seated himself inside her. "I knew there was a reason I fell in love with you," he said, then he took her mouth, smothering her sighs and breathing in her shallow pants.

Paige's eyes fluttered shut once again as she let the sensation of being full of Mitch consume her. The subtle stretch inside her was a welcome ache that she felt all the way down to her toes, while the way his pubic bone rocked against her clit had her seeing stars and biting her lip to stifle her cries.

His thumb on her bottom lip had her opening her eyes.

"I want to hear every moan," he said hoarsely. "Every cry. Every plea. Don't hold back, Paige." He thrust harder, hitting her deeper inside. She arched her back, and he drew a taut nipple into his mouth, laving at her tender peak until it was so tight it hurt.

"Open your eyes," he ordered.

She loved it when he got bossy.

She hadn't even realized her eyes had closed, but she did as she was told, watching as his eyes seared her face, his mouth set in a determined frown, brows pinched in concentration.

She ran her hands over the tight muscular bulges of his biceps and chest. Mitch had mentioned that he'd joined the same gym as the rest of the single dads, the one that Adam's brother Zak owned. Paige used to belong to the gym too.

Leaning forward, she bit his pec, enjoying the sharp inhale of his breath as she scraped her teeth over the bunching muscle. Her nails dug into his flexing biceps and her heels into his contracting ass cheeks. Whatever he was doing at the gym was paying off. She liked what she saw. She liked what she felt.

The man was a well-oiled, powerful machine.

Pistoning in and out of her with slow, measured thrusts, he brought her closer and closer to that sweet peak of ecstasy, to the pinnacle she'd come to strive for once again since meeting Mitch Benson.

He wedged a hand between them and rubbed rough, erotic circles around her clit, heightening her pleasure, bringing her to the clifftop quicker so that she suddenly found herself teetering on the edge. Her lips roamed across his heated flesh, sprinkling soft kisses to his chest, neck and shoulders. He pinched her clit between his thumb and forefinger, causing a gasp to break free from her lips. She bit his shoulder in response, loving the way he responded by bucking into her harder with a surly, masculine growl. Her heels dug more firmly into his muscular ass cheeks, the feel of them tightening and relaxing with each deep pump turning her on and giving her that gentle nudge she needed to tip off the mountain.

She clamped down hard on Mitch's shoulder and let go.

He didn't stop.

He just kept going, coaxing out her release at the same time he found his own.

She contracted around him, squeezing her muscles tight as the waves of bliss crashed through her. He pinched her clit again, and another orgasm blended with the first, taking her back up to the top of the hill and flinging her off the highest peak one more time.

Her toes curled, and her fingers bunched on his biceps, digging deep wells into his arms with her nails.

Mitch grunted, but she didn't think it was in pain. He brought his head up from the crook of her neck and took her mouth, thrusting his tongue in and out to mimic the pace of his cock inside her. He stilled and then relaxed as his cock pulsed and he found his release. She squeezed him, though she hardly had enough energy after those two back-to-back orgasms, but she did the best she could, milking him, doing what she could do to increase his pleasure the way he did for her.

They stayed there for a moment, their breaths ragged, chests heaving, bodies covered in a thin layer of sweat.

Paige opened her eyes and lifted her head up. Mitch was looking at her. She batted her lashes and attempted to look away. The intensity in his stare unnerved her.

"Don't," he whispered, though the edge to his tone was unmistakable. "Don't look away."

The grip of his hands on her butt cheeks tightened, and he picked her up off the table and carried her over to the couch, plopping her down and pulling out of her in the process. He removed the condom and tied it before he tugged his shorts back into place. Then he disappeared, returning seconds later with a washcloth and a glass of water.

She was still naked, and a breeze from a fan in the corner of the room made goosebumps rise on her skin as it cooled her heated body. Mitch grabbed a blanket from on top of a small trunk across the room and draped it over her. "Warm?" he asked, sitting down on the couch beside her, gauging her reaction with a wary look in his eyes.

She smiled lazily at him and took a sip of her water. "I'm perfect, thank you."

He seemed to relax after that and accepted the water when she offered him a sip.

"Use whatever photos of me you like," she said after a few minutes of quiet. "They're all stunning and do showcase your talent."

"And your beauty," he replied.

She still had a hard time believing him when he said she was the perfect model and continuously called her beautiful, but she also wasn't in the mood to argue. She looked good in those photos because he knew how to wield his camera like a wizard with a wand, she was sure of it. He could probably make a bag of garbage look like a million bucks with the right lighting.

She'd been staring off at a spot on the wall in thought when his knuckle tucked under her chin and he turned her to face him. "It's my new mission in life to convince you that you're beautiful. To love yourself again."

She rolled her eyes and tried to look away, but he wouldn't let her.

"Roll your eyes like that at me again, and you'll find yourself over my knee faster than you can blink, with a red handprint on that sexy ass of yours."

Paige's eyes flew open wide.

Mitch's face split into an even wider grin. "You think I'm joking? Go on and test me."

She took another sip of water, finishing the glass but wishing that he'd brought her a big bucket. She was parched.

He tossed his head back and laughed. "Oh Paige, if only you could see your face right now." He got up and grabbed his camera off his desk.

Click.

Click.

Click.

She wanted to roll her eyes again but fought it.

Mitch sat down on the couch again and scooted in close to her, bringing the screen of his camera between them and pressing a button until images of her sitting on the couch right where she was now popped up on the screen. "See how gorgeous you are? Look at the flush of your skin, the brightness of your eyes. You can try to convince yourself all you like that the thought of me spanking you doesn't intrigue you, but you'd be lying. It's written all over your face, all over your body."

Paige swallowed and studied the image of her on the screen again. Her hair was coming out of her bun, a mass of wisps and tendrils around her face, neck and temples. Her cheeks were rosy, her lips puffy and a deep red, and her brown eyes bright. The blanket was tucked under her arms, leaving the top of her chest and collarbone bare. Anybody who saw this would know the woman in the picture had just had amazing sex, but that didn't detract at all from how content she looked. How at peace and happy she seemed. Her muscles were relaxed. There were no lines on her face. She was enjoying the blissful aftereffects of a being with someone who made her feel beautiful, and in turn, that beauty shone through to the world.

"See," Mitch said, interrupting her thoughts. "See how beautiful you are?"

Slowly, she nodded. She did see it. For the first time in a very long time, she could see what Mitch saw. She was beautiful.

"It's not all tricks with good lighting and camera angles. Sometimes the subject makes the photo. All I have to do is point and shoot."

All I have to do is point and shoot.

Worrying her lip between her teeth for a moment and contemplating what she was about to do, she set the water glass down, stood up and brazenly let the blanket fall to the floor. "Then point and shoot."

15

UNLIKE THE WINTER MONTHS, which can seem to drag on, blending together until they feel like one dark, cold, dreary day that's never-ending, the summer was flying by. Plenty of sunshine, warm breezes, days spent at the beach and evenings spent chasing butterflies. It seemed like one minute, Paige was facing her fear and dancing for Art in the Park on the Fourth of July, and the next, she was menu-planning in her new restaurant space with her staff in the middle of August.

Mitch had set his studio opening for the last weekend in August, and Paige had agreed to cater it. She wasn't going to open Lilac and Lavender until Labor Day, but they needed their space ready for production and their menu set by the time they catered for the studio opening.

"What about doing a take on a Yorkshire pudding, but instead of making it savory, you make it sweet and then fill the center with a Boston cream or hazelnut filling?" Jane suggested, as she and Paige sat in the restaurant one Tuesday afternoon and mulled over the menu.

They'd been doing this for a few weeks now. They'd

discuss menu items, banter them back and forth and then make them, perfect them and add them to the list or cull them altogether. They were pretty much done with the savory dishes they would offer for breakfast and lunch. Paige was almost done the catering menu, but she was struggling for *wow* items to add to her bakery case.

Paige nodded mindlessly and hummed, trying to envision a sweet Yorkshire pudding. "Yeah, that might work. They're really oily though, and I worry about them getting too hard too fast. I like where your head is though. I just want something that we're known for, you know? Something that will put The Lilac and Lavender Bistro on the map. Something that will make people line up around the block, like the cronut."

"Like your banana-bread bread pudding at Narcissus?" Jane asked. "Or your white chocolate pound cake?"

Paige drummed her fingers on the table absentmindedly and nodded. "Yeah, but I want new recipes. I'll wait a bit to introduce those menu items back into my own restaurant."

Jane's smile was devious. "Unless customers come begging for it. Since you took your recipe books and poached all her staff, Marcy's menu is royally fucked. Word will get out that she's a twat to work for, and she won't be able to hire a damn soul with a worthy recipe book within six months."

Paige was still waiting for the other shoe to drop. So far, since Paige left Narcissus, taking four of the kitchen staff with her, she hadn't heard a peep from Marcy. She knew she would eventually, she just didn't know when or how that bitch was going to rear her ugly head again.

"We're taking bets. You want in?" Jane asked.

"Bets on what?"

"On when Narcissus goes under. I say she'll be scrambling by Christmas. Dani says Valentine's Day; Theo says by March."

"And what about Jill?"

Jane snickered as she tucked a strand of purple-streaked blonde hair behind her ear, revealing a sleeve of tattoos beneath her open chef's coat. "Jill is the biggest cynic of us all, you know that. She doesn't think Narcissus will be open by Halloween. Says that Marcy's going to run that place into the ground by running off the staff."

Why did Paige feel sorry for Marcy?

Jane squinted at her. "Don't you dare feel sorry for that bitch. She deserves everything she has coming to her. After what she did to you for all those years, she should be in fucking prison."

"Yes, well ... " Paige hit her pad of paper with her pen a few times. "I don't disagree with you, but I'd hate to see the restaurant close. Narcissus was a beautiful place to eat and work."

"For a while. Until it wasn't. Now Lilac and Lavender is going to be *the* place to get your lunch and your events catered."

"It won't be if we can't come up with a signature pastry." Paige sighed.

Jane's lips twisted, and her nose wrinkled in thought. "It's easy enough to put lavender in a bunch of our pastries. Your lavender scones are the fucking bomb, but could we make a lilac out of pastry?"

Paige exhaled. "I've thought about that, but I keep coming back to chocolate, and I'm not a chocolatier. I can and do work with it, but it's never been my forte. I'm all about the flour, the butter, the lard and the frosting."

Jane grinned. "And you do it so well." She took a bite of the caramel apple fritter Paige had made that morning. "This is a winner. We definitely need to add this to the menu." She licked a blob of caramel off her thumb. "I mean I could drink this stuff."

Paige snorted before turning her attention back to the pad of paper in front of her. "I just don't know. A lavender fritter? A lavender pavlova? Small, personal-size lavender pavlovas with berry compote? With lavender jam?"

Jane's eyes lit up as if Paige was finally on to something, but a knock at the door had them both swiveling in their chairs, breaking their creative process.

Right! Mitch's mother.

Paige stood up and made her way to open the lock. "You must be Mrs. Benson. Mitch and Violet have told me so much about you. Please come in."

She was a striking woman, with green eyes the same shade as her children's and short-cropped, straw-colored hair with strands of silver throughout. She could see where Mitch and Violet got their good looks. She could also see that both of them would age well.

"Call me Greta, please," she said with a slight shake to her voice as she stepped inside and followed Paige deeper into the restaurant.

Paige nodded. "All right then, Greta. Thank you so much for agreeing to come and meet with me. It means a lot. I'm also so happy to finally meet you."

Slowly, Greta's eyes roamed over the space and then over Paige. Paige couldn't tell whether the woman was simply a cautious observer, taking in her surroundings and company before speaking, or if she was passing judgment and quietly ridiculing what she disapproved of.

"Caramel apple fritter?" Jane held up a pan with the sticky confections in front of Greta's face. "Paige just made them, and they're fucking awesome."

Paige shut her eyes and winced. She loved Jane, but the woman had the vernacular of a sailor. She noticed Greta stiffen slightly from the abrasive word. But surprisingly she took one, her eyes widening and her mouth splitting into a big smile the longer she chewed.

Paige let out a small sigh of relief.

Jane was all smiles. "See, what'd I tell you?"

Greta nodded. "These are fantastic." She turned to face Paige. "You made that?"

Paige nodded, wanting to dip her head and look away, but she knew she couldn't. She not only wanted Greta to take the commission but she also wanted Mitch's mother to like her. She couldn't let her shyness get the better of her and ruin this very important first meeting.

The frosty exterior that seemed to have followed the older woman inside slowly began to melt away when she smiled again and set her sketch pad down on the table. "Well, if all your dishes are like that, then I think this place will be a huge success."

"Thank you."

Greta turned to face the big blank wall next to them. It was the only wall that ran the entire length of the space without any interruption, besides the door leading to Mitch's studio. Right now, it was a blinding white, but Paige hoped they could change that. Paige hoped Greta could change that.

Once Paige told Greta what she wanted, the two chatted a bit before Greta asked for some time to measure and sketch on her own. Paige was just glad she'd agreed to take the job and sat back down with Jane again, her workload and stress level a touch lighter than before her boyfriend's mother had walked in.

How many women could say that? That their boyfriend's mother *lightened* their stress load.

She chuckled to herself as she picked up her pen and paper once again and wracked her brain for an epiphany.

"That seems to have gone well," Jane whispered, leaning

in over the table so that Greta couldn't hear her. "I was a bit worried when she walked in with a frown on her face."

Paige nodded. "Me too. Maybe she's just shy like me, and that's misinterpreted as frosty."

"Could be." Jane took another fritter off the plate and dove in. "I wouldn't know what that's like. I've never been shy in my life."

Paige giggled. "Don't I know it."

"So back to the signature dessert ... "

Paige sighed, pulled her bun out and ran her fingers through her hair. She was about ready to pull it all out strand by strand from the stress of coming up with a signature dessert. "I know. I just can't figure out what to do. I mean, do I do a chocolate flower? Do I do a pastry? I want it to scream The Lilac and Lavender Bistro, but I just can't figure out what will do that."

"A churro?" Jane offered, getting up to grab her water bottle off the counter.

Paige paused. "As in the stem?"

Jane lifted a shoulder. "I dunno. I just love churros."

"You know lilacs are edible, right?"

Paige spun around in her seat to face Greta, who was now standing right behind her. Jane's mouth dropped open.

"They are?" Jane asked.

Greta nodded. "And they're actually quite delicious. You can candy them or crystalize them with egg whites and sugar."

"You've done this?" Paige asked, her mind gathering ideas like a squirrel gathers nuts for the winter.

Greta shook her head. "No, but in the last few months I've watched a fair bit of television, and I saw them do it on a baking show."

Jane and Paige stared at each other, a smile spreading across both their faces.

"Are you thinking what I'm thinking?" Jane asked.

Paige nodded. "A churro as the stem, crystalized or candied lilac flowers adhered to the stem with white chocolate?"

Jane nodded. "We could do other flowers too." Her eyes grew wide. "Fuck, a lavender churro would be amaze-balls."

Paige turned back to face Greta, her brain now bursting with new ideas. "You're a genius. Thank you."

As if a light switch went on inside her, Greta's smile erupted, her eyes turned bright, and an entirely new glow seemed to radiate off her. "You're very welcome." She put her head back down to her sketch pad but not without that big smile still on her face.

WHISTLING A TUNE TO SOME KIDS' movie Jayda was currently obsessed with, Mitch opened the door to Liam's house Saturday night. They were two weeks away from the opening night of his studio, and although he should have been spending his time finalizing things and working on the edits for a photo shoot he'd done last week—it was poker night. And nothing got in the way of poker night.

The sound of heavy footsteps and a friendly "Yo" had him holding the door.

Adam nodded and smiled, a six-pack of beer in one hand and an envelope in the other. He handed the envelope to Mitch. "In case you see her before me, can you give this to her?"

Mitch took it from Adam. "These the custody papers?"

"Yeah, had Liam draw them up yesterday. I signed them, and now Paige just needs to sign them."

They made their way into the kitchen, where a cacophony of other male voices laughing and murmuring greeted them.

Paige and Adam had had a big sit-down conversation earlier in the week, and they'd invited Mitch and Violet to sit in on it, seeing as they were now the significant others in Adam and Paige's lives. Paige had revealed to Adam that she was ready for a more active and influential role in Mira's life again. Obviously, Adam had been thrilled, but he'd also been concerned about Paige's new job and the stress it was going to put on her. She'd reassured him that yes, her job had stress, but so did his. However, unlike her old job, where she was only allowed to be so creative, as her own boss she had no ceiling on where her imagination could take her. She was finally, after a very long time, happy again. She was creating and innovating, and she wanted to share her joy with her daughter and not just as a weekend parent.

Mitch was so proud of her for standing up for herself, for putting her needs and the needs of her daughter ahead of everybody else.

They'd had their conversation at Adam's home, which had been Paige's home. Violet was going to move in with Adam, seeing as they were now having a baby together, which made Mitch wonder whether Paige would eventually move in with him.

Oh, what a tangled web. Musical houses.

But at the same time, it was kind of wonderful that they all got along so well and that Jayda and Mira had already bonded. They were all going to be in each other's lives for the foreseeable future, raising the girls together. They might as well be friendly about it.

"My therapist thinks it's a great idea," Paige had said, calmly taking a sip of her iced tea. "I'm no longer a risk to myself. The creative outlets of dance and baking are working wonders for my moods and all the intrusive thoughts. I'm in a good place, Adam."

Mitch squeezed her leg and gave her a reassuring smile.

Adam and Violet sat on the opposite couch. Mitch's sister looked pale and sickly. The pregnancy was certainly taking its toll on her.

"That's awesome," Adam said. "I'm willing to call up Liam now and have him draw up new custody papers if that's what you want. I just want to know that you're okay. I don't want you to feel ashamed or embarrassed for saying you need a bit more time to take care of yourself."

The sexy line of Paige's throat moved as she swallowed. "I appreciate that, but being more involved in my daughter's life is exactly what I need right now. Besides, with the new baby coming, won't it be nice to have only one kid to worry about half the time?"

Violet and Adam made similar faces of unease.

Mitch wasn't sure if they were holding back their joy for Paige's sake or if they were both still a little shell-shocked from the baby news.

Adam slapped his thigh and stood up, dragging his phone out of the back pocket of his shorts. "Then I'll call Liam right now."

A hard slap on Mitch's back brought him back to the present, where he and Adam were standing in Liam's kitchen. He turned around to find their host with a slightly irritated expression on his face.

"What the fuck, man?" Liam said. "I open my home up to you, feed you, and you repay me by having your studio opening on poker night?"

Mitch paused, his mouth open, his eyes darting around the place to gauge the reactions of the other guys.

Was Liam joking or was he serious? It was so hard to tell with the guy sometimes.

"Uh … I'm sorry?"

Liam's mouth split into a big grin, almost too big, and he slapped Mitch on the back again. "Ah, I guess I won't hold it against you. As long as there is free food and booze at this thing, I forgive you."

Phew.

The last thing Mitch wanted was to piss off their host and founder and be kicked out of the club for double-booking everyone. This club had become his second family.

He was all nods, popping the top on his beer and downing half of it before speaking. "There will most definitely be both. The temporary event liquor license just got approved this morning, and Paige is catering."

Liam's eyes swiveled to Adam. "Your ex?"

Adam nodded. "She's a killer cook and an even better baker. Opening up her own restaurant."

Liam wandered into the dining room, where Atlas, Scott, Zak and Mark were setting up the poker table, chairs and food. Scott, Liam's brother, was behind the big leather-top bar, a very expensive bottle of scotch in his hand.

Adam and Mitch each grabbed a bowl of potato chips off the kitchen counter and followed Liam.

"So you're still dating Adam's ex, then?" Liam asked, taking a seat at the table next to Zak.

Mitch nodded, sitting down beside Mark. "I am. Going great. Her restaurant and my studio are next door to each other."

Liam tossed his head back and laughed. "Oh, that's going to make it *so* easy when things go south." He snorted and tossed a handful of pretzels into his mouth, shoving them into his cheek so he could talk. "I've got a good real estate agent. When you need a divorce, I'll be your man. When you need to rent a new space so you're not staring at your ex every minute of every goddamn day, I'll hook you up with Klein."

Both Mitch and Adam glared at Liam and said "Watch it" at the same time.

Liam's laugh was diabolical.

As nice of a guy as he was, he could also be a real tool.

Mitch had only been part of The Single Dads of Seattle for a few months, but he'd already heard Liam's anti-love, anti-marriage tirade more times than he could count. The man was a cynic.

Early on, after Liam's first soapbox announcement condemning love and marriage, Adam explained to Mitch that Liam's wife had put him through the wringer during their divorce. Liam was jaded and preferred to have a friend with benefits but no commitment because, according to Liam, commitment was just another word for "handing your balls over to a woman so she can crush them in the palm of her hand."

"You're a prick," Atlas said, shuffling the cards and dealing them out. "Just because your wife turned out to be cold-hearted doesn't mean all women are like that. Some of us married incredible women. They were just taken from us too soon." Atlas's voice wobbled toward the end, and he swallowed hard. Mitch watched as his jaw grew tighter by the second. Mitch knew exactly how the man felt.

Liam held up his hands in surrender. "I never said any of them were. I happen to love women. Particularly ones who don't try to take me for half my money."

Atlas rolled his gray eyes. "You're still a prick."

16

SUNDAY MORNING, Mitch and Jayda pulled into Paige's parents' driveway. Mira had spent the night with her mother, as Adam was at poker night with Mitch. Now the four of them were going out for breakfast and then the Seattle Aquarium.

"Do you love Mira's mommy?" Jayda asked, batting her father's hand away and unbuckling her own seatbelt. His daughter was far too grown-up, far too independent and mature for six years old. He missed his baby.

Mitch offered her his hand, and to his delight, she took it. "What makes you ask that?" he asked cautiously as they approached the side gate that led to the backyard and pool house.

"Because Mira says you do. And I see how you look at her mom. It's how Mira's daddy looks at Aunt Violet." She blinked up at him with such wide-eyed innocence and curiosity, Mitch felt his entire chest tighten.

"Would it bother you if I did?"

Frowning slightly in thought, she finally shook her head. "No. I like her, and she makes you happy. I like it when you're happy. When Mommy died, you weren't happy for a really long time."

Mitch swallowed down the hard lump in his throat and opened the gate, letting Jayda in through first. "Are you happy?"

She nodded, her long, thick blonde ponytail swishing behind her. "I miss Mommy, but I know she's still with me." She touched her heart. "Just like Grandpa. And Uncle Jean-Phillipe is in Aunt Violet's heart. They're not gone, they're just not with us."

Holy shit.

Mitch paused on the stone path in the garden, staring down at his daughter. "Who told you all of this, sweetheart?"

She squinted up at him, the sun in her eyes making the vibrant blue irises glow like the sea at high noon. "Aunt Violet. And also my friend Alice at school. Her daddy died right before summer, and that's what she said."

Right. He'd received an email shortly before the end of school in June that one of the student's fathers had been in the military and was killed overseas. He'd talked about it a bit with Jayda, but she seemed less affected by it than he was.

"I talk to Mommy sometimes," she said softly, brushing her small thumb over the delicate petal of a rose before letting go and looking down at her feet. "Grandpa too. I try to talk to Uncle Jean-Phillipe, but he mostly talks French to me or is off dancing in the clouds, so we don't talk much."

Mitch hadn't been prepared for this. He knew that eventually Jayda would begin to ask questions about her mother and grandfather and that Mitch would have to tell her what happened, how they died and where they were now. He'd had a brief conversation about death with her when her mother passed, but she was four and a half at the time, and he wasn't sure how much of it she understood. Apparently, he hadn't given his daughter enough credit, because she understood more than some adults.

"What do you talk about with Mommy?" he asked.

She shrugged, her eyes lifting up to the sky and following a hummingbird as it zigged and zagged above them. "All kinds of stuff. I mostly talk to her before bed or when I wake up in the morning. That's usually when she's there. Grandpa only pops by when I'm playing with Play-Doh."

So that was why she'd been asking to play with her Play-Doh more often in the last few months. Interesting. He wondered why his father only appeared to Jayda when she brought out her Play-Doh.

"Is your Mom okay?" he asked, wanting more than anything to feel some kind of a connection again to Melissa. She'd been taken from him so quickly and in such a harsh and unforgiveable way, he'd been denied the chance to say goodbye.

She nodded again and stuck her finger out when the hummingbird dipped low and flitted around her face. Mitch didn't think it would land on her, as there was no feeder around.

"She misses you. Misses me. But she's with my brothers, and they're happy." She giggled as the hummingbird landed on her finger. "She's here now."

Mitch stared down at his daughter in complete shock. His heart raced inside his chest, and a freaky cool breeze shot down his spine. It was the middle of August and the trees were standing stock-still. There wasn't a breath of wind, and it was hot as the earth's core, and yet goosebumps chased across his arms and down his legs.

Melissa?

How did Jayda know about the babies? They hadn't told her they were pregnant again. Let alone that it was twins. They hadn't told a soul.

How on earth did she know it was twin boys? They hadn't even been told that.

The hummingbird lifted off her finger and buzzed away. "Mommy says she's happy you're happy again. She likes Mira's mommy."

The sound of a sliding door opening and shutting, followed by footsteps and a happy whistle, had Mitch and Jayda walking again. He glanced down at his daughter and took her offered hand once again. "I love you so much, sweetheart, and I'm glad you're talking to your mom."

Jayda grinned up at him. "Me too." She let go of his hand and began to skip toward a smiling Mira, but then she stopped and turned back to face him. "Oh, and Eli and Easton say hi." Then she turned back and ran to Mira.

Mitch nearly fell into the pool.

How on earth did she know what they were going to name the babies if they turned out to be boys?

JAYDA ROLLED her eyes and smiled at Mira across the breakfast table in the restaurant.

Paige stifled a laugh and ran her hand over the back of Mira's head. "All right, sweetie, that's enough whistling. Let's wait to practice more when we get back outside."

Mira made a pouty face. "But I just learned to whistle last night, and I need to practice." She pursed her lips and blew again.

Jayda growled. "Whistling is great, but not at breakfast."

Mira's bottom lip shot out, and she looked up at her mother for help. Paige hid her smile, nodding and taking a sip of her coffee before answering. "Jayda's right, sweetie. It's already pretty loud in here. Let's wait until we're outside."

Sighing dramatically, the way four-year-olds were known

to do, Mira reluctantly nodded. "I'm very good at whistling now. Everybody needs to know." She dug into her raspberry pancakes, getting whipped cream all over her face.

Everybody needs to know.

Where did she learn this stuff?

Mitch chuckled softly next to Jayda. His eyes were warm, but his smile was small. He'd been off all morning. Not distant or anything, just *off*.

Mira and Jayda chatted quietly, each of them blowing bubbles in their chocolate milk until giggles took over the table. Paige had been staring at Mitch, waiting for him to lift his eyes from his plate, but it almost seemed like he was deliberately avoiding her gaze.

What the heck was up?

She knocked his foot with hers beneath the table, and finally he lifted his eyes.

"You okay?" she asked, unease drifting into her belly.

He nodded. "Yeah, sorry, just a lot on my mind."

She lifted her brows. "Care to share?"

His eyes darted to the girls, who were still giggling. "Once little ears are no longer around." Then he smiled tightly and put his head back down, picking at his fisherman's breakfast of poached eggs, toast, sausages and haystack hash browns.

Paige swallowed and stared at the top of his head, wondering if this was not only technically their first date but also their last.

AFTER A FUN-FILLED morning and afternoon of breakfast, the aquarium and ice cream, Mitch pulled into his driveway.

Paige gave him a quizzical look. Why were they here? She thought he was going to drop her and Mira back off at her parents' house.

He turned off the car and faced her. "I texted Adam a little bit ago and asked him if he'd take the girls so you and I could have some alone time. We're going to go get dinner, and then I can take you home."

Oh.

Butterflies and dragonflies and a bunch of other winged creatures took flight in her belly. She nodded her head and opened the car door to help Mira out of her car seat, unsure how to respond to Mitch, because despite this lovely surprise date, he still seemed off.

Was he planning to dump her over dinner? Soften the blow with food?

"I can do it, Mommy!" Mira whined, unbuckling her own car seat. "Jayda can do her seat. I can do mine. I'm a big kid, just like Jayda." She pushed her mother's hand away and jumped out of the car, racing to the front door and flinging it open, not even bothering to knock or say goodbye to her mother.

Paige rolled her eyes before climbing back into the front seat. "Well, goodbye to you too," she said dryly.

Mitch had walked the girls to the front door, so Paige was left to her own plaguing thoughts, and all of them involved Mitch and why he was being so weird.

Was this a breakup date?

Had he realized she was too much work and he wasn't ready for the drama that surrounded her?

Had Adam said something to him?

She was lost in thought, and not all of it good, when the door opened and Mitch slid behind the steering wheel. "Ready to go?" he asked, turning on the ignition.

"Mhmm." She glanced out the window and watched her old neighborhood zip by as they headed back out of suburbia and down toward the water once more.

"I was thinking we could grab takeout from that fish taco

place near the Ballard Locks and then go eat down on the beach. What do you think?"

She didn't bother to turn her head toward him. "Sounds good."

A hand landed on her thigh and squeezed. Finally, she moved her gaze from outside the car to inside. They'd stopped at a red light, and Mitch was looking at her.

He offered her a smile, still not as big as the ones she'd grown used to seeing, but it was genuine at least. The light turned green, and he removed his hand to move the stick shift into the next gear, his eyes leaving hers and focusing back on the road.

They drove the rest of the way in silence.

Deafening silence.

17

SANDALS OFF and sand between their toes, they lazily made their way down the beach. The surf gently sloshed at their ankles, and gulls and shore birds rode the sea breeze, searching the shallows for dinner. The sun was hot but no longer high as it slowly started to sink behind Bainbridge Island to the west.

It was the perfect date night.

The perfect date.

Or at least it would have been.

Mitch held their dinner in one hand, but the hand that was next to Paige remained at his side. She wanted to grab it, but after his odd behavior this afternoon and the continuing quiet between them, she wasn't sure how he'd respond and whether her hand was welcome.

She hated this unsureness. She hoped once they found some privacy he would open up because she couldn't take much more of Mitch's sudden blockades and the fact that they all seemed to be put up in front of her.

"Here?" he asked, gesturing to a couple of large pieces of driftwood they could use as a bench. They were behind a small outcropping of boulders, protecting them from the throng of other people aimlessly wandering the sand, taking in the beautiful summer evening.

She nodded and headed up toward the logs, sinking down on her bottom and burying her toes in the cool sand.

Mitch sat down next to her, close enough for their thighs to touch, and opened up their takeout bag. He passed her tacos, drink and a few napkins before grabbing out his own.

They ate in silence.

More silence.

It was killing her.

After about ten minutes of the two of them just sitting there, eating and watching a seal dive for his supper, she crumpled up the empty taco paper and stuffed it into the takeout bag. Then she took a deep breath, swallowed and turned to face him. "What is up?"

He'd been taking a sip of his root beer, but his eyes held a look that said he wasn't surprised at her question. Perhaps he'd even been waiting for it.

He had said, after all, that they could talk when little ears weren't around. So now he needed to keep his promise.

"You've been off all day," she went on. "You haven't been rude or mean to me, but you've been unusually quiet, unusually sullen. Is everything okay?"

He set his drink cup down in the sand, crumpled up his own taco paper and put it with the rest of the garbage before turning to face her. He took her hands in his. Their knees touched.

His hesitation was torture. Surely he had to know what he was doing to her, that the waiting was excruciating. If he was going to dump her, why wasn't he just getting it over with? Why drag it out? Why treat her to a meal and walk miles away from the car? They'd just have to walk back to it together in even more awkward silence than when they'd walked there.

"Jayda asked me today if I loved you."

Her palms had grown sweaty in his, and as much as she wanted to wipe them on her denim shorts, she also didn't want to let go.

She nodded, encouraging him to go on.

"I asked her what she would think if I did love you, and she seemed okay with it."

"Okay ... "

"She also started talking about her mother ... Melissa. She said that she talks to Melissa."

Paige lifted an eyebrow. Where was he going with this?

"We were in your garden this morning when Jayda stopped and a hummingbird landed on her finger. She said that her mother was there, and then when the hummingbird flew away, she said Melissa liked you."

Paige pulled her hands from Mitch's grasp and wiped them on her shorts. She couldn't take it anymore, and she needed some distance. She stood up and stepped away a few yards in the sand. She spun around to face him. "Why are you telling me this? Did Jayda telling you that Melissa liked me make you realize that you didn't like me? Are you ending things between us?"

His face fell, confusion clouding his bright green eyes. He was up off the driftwood log in less than a second, once again taking her hands in his. "No, not at all."

She pulled her hands away again. His touch muddled her, and she needed to keep a clear head. "Then why have you been so weird today? I honestly thought you were planning to dump me."

He shook his head and stepped away, pacing in the sand, running his hands through his thick, dark hair and then scrubbing them down his face. "All that stuff with Jayda today just got me thinking."

"About?"

"About everything. About Melissa. About you. About the kids. I didn't think I was ready to start dating." Her eyes must have betrayed her hurt, because he immediately began to backpedal. "What I mean is, I hadn't planned to start dating. I wasn't looking. But I wasn't closed to the idea either." He exhaled and turned to face the sea. "I told Violet when she started seeing Adam that I was open to the idea of seeing someone, but I wasn't looking, that I wasn't ready, but the right person coming along could change all of that. I figured that if I was meant to date again, the right person would show up in my life, otherwise I was going to focus on my daughter, focus on work. And then *bam!*" He clapped his hands loud. "You danced right into my life."

"You pursued me, remember?"

He faced her again. "I know. Because once I saw you, once I met you, I couldn't get you out of my head. Your strength, your kindness, your raw emotions and how passionately you convey them with everything you do burrowed deep under my skin, and the only relief was to make you a permanent fixture in my world. I can't imagine my life without you anymore. We've only been seeing each other for a month or so, and already I've said the *L* word and I ... " His throat undulated on a hard swallow. "I've already lost one woman I loved."

Oh.

Paige's heart softened, and she stepped toward him, taking his hands in hers. "And you're worried that now that you've opened your heart up to another, you could lose her too?"

He nodded solemnly. His jaw tightened, and a strong, masculine muscle ticked on one side. He was struggling to keep it all together. "Vi going to the hospital was torture. My sister is my rock. With our mom struggling with the loss of our dad, Vi was the person I turned to. But now I have you. I'm in love with you, and I can't imagine my life without you, but it's also terrifying. I don't want to lose you. I couldn't bear it. I can't ... " He exhaled through his mouth and turned back out to sea, his bottom lip now wobbling slightly as his jaw jutted forward.

She didn't turn him to face her but instead stood next to him and laced her fingers through his. "I don't plan on going anywhere," she said softly. "I can't imagine my life without you either. You've turned my world upside down and in the best possible way. I know you think I'm strong, but I only feel strong because of you. You've helped me find a strength I didn't know I had left inside me, and I don't want to lose it. I don't want to lose you."

"This happened really fast," he breathed. "I didn't expect to meet someone and fall for them as fast and hard as I've fallen for you. And the fact that our girls love each other ... I know it was meant to be, but ... "

"It all happened really fast," she finished. "I feel the same way. Our romance was a whirlwind and yet this is our first date."

His head snapped around from the sea to her face, his mouth open in surprise.

She chuckled and shrugged. "Well, it is. Technically. I mean we sleep together, hang out together, but we've never really *been* out together."

He faced the water again and hung his head, shaking it slightly. "Fuck."

She shrugged and squeezed his fingers. "Don't sweat it. Sometimes the best relationships are unconventional ones. But if you're worried that we're going too fast, we could always slow down."

He faced her again, grasping her arms. "No. I don't want to slow down. Everything that's happening between us is happening for a reason, happening at the pace it's supposed to. What we have is amazing. It's just ... " He sighed. "Jayda's words today just rattled me. I don't for a second disbelieve that she's talking to her mother. She's always been a very spiritual child. She said that my dad visits her when she plays Play-Doh and Violet's partner, Jean-Phillipe, only speaks French to her, but he's usually too busy because he's off dancing in the clouds."

"Wow, that's specific. Mira's not there yet when it comes to the discussion of death. My grandmother died about four months ago, and she talks about great-grandma, but she doesn't say she talks *to* her. She actually did something a little odd the other day."

His eyebrow lifted.

She continued. "She was playing with chalk with my mother out on the driveway and had my mother draw everyone in the family, including my grandmother. Then Mira picked up a piece of chalk and scribbled all over my grandmother, saying that she was gone. She was dead, so she needed to be scribbled out."

Mitch's eyes widened.

Paige's chuckle was forced. "Yeah, she's processing in a very interesting way. We talk about my grandmother a lot, which I think helps. She also left Mira a garnet ring as both their birthdays were in January and that's their birthstone, but I'm still not sure how much Mira understands death."

"Kids understand more than we think. I didn't think Jayda understood half as much as she does about death. She's teaching me."

Paige took a half step toward him. His fingers on her arms loosened.

"We always learn more from our children than they learn

from us." She looped her arms over his shoulders and clasped her hands behind his neck. "That was the best piece of advice my mother ever gave me."

His fingers tickled along her arms before encircling her waist. "Solid advice."

"I'm scared too, Mitch. I haven't been with anyone since Adam. I don't even know how to date anymore. Am I doing this right? Am I being a good girlfriend?"

His smile had her moving into his arms. "You are."

But his behavior had sparked an unease inside her that she'd been ignoring for a while now. Perhaps he was right. Maybe they were going too fast. Should they slow down? She shook her head, her eyes darting across his face in search of something she wasn't even sure of. "I don't even know if getting involved with someone right now is healthy. I mean I've told my therapist about you, and she's supportive, but is it really the best idea? I know I'm happy when I'm with you. I'm glad you pushed me and pursued me. I don't want to go slow or lose you from my life, but is it right? Is it healthy?"

"We're spiraling," he said, pulling her body tighter against his. "We can't spiral. Especially not both of us."

She shook her head. He was right. They were spiraling. Spiraling was bad.

"If it feels right, we need to go with it. We can't second-guess ourselves. We can't second-guess us."

She nodded. "Can't second-guess us."

He pressed his lips to her forehead. "I'm sorry for today. I'm sorry I was weird and distant. It's just what Jayda said jarred me, and I was struggling to process. I didn't think I'd ever feel this way about someone again, and it just ... it's—" Instead of finishing his sentence, he pressed his lips to her forehead again.

She could fill in the rest for him. s

It's scary. It's overwhelming. It's startling. It's exciting. It's confusing.

Boy oh boy, was it confusing.

Something out of the corner of her eye caught her attention. She turned her head to see a lone hummingbird hovering just a few feet beside them.

Mitch's gazed followed hers.

They both watched the hummingbird which seemed to be staring straight at them.

Paige's breath snagged in her throat. Melissa?

Mitch must have been thinking something similar because she could tell he was holding his breath as well.

Then, just as quickly as the hummingbird arrived, it flew away. Leaving Mitch and Paige alone—together. Just the two of them.

Mitch turned back to face her and she met his gaze.

He went to open his mouth to say something, but she cut him off, "I know," she said with a small smile, playing with the nape of his neck and pushing his head down so that his lips hovered over hers. Her tongue flicked out to graze his lips. "I feel it all too. But we can feel it together, explore the emotions, the newness together."

He licked her lips. "I like that idea. Together. We're in this together." Then he sealed his lips over hers, pushing away all her worries and doubts from earlier, only to replace them with shiny, happy thoughts of the future.

18

It was the Friday night before the opening night of Mitch's studio, and Paige opened up the door to her restaurant to take a peek at Greta's paint job. She'd left her to her own devices, giving her a key and letting her come and go at her leisure. As long as she was finished with the mural by opening day on Labor Day, Paige didn't really care when she painted or how long it took her. She was just grateful she'd found someone whose art she liked and who wasn't going to charge her an arm and a leg to paint a bunch of lilacs and lavender on the walls.

The restaurant smelled like fresh paint. Drop cloths were draped all over the tile floor, and a ladder sat next to a half-finished deep purple lilac bush. The outline of a dragonfly hovering over the flower was penciled on the wall, along with more flowers and foliage. She couldn't wait to see the finished product.

The sound of music from next door in the studio had her turning off the lights in her own little haven and opening the door to see if her neighbor could lend her a cup of sugar. Or something.

She knocked gently as she turned the latch, but he hadn't heard her, and rightfully so, because not only was the music extremely loud; Mitch was also singing.

She wandered around the corner to the section of the studio where he took the portraits and where she'd let him photograph her naked. She found Mitch with his back to her, his hips wiggling in time with the beat, and his voice competing with the small speaker he had set up in the corner. She couldn't place the band that played, but she'd heard the rock song on the radio once or twice. It wasn't the top-forty hits she was used to, but it wasn't terrible either.

Smiling, she leaned against the wall, crossed her arms and watched him. Watched him wiggle that delicious ass as he fiddled with a photography light in the corner.

Damn, her man was fine.

Mitch's big camera on the corner of the end table next to the couch caught her eye, and she picked it up.

She wasn't nearly as versed in the ways of cameras as her shutterbug boyfriend, but she knew her way around a DSLR. She hung the strap around her neck, turned it on, adjusted the focus and started to shoot.

Careful not to alert him of her presence, she quietly moved around behind him, taking pictures, mostly of his back and butt but a few of his profile as well. He was still too busy with the cords and the words of the song to take notice.

Good thing the front door was locked, otherwise the man could be robbed blind and be none the wiser.

She wanted to get a better shot of his face and those full lips of his, but she also didn't want him to see her. Candid was always best. Even the novice photographers like herself knew that.

She kicked off her flip-flops so they didn't impede her stealth, crouched down and moved in closer. Perhaps if she crept up to him, just behind him, and she popped up, she could catch him unaware.

Like a puma, she stalked her buck as she approached him, her trigger finger poised ready on the button.

She was close enough to smell him now, and like always, he smelled incredible. Manly and fresh, but also earthy. Whatever his deodorant or body wash was, it worked for him.

Abandoning her stealth mode for just a moment, but not standing up from her crouch position, she took a deep inhale and shut her eyes, letting the heat from his big frame and sexy scent wash over her and fill her up.

She opened her eyes once again only to come face to face with Mitch staring down at her, a big, goofy grin on his face.

Paige hit the button on the camera and then fell back on her ass with a loud and painful *oof*.

Click.

Click.

Click.

She made sure to let her butt take the majority of the impact, cradling Mitch's precious Canon next to her chest like it was a newborn lamb, and all to the laughter of her handsome boyfriend.

She sat up and huffed out a breath in despair. So much for being a photography ninja.

Mitch placed his hands on his hips, his mouth twisting and twitching as he struggled to contain more laughter. "What were you up to?"

She rolled her eyes and took his offered hand so he could help her stand up. She rubbed her sore butt cheeks before unslinging his camera from around her neck and handing it to him. "I was trying to get some shots of you singing and dancing. All the ones I got were of your butt."

He wiggled said gorgeous cheeks of lusciousness with a wily grin. "You want me to pose for you?" He handed her back the camera and grabbed a big level with the bright yellow bubble in the middle and held it up to his mouth like a microphone. He began to sing along with the song playing out through the small but powerful speaker.

Shaking her head at the man in front of her but not denying how much happiness flowed through her, or the perma-grin on her face, she grabbed the camera from him again and started dramatically snapping photos. She bent down and tilted the camera. "That's right, baby. Work it. Work it."

He lifted his shirt up just a touch to reveal his stomach, then threw his head back and closed his eyes.

She chuckled. "The camera loves you. You were born for it, baby. Yeah, yeah, that's it."

She spotted the small stand fan in the corner and grabbed it, pointing it directly at him and turning it on. His hair wasn't really long enough to get that *wind-blown look*, but these photos weren't for anybody's eyes but hers anyway. She'd know there was wind.

He continued to pose, pursing his lips and cocking his hips just like every third model on the side of a bus.

"Shirtless, baby, shirtless. Show me what you've got hidden under there. Don't hide it from the world. You worked hard to get it; show it off."

His eyes flashed open, and he pinned that soulful green stare right on her. Gooseflesh rippled along her arms. Without removing his gaze, he peeled his shirt provocatively over his head and tossed it at her. It landed on her head. She rolled her eyes and pulled it off, setting on the couch behind her.

He went for his belt buckle.

Had she blinked?

Probably not.

Saliva filled her mouth as he painfully fucking slowly

released the buckle on his faded, well-worn, ass-hugging, panty-soaking, perfect-fitting jeans. A small trimmed crop of hair from beneath his boxers peeked out, teasing, tempting. She could easily make out the thick line of his erection as it lay heavily against his muscular thighs.

He cocked one eyebrow, asking for her permission to continue undressing.

She swallowed hard and nodded. "Take it all off. Ain't nothin' wrong with what God gave you."

Ain't nothing wrong at all.

His smile was wicked and cocky as hell as he pushed his jeans down his thighs, letting his boxers take the journey too.

Her heart thumped heavy in her chest.

Click.

Click.

Oh, she would need copies of these FOR SURE.

Mitch's jeans dropped to his ankles and he kicked out of them, relieving his big sexy man-feet of his sandals at the same time.

Unlike Paige, who remained conscientious and unsure of her appearance every minute of every day, not wanting to draw attention to herself or her flaws, Mitch stood tall, proud and hard as granite in front of her, grinning like he'd just won the lottery.

Click. Click. Click. Click. Click. Click. Click.

Her finger was beginning to cramp from pressing down so hard on the camera button.

But this man was a work of art. He needed to be captured.

Hell, he needed to be sculpted and put in a freaking museum.

And then it hit her.

Was this how Mitch saw her?

Flawless?

Because even though she knew Mitch had flaws and scars

and quirks, to her, standing there vulnerable but also proud and naked as a bushman, only not nearly as hairy, he was perfect. She was driven to capture him on camera because something so beautiful, so perfect should not go unappreciated, should not go uncaptured.

She'd stopped taking photos and was standing there, mulling over her revelation, when a big, warm hand wrapped around her waist and another one pulled the camera from her, his fingers firm as they grazed hers.

"Stunned by what you see?" he purred.

"Mesmerized," she whispered back, looking up into his eyes.

He set the camera down on the work bench he had set up against one wall and walked them backward toward the couch. Smiling up at him, she wrapped her arms around the back of his neck, feeling his erection bob against her hip as they backed up.

Her calves hit the couch, and he fell on top of her, her body instantly relaxing when he placed all his solid weight over her.

"Going to have to put a warning on those photos," he said, settling between her legs. "Or delete them."

She shook her head and wiggled her hips beneath him. "Nuh-uh. No deletes. Those photos are a work of art. Some of the best photos I've ever taken, I'm sure. I bet we can get them blown up and framed in time for opening night tomorrow too. Put a few on the wall next to that wedding you shot in Italy."

The twinkle in his eyes stirred tendrils of need inside her. "Sounds good to me." With his own ninja skills, he divested her of her shirt and bra easily, leaving her topless beneath him, her nipples painfully hard.

His eyes flicked down between them, and with another impish smile, he latched on to one of her tight peaks, sucking it hard into his mouth to relieve her ache but add a new one, a more pleasant but much more demanding ache that sprinted down her body and settled between her legs.

Paige raked her fingers down his back and gripped his fine ass in her palms, digging her nails into the taut muscle, tossing her head back in a laugh when he clenched the muscle until it was hard as stone.

"I like this side of you," he said, planting kisses over her bare chest and down her belly, forcing her to release the death grip she had on his ass. "I like to see you smile, hear your laugh. You have the best laugh." He slipped off the couch onto his knees and pulled her around so that her legs, still clad in her denim shorts, were parted on either side of him. He made quick work of her bottoms, unfastening them with deft precision, but he left on her panties.

Paige licked her lips and stared down the line of her body at his head as he leaned forward over the couch and shoved his nose between her legs, inhaling.

He tugged at the spot on her panties right over her clit with his teeth, and she damn near had a heart attack when it bounced back against her tender nub. It was wet, and not just from his mouth.

His long fingers hooked into the side of her underwear, and he drew them down over her legs as well. He brought the panties to his nose and inhaled again.

She squirmed on the couch as she watched him. She should feel weirded out by that, right? She wasn't particularly fond of her feminine scent, her *essence* as some romance novels called it. Not that it was bad or an unhealthy smell, but she certainly never put her underwear to her nose and took a whiff. She also couldn't say she'd do that with Mitch's boxers if given the chance.

But watching Mitch do it, watching his eyes become hooded and filled with lust, his erection dripping a bead of precum onto the top of his thick thigh, it made everything inside her clench. It turned her on something fierce and made her want to watch him do it again.

"Gonna put those photos into your spank bank?" he asked, bringing one of her legs over his shoulder and nipping at her inner thigh.

"Shouldn't need a spank bank with you on the ready," she breathed.

His other hand reached up her body and began to twist and twiddle her nipple. "Good answer."

She wriggled beneath his touch, squeaking from the nibbles up her leg. "As long as I've got you on the ready, twenty-four seven, I'll just use those photos for my side business. Sell them to all my girlfriends for their spank banks."

He sucked on one of her folds, forcing her to shut her eyes and sink her top teeth into her bottom lip. "I kind of like that idea. All your friends flicking their bean to images of me, meanwhile I'm the only one who gets to flick"—he flicked her clit with his finger—"and suck"—he sucked her clit into his hot, wet mouth—"and lick"—he swept the flat of his tongue all the way across her clit, making her shiver—"*your* bean."

"Until you go away on a photo shoot. Then I'll have to make a withdrawal from my spank bank." Her hips leapt off the couch, and she pressed her pussy against his face.

He buried his face between her thighs, and she ground up against him. She was already super-close, but she wanted more than this. She wanted what she'd taken pictures of. She wanted what was currently peeking out at her from the floor where he knelt and his cock lay heavy against his belly.

He released her clit and kissed the inside of her other thigh. "The thought of you touching yourself to pictures of me will get me through our time apart, then when we're finally together again, I'll make up for lost time." He grabbed her other leg and swung it over his shoulder so both her legs were now resting on him, then without so much as a deep breath or a wink, he dove in between her legs and made her come harder than she'd ever come before.

Moments later, after she'd found her head and caught her breath, Mitch sat back up on the couch, a condom in his hand. He rolled it over his length and Paige climbed on, straddling his lap and sinking down immediately to take him inside her.

He cradled her ribcage in his big palms, and they each let out a contented sigh when he hit the end of her.

She began to ride him.

"Thank you for everything," she said, lifting up high so that just the tip of him remained inside her. She could see the frustration begin to grow on his face. She did a sultry little hip swirl before dropping back down. "You encouraged me to chase my dream, and now, tomorrow, that dream is becoming a reality. I'm catering my first gig. The first gig in my very own restaurant."

"It's all you, baby," he replied, his voice a deep and masculine rumble next to her ear as she bent her head and licked along the roped muscles in his neck. "Can't wait to watch your star just get brighter and brighter. You're going to be the talk of the town in no time."

She lifted her head and stared down at him, loving the way his face transformed when they made love. He was usually such a happy guy, with a smile on his face and a brightness to his eyes that spoke of not only intelligence but of passion. But when they fucked, when they made love, when he was buried deep inside her and they became one, all of that vanished.

Instead Mitch became this heavily focused, brow-pinched, scowl-faced fucking machine. He was primed and ready to fuck. He was primed and ready to fuck *her*. His only train of thought, his only objective was to fuck, and like hell if he was going to mess it up or get distracted.

And it turned her on.

To know that she made him that wild, that primitive and that fixated on her and only her made her feel like the most desirable, beautiful, sexual woman in the world. He transformed when he was with her, and it was the transformation most women only dreamed their man to make—from the sweet, devoted man who loved his kids, worked hard and was everyone's favorite neighbor to the sex god with a one-track mind and an insatiable hunger for her and her alone.

The dream was now her reality.

Mitch was her reality.

Mitch was hers.

"So proud of you, babe." He grunted, gripping her ass cheeks hard and rocking her against him until his lower abs hit her clit and her leg spasmed. "Gonna show you how proud." He captured one of her nipples in his mouth and sucked hard, wedged a hand between them and rubbed rough circles around her clit. With his other hand, and one single, very long finger, he pushed against her anus.

"Let me in."

She relaxed.

He pushed harder, past the tight ring of muscle, until all she felt was full and amazing. She lifted up on his lap again. His finger went with her, pushing in even deeper when she dropped back down.

She was really close now. Damn close.

He released her nipple between his teeth and lifted his head. She took his mouth, wedging her tongue between his lips with a force that probably surprised both of them. He pinched her clit, and she came.

He pushed another finger into her tight hole, and she came harder.

He surged up, and she clenched around him and came a second time.

Two orgasms crashed into each other like opposing waves, creating one big super wave. It ripped through her body from end to end and back again, reaching the crescendo just as Mitch poured himself inside her, taking her mouth once more and swallowing her gasps and cries, mixing them with his own.

After what felt like hours of sitting in his lap, listening to their mingling breaths and the beat of her pulse in her ears, Paige slipped off Mitch's lap and ducked into his small bathroom to clean up. She returned seconds later to find him standing there with his jeans on and a bouquet of flowers in his hand, along with a bottle of champagne.

She quirked her head to the side as she made her way over to her clothes and quickly got dressed. "What's all this?"

Once dressed, they sat down on *their* couch.

"It's a small thank-you and congratulations gift," he said, handing them to her. Along with a small wrapped box. "You did it. We did it. I couldn't have made this happen without you, and I'm so glad and proud of you for taking the plunge and starting up your own business. You are going to be a huge success, Paige McPherson. Seattle won't know what hit it."

She smelled the flowers, then began to open the gift box. Mitch deployed the cork from the champagne, grabbed two cups from the glass and chrome trolley he had set up with coffee mugs and a Keurig, and poured them each a cup.

He handed her her cup, then sat down next to her just as she pulled out a framed photo of the two of them.

"Who took this?"

Her curious expression prompted his reply. "Jayda took it. I gave her her own camera for her sixth birthday, and she had it at the dinner you made for us all at your parents', remember?"

Paige shook her head. "I was probably so focused on the meal. I've also stopped paying attention to the sound of a photo being taken because you take so many."

His smile was knowing. "I don't even know when she took this, but she did, and she gave it to me the other day. I guess she secretly had Violet get it printed and help her buy a frame. She wanted me to give it to you."

Emotion clutched at Paige's heart.

"She wants you to know that she likes you, she's okay with you being in my life, and she's really excited for your new restaurant. She hopes that one day you'll hire her to be a server. When she's old enough."

Paige hiccupped a small sob and then laughed, wiping the back of her wrist beneath her nose. "I don't know what to say." She ran her hand over the beautiful photo of Mitch and Paige standing in the kitchen at her parents' house. His arms were around her waist, her hands over his shoulders. They were both smiling, staring into each other's eyes and already appearing as in love as they were now. Because she did love him, she hadn't said it yet, but she knew it to be true.

She loved Mitch.

They were in love.

They were happy.

"You have a remarkable little girl," she said, lifting her gaze to Mitch and batting a tear that rolled down her cheek. "And quite the budding photographer."

Mitch smiled and pulled Paige back into his lap, planting a big kiss to the side of her head. His arms around her felt good. "That I do. She also told me to get a good night's sleep tonight—both of us, because we have big days tomorrow."

Paige giggled. "I guess that means round two is out of the question?" She turned in his lap and nipped at his chin.

She was beneath him in seconds, his growl vibrating through her in pleasant waves that made her tingle all over.

"Oh baby, I'd rather have a good fuck with you than a good night's sleep any day of the week. Ain't nothing more therapeutic." Then they went at it again and again until it was the wee hours of the morning.

The morning of the grand opening.

19

MITCH AND PAIGE stood in the small bathroom of his studio. She turned to him and adjusted the collar on his navy button-down shirt, running her hands affectionately over his shoulders. "You look hot," she purred, standing up on tiptoe and kissing his cheek. "I'd book a photo shoot with you just to stare at you."

He growled and wrapped his arm around her waist, tugging her against him. She felt so good in his arms. "You don't have to book a thing. Just be you. My muse." His smile widened, even though the butterflies in his stomach made him feel nauseous. "And if *you* would like to get naked as I take pictures, who am I to stop you?"

She rolled her eyes and nipped his chin. "Maybe once the people are gone and the doors are locked. I have a *very* important catering gig I need to get ready for. Big client. I really want to impress him."

She was all smiles. He loved it when she got playful. It was becoming more and more common as their relationship progressed and Paige slowly came into her own. Since meeting her on the Fourth of July, he'd watched her confidence double, if not triple. She still had insecurities, which she carried around with her like a balloon tied to her belt loop, but they were no longer a bouquet of balloons in a bunch of bright colors that distracted everyone from the person in front of them. Instead it was a single balloon, without helium and the same color as the sky. You'd miss it if you weren't looking for it.

She was finding her calling, finding herself again and embracing it. And he loved that he had a front-row seat to her transformation.

A knock on the bathroom door had them pulling apart as if they were two tweens in a closet doing seven minutes in heaven.

"When you're done having sex in the bathroom, I could really use your take on plating the canapes," Jane called through the door, humor in her tone.

Paige rolled her eyes again and opened the door. "We weren't having sex."

Jane grinned. "Yeah, right. Nothing like a little pre-opening quickie to get the endorphins pumping and put you both in a good mood." She turned her back and headed toward the restaurant.

Paige stuck her tongue out at Jane's back, which made Mitch laugh. He looped his arm around her waist and followed her. "I like the way she thinks." He squeezed her butt. "I could use some endorphins to chase away the jitters. Feel like ducking back in there for a couple of minutes? Boost my confidence."

She glanced up at him with shock in her eyes. "Just a couple of minutes?"

"For the first round. Next round, I'll take my time." He bobbed his eyebrows up and down.

They stepped over the threshold that led from his studio into her restaurant. It wasn't quite finished on the dining side yet, but the kitchen had been up and running for nearly two weeks.

Decadent aromas wafted toward him as they made their way to the kitchen. A timer started going off on the oven, and steam rose from a pot on the stove. Yet everyone in the kitchen, all four members of Paige's staff, seemed calm, collected and competent. There wasn't a frazzled face or nervous person among them.

It was because they had a capable leader who not only led with her heart and her head; her recipes were flawless.

Mitch could attest to that last bit firsthand. Last week, when Paige was finalizing the menu for the opening night, she had forced Mitch to taste-test everything.

Not that she really had to *force* him at all. He'd been a willing guinea pig, squeaking for more. He'd never tasted anything so good in all his life.

Incredible dish after incredible dish graced his plate, only to wow his taste buds moments later. He had not one negative piece of feedback, not an ounce of criticism.

Well, except that she was still wearing clothes when she served him. But that wasn't a complaint about the food, just the service.

Paige hadn't believed him. She thought he was just being kind and had badgered him for critique and suggestions. But he'd truly had none. Everything she'd made had been perfection.

And now that perfection was being executed on a grander scale and by competent people Paige trusted to do her recipes proud.

She stepped out of Mitch's grasp and approached the counter, where Jane had a big tray of little cracker things with what looked like salmon on them all spread out.

Paige flicked her eyes up to Mitch's. "I'm going to make

sure everything's ready here, okay? Let me know when you're opening the doors, and I'll come stand with you."

That was her kind way of telling him to get lost because she had work to do, and she didn't need his incompetent ass in the way.

Message received.

Snickering, he made his way back over to the studio.

His watch said ten minutes to four. The doors opened at four. He hadn't even been paying attention to the sidewalk beyond the front door until a wave and cocky smirk, followed by a subtle knock and more cocky smirks, had him heading to the front door and unlocking it early.

Liam waved a bottle of scotch in the air. It had a big red bow on it. "I came with celebration gifts," he said, handing it over and wandering into the studio, his brother Scott in his wake, along with Zak, Adam's younger brother; Mark and his girlfriend, Tori; Emmett; and Atlas.

He'd never say it, but it meant the world to him that the single dads had come to his opening night to support him. They really did have each other's backs. They really were a family.

Zak slapped him on the shoulder, his smile wide and his blue eyes twinkling. "Glad things with you and Paige are working out." Zak didn't let go of Mitch's shoulder. Instead he squeezed, just a little. "I hope things continue to work out." Zak's smile grew even bigger, showing off perfectly straight white teeth. At the moment, he reminded Mitch of a redheaded wolf, as the man was far too big to be a fox.

Mitch shrugged Zak's hand off and smiled back. "They're working out great, man. No need for the strong-arm."

Zak tossed his head back and laughed. "I like you. You're funny."

"You being my big protector again, Zachary?" came Paige's voice. She made her way toward them and stood next to Mitch, cocking her hip and crossing her arms in front of her chest, glaring up at Zak. "I can take care of myself, you know?"

Zak's smile never shrunk a bit. His pupils dilated, though, and his nostrils flared just slightly. Did he have a secret crush on his brother's ex-wife? Was he hoping for something between him and Paige when Paige and Adam got divorced? He was certainly regarding Mitch's girlfriend with an appraising look of admiration and intrigue.

Paige's foot tapped on the floor. "Hmm?"

Zak scratched the back of his neck and laughed. "Ah, Paige, I'm just looking out for you. You'll always be family." He bent down and gave her a big hug, picking her up so that her feet dangled and a black flat shoe dropped. A frisson of unease weaseled its way up Mitch's spine as he tried not to notice the bunch and flex of Zak's tattooed arms as they squeezed around Paige.

Both Paige and Zak laughed as he set her back down on the ground. She swatted his chest. "I appreciate it. But be nice to Mitch. He's one of the good ones."

"You only date the good ones," Adam said as he and Violet walked in the door, Adam's smile wide and joking.

Paige rolled her eyes. "That's true. My standards are quite high."

Violet embraced her in a hug. "As are mine. Nothing wrong with that."

Paige laughed and agreed. The two women stepped off to the side to chat.

Adam slapped Mitch on the shoulder. "Looks great, man. You did a fantastic job."

Mitch beamed. "Thanks."

All the single dads had spread out around the studio, studying the photos Mitch had carefully selected and hung on the wall. Paige's staff had already started setting up the tables of food, and Mason, Mitch's buddy from high school and a bartender, was almost done setting up the makeshift bar. Mitch was excited because Mason's surrogate was due with Mason's baby any day now. Then Mason could join The Single Dads of Seattle.

It'd be nice to have an ally from the old days around the poker table. As much as he knew he was now an accepted member, once in a while he still felt like an outsider, especially when all the men started talking about their ex-wives and their days *off* when they didn't have their kids. Mitch couldn't relate to that.

He spotted Emmett out of the corner of his eye, as well as his mother and Paige's parents, who had both Jayda and Mira with them.

Everyone who was nearest and dearest to him was now here.

Supporting him.

Celebrating him.

Helping his dream, and Paige's dream, become a reality.

"Drink?" Mason asked, bumping him in the shoulder and bringing a cool, drippy bottle of beer in front of Mitch's face.

Liquid courage.

"Ah, thanks." Mitch accepted the bottle and immediately took a sip.

"Your lady's something special," Mason said, tipping back his own beer and practically emptying half. "A looker and one hell of a cook. You hit the jackpot right there."

Mitch grinned as his eyes followed Paige around the room as she and Violet, now joined by Tori, Mark's girlfriend, wandered slowly around the gallery, looking at all the photos Mitch had taken of Paige. He was sure she was being modest and deflecting their praise. They were still working on her self-esteem and self-love. She'd get there.

Mason snickered next to him. "You've got it bad, man."

Mitch exhaled, shifting his gaze from his woman back to his best friend. "That I do. She's the whole damn package."

Mason held up the hand cradling his beer bottle and used one finger to point at a very sexy, very captivating photo he'd taken of Paige. "That one is *hot*."

He had that right.

Paige wore her black dance bodysuit. Her hair was wild around her, and she had some very seductive bedroom eyes going on. Her smile was small and knowing, as if she had a secret to tell, but the only way she'd reveal it was if he revealed a secret of his own.

"You selling any of them?" Mason asked, admiring another one of Paige. This one was of her using the pasta roller on her mixer to roll out her sfogliatelle dough. Flour dusted her cheeks. Her eyes were bright and her lips set in a thin line as she concentrated on the task.

Mitch shook his head. "Not any of the ones with models. I'll part with prints of my landscapes or wildlife, but most of these are just to showcase what I can do."

Mason nodded, wandering up to the photo Mitch had taken of a blue heron standing in a marsh at sunset. The sky colors behind the bird were a watercolor of pinks and purples, yellows and oranges. The bird held a small fish between its beak, but instead of swallowing it, it simply stood there, staring up at the sky.

"I'll buy a print of that," Mason said. "Lemme know how much. I'll take it in this size, too. It'll look great in my dining room."

A line forming at the door caught Mitch's eye.

The public was here.

It was showtime.

He rested his hand on Mason's shoulder. "I'll give you the friend discount. A painting for booze. How does that sound? I come to your bar, you hook me up with a pint."

Mason was all smiles. "You got it."

Mitch found Paige at his side, and he wrapped his arm around her waist. "Everyone, could we have your attention, please?"

Murmurs and conversations came to a halt, and all eyes fell to Mitch and Paige.

They both took deep breaths.

"We'd just like to thank all of you for coming tonight. This studio has been a big dream of mine for a while, and thanks to all of your love and support, it's finally become a reality. I'm looking forward to taking family, wedding and holiday photos for all of you, and now that I have the proper studio space, I won't be editing those photos in the dark and noisy corner of my kitchen."

Chuckles drifted through the small crowd.

"We have a line forming outside, so we will keep this short. Paige's dream began long before mine. She knew she wanted to cook, to bake, to feed people incredible food since before a lot of us had even had our first kiss. She has worked harder than any person I've ever met, overcome more obstacles than any person ever should, and she has so much to show for it. I know that you're all as proud of her as I am and all that she's accomplished. The Lilac and Lavender Bistro is going to become a Seattle hotspot by year's end, so let's all hope she just takes note of everyone in this room and puts us to the front of the reservation book when we call."

The woman in his arms laughed quietly, but he also heard her hiccup a sob. He didn't look down at her, but he squeezed her tighter against him.

"So please, without any further ado, welcome to Mitchel Benson Photography, and please enjoy the incredible food we have here tonight, courtesy of The Lilac and Lavender Bistro." He nodded at Liam and Scott, whom he had designated as official door openers. "We are open for business!"

20

PAIGE'S FACE hurt from smiling and laughing so much.

They were two hours into the studio opening, and the place was packed to the rafters with friends, family, admirers and photography enthusiasts.

Her food was a huge hit—thankfully—and she'd noticed several people not only entering to win the free photo shoot Mitch was offering but also buying prints and booking photo shoots.

Finally, with a moment to herself, she stole to an empty corner, grabbed a bottle of water and chugged. It was a sweltering August evening, and although the air-conditioning was on full blast, the number of bodies packed into the confined space made for a sauna-like feeling to Paige, who was wearing her black chef's coat.

"Hey, chef." The man Mitch had introduced as Liam sidled up next to her, his plate loaded with her food. Zak and Liam's brother Scott joined him.

"Hey, guys. How's the food?" She scoped out their plates. "Be honest."

They all had mouthfuls, but Zak was the first to speak.

"You know I'll always lick the plate of anything you make, Paige. You're the best cook ever." He pretended to whisper. "Don't tell my grandma that."

Paige smiled. "You know you can go back for seconds, right? You don't have to pile everything on to your plate at once."

He shook his head and picked up a chickpea flour breaded Moroccan spiced chicken tender and dipped it into the mint yogurt it was meant to be paired with. "I took two of everything. I don't want to miss out." He took a bite of the chicken tender. "These are fucking awesome."

Liam and Scott both nodded.

Zak double-dipped his chicken into the mint yogurt again. "Besides, I'm carb loading. I'm running a half marathon tomorrow, need to fuel up."

Paige rolled her eyes. "Sure. Fuel up. Sorry I don't have any fettuccini alfredo for you. I know that's your favorite."

He shrugged, then dove into the pea shoot and Thai peanut mini wrap. "I think I can manage."

"I'm doing a full marathon tomorrow," Scott piped up. "Have to drive twenty-six miles to go pick my kid up from his grandparents tomorrow. Gonna need some fuel for the drive."

Liam snorted. "I just fucking love food. If I gain five pounds from this tonight, I won't give two shits." He swirled his pinky finger into a dollop of apricot chutney on his plate and stuck it in his mouth. "I could fucking drink this shit."

Paige took a sip of her water. "I'll send you home with a jar of it. Just remind me before you leave."

His dark brown eyes went wide. "Oh, I like you." He wrapped an arm around her shoulder and squeezed her into his frame. "Photogenic and a killer cook. If I didn't believe in love, I'd say I loved you."

Zak and Scott groaned and rolled their eyes.

"Not today," Zak said blandly. "We don't need your cynical

diatribe tonight, please. Save it for poker night. Hell, save it for when you're alone in your car, because I'm pretty sure you're the only person who wants to hear it."

Liam released Paige and straightened up, picking up a canape off his plate and popping it into his mouth, shoving it into his cheek before he spoke. "I'm just saying—"

"Yeah, but don't," Zak cut him off. "Just don't."

Liam's face scrunched up before he shrugged and continued eating. "I'm just saying ... "

"Always the last word," Zak grumbled. He directed his attention back to Paige. "How's it all going?"

She nodded. "It's going all right so far. My staff is very competent. They've been replenishing the trays and clearing dirty plates left behind. They're a well-oiled machine. I'm very lucky."

"But how are *you?*" Zak probed. "I mean, your face is plastered all over these walls. Every picture is incredible, but it has to be a bit overwhelming to watch people fawn all over your images."

She'd been trying not to think about that. Whenever she was forced to walk past a photo of herself—which was a lot—she put her head down or looked in the opposite direction. As much as she had okayed Mitch hanging the images of her, she wasn't keen on staring at them.

"It's a little weird," she admitted. "But Mitch says they're some of his best work, and I want him to put his best work out for the public to see, so ... " She toed at a speck on the tile floor. "I guess I have to suck it up and be modest in other ways."

"Or you embrace it and hold your head high," Scott offered, wrinkling his slightly crooked nose. "Those photos are beautiful, you're beautiful, and your food is incredible. No need to be modest about any of it. Be proud."

A warm hand encircled her waist, and lips touched her temple. "I couldn't agree more."

She glanced up and smiled at Mitch.

"The boys keeping you company or driving you nuts?" he asked, offering her a glass of wine. She shook her head. She was still on the clock and wanted to keep a clear mind. She'd celebrate once the doors were locked and it was just her and Mitch left to clean up and decompress for the night.

"They're keeping me company," she assured him. "Making me laugh."

"I hope not at my expense," he joked.

"You came over too soon," Liam added. "We were just about to tell her how terrible you are at poker."

Mitch pretended to look offended. "It's because I have an honest face. Can't lie to save my life."

She wrapped her arm around his waist and rubbed his lower back. "Nothing wrong with that."

"Unless you're betting money," Scott corrected.

"Mitch is going to have to toss in twice as much into the pot now too," Liam added. "Once you've got a lady in your life, your buy-in doubles."

Mitch rolled his eyes. "So Mark and Adam have told me."

Paige spied Jane out of the corner of her eye. Her number two was trying to get her attention.

"Excuse me, gentlemen," she said, squeezing Mitch's muscular back with one hand and Zak's powerful forearm with the other before taking her leave and being whisked off to the kitchen by a nervous-looking Jane. "What's up?" she asked, once they were out of earshot of the masses.

"A food blogger."

Paige squinted in confusion.

Jane's eyes went wide. "A big-time Seattle food blogger and restaurant reviewer is here, and he wants to talk to you."

Dread filled Paige's stomach. "Does he have a complaint?"

Jane shook her head, excitement filling her still-wide eyes. "The opposite. He has nothing but praise. Wants a quote from you."

Tingles raced up and down Paige's arms.

Nothing but praise.

She let out a deep breath and nodded. "I need to just check my hair in the mirror, and then I'll go talk to him." Then she took off toward the restaurant bathroom to go and collect herself, unable to wipe the smile off her face if she tried.

ON CLOUD nine after speaking with the food blogger and reviewer who had introduced himself as Will Gorgehimself, Paige floated around the full studio, checking in on guests and making sure everyone was still enjoying her food. She perused the biggest table and noticed an empty canape plate. The saying shouldn't be *going like hotcakes,* it should be *going like canapes.* At least Paige's canapes. Smiling, she grabbed the empty plate and spun around to head next door again and grab more smoked salmon cucumber canapes when a blast from the past—a blast from high school—blocked out the sun in front of her.

His smile was wide, just like his shoulders, and his big, muscular arm was casually draped around the waist of an attractive redheaded woman.

He walked right up to her.

Paige swallowed.

"Hi, Paige!" He released his wife and didn't bother waiting for Paige to respond before he drew her in for a big hug.

"Garth! Wow, uh, what are you doing here?"

He pulled away, still smiling, and drew his wife back into his embrace. "Our daughter, Lizzie, goes to dance class at

Benson School of Dance. Violet extended the invitation to all the parents."

"Oh!"

Seeing that Garth and Paige were getting caught up after all these years, his wife smiled shyly, then took off in the direction of the makeshift bar in the corner.

"So, how the heck are you?" Garth asked, shoving his large, meaty hands into his pockets. "Looks like you're doing well. You look great." His eyes roamed her body from head to toe, but it wasn't in a creepy predator way, more in just a friendly, long-time-no-see way.

Paige blew out a slow breath. "I am, thanks. Yeah, I just started my own restaurant and catering company." She hooked a thumb over her shoulder. "Next door, actually. We open in a couple of weeks for breakfast and lunch, but I already have a great staff, and we decided to cater this event to test the waters and get people talking about the food."

He grabbed a couple of appetizers off the tray of a passing waiter. "Well, they look amazing. I'm sure your restaurant is going to become the hottest spot in Seattle."

"From your mouth to the ears of the masses."

Paige nibbled on her bottom lip as Garth's dark-blue eyes grew serious. He leaned in closer before he spoke. "I heard you worked with Marcy."

"*Worked* being the operative word. Emphasis on the past tense," she said with a snort before cocking her head to the side in curiosity. "How did you know?"

"Facebook."

"What!"

"She posted about how she was your boss, and then when you quit, she badmouthed the crap out of you."

Ice dripped down Paige's spine. "She what?"

"Don't worry, enough people jumped on her and defended you that she took the post down. We all know the hell she put you through during school. Nobody believed for a second the things she posted."

"What did she post?" Had she spread horrible rumors about Paige? Made fun of her?

Garth shook his head. "It doesn't matter. Nobody believed her, and nobody supported her. Her fall from grace is going to happen, Paige. A little later in life than any of us would have hoped, but it will, trust me. She never had to work for a damn thing in her life. Everything was handed to her, including the money to buy the restaurants. When her dad died, he left her a bunch of cash, and because she had a business management diploma, she thought she could run a restaurant. The one she bought where you worked is her third. She ran off all the staff at the other two and had to close."

Paige's eyes went wide. "They all quit?"

He nodded. "You're not the only person she treats like garbage." He made a face of regret. "You were just who she treated like garbage the longest ... and the worst."

Bile burned the back of Paige's throat. She really didn't want to rehash the past right now. She'd been happy and reveling in the praise of all her admirers before Garth walked in. And yet, the curiosity was overwhelming. Why had Marcy hated her for all those years? Why did she torture her so, try to ruin her life again and again? What had Paige done to warrant such blatant hatred?

Her need to know got the better of her, and she asked the question that had been on her mind for far too long. "Garth, do you know why she hates me? What did I do to her?"

His eyes flicked up to an image behind Paige, and he wandered over to it, encouraging Paige to follow him with a hand at her elbow. "You have a natural beauty," he said quietly. "A smile that just lights up a room." His eyes fell back down to hers, and heat wormed its way into her cheeks.

Garth was still a very handsome man. He had a way of just looking at a person and putting them at ease. Despite his popularity all through school, he'd never been a jerk or a bully. Not only was he popular, handsome and a star athlete, but he was also a really nice guy.

She nibbled on the inside of her lip before speaking. "Thank you."

"That's part of the reason why she went after you the way she did."

She didn't understand, and it must have shown on her face.

"You had the perfect life. Your parents were devoted and there for you. You were sweet and kind, polite and generous. Parents and kids, teachers, they all liked you. They all liked your parents. You were smart. You *are* smart. And you're beautiful. You don't have to wear an ounce of makeup, and you still look like a cover model."

"She told you all of this?" Paige found it hard to believe. Garth had to be embellishing.

His eyes drifted back up to the photo of Paige in the kitchen. "She complained about you all the time to me. How perfect you were. How perfect your life was. She was jealous. Her jealousy fueled her hatred. You had everything she wanted. Her parents never came to her recitals or competitions. She was raised by various nannies and put in day cares. She was given everything but what she wanted most—love, attention, nurturing. So she lashed out, and you were an easy target."

Paige's mind reeled. "I find it hard to believe that Marcy was deep enough to know why she behaved the way she did."

"She doesn't understand *why*, deep down anyway. Marcy isn't a deep person."

"About as deep as a puddle," Paige murmured, averting her eyes.

Garth chuckled, scratching the close-shaved dark beard on his strong jaw. "True enough. No, though. She complained about how perfect you were, your grades, your parents, your life, but she never said that she was jealous of you. But it doesn't take a rocket scientist to figure it out."

Paige's lip twitched. "What did you ever see in her, Garth?"

He rolled his eyes and shook his head. "She was a cheerleader. I was a football player. It was like we were betrothed by the powers that be. I really didn't feel like I had much of a choice."

"Until you did."

"She made it pretty easy."

Paige exhaled. "That she did."

"I hate that I stayed with her that long. That I let it get that far." He dropped his head and shook it, shuffling his feet and shoving his hands back in his pockets. "I'm sorry, Paige."

As nice as it was to see Garth and catch up, Paige would rather talk about the present or the future than let the past bring her down anymore. Her food and Mitch's photographs were an absolute hit, and they were both riding the waves of success. She wanted to keep her high as long as she could.

"What are you up to these days, Garth? Where are you working?"

He lifted his head and pinned her with that dashing smile that had won the hearts of far too many freshman girls to count. "I'm a contractor."

"Oh, cool, and your wife?"

"Deb is a psychologist."

Paige nodded. "Ah, hence the in-depth breakdown of *She who I'd rather not name.*"

His smile said it all. "Guilty."

"Well, I appreciate you guys coming, and it was so nice to see you and catch up." She rested a hand on the side of his shoulder. "Mingle, eat and enjoy. Thanks again for coming, Garth." Then without waiting for him to delve any deeper into Marcy Thibodeaux and why she'd treated Paige like a punching bag for twelve years, Paige took off next door to go and grab more food.

21

HUMMING in time with the music playing in the studio, Paige placed more canapes on the tray in her kitchen. Her belly rumbled, and that's when she realized she hadn't eaten anything since breakfast. Too worried about making sure everyone else had enough food, she forgot to take care of herself.

"No time like the present," she murmured, cramming a canape into her mouth and giggling at her puffy cheeks.

"My sentiments exactly."

She leapt about ten inches off the floor at the sound of a familiar voice behind her.

Tristan.

As happy as Paige had been all day at the success of Mitch's opening, and the crowds enjoying her food, she couldn't mistake the weird niggling sensation that had been going on at the back of her neck all day. As if there was someone out to get her, plotting. Planning to ruin their night in some way. She'd been on alert all night, watching the door for signs of Marcy and any one of her minions, because who was she kidding? If there was anyone who was out for Paige's blood, out to ruin her, it was Marcy Thibodeaux.

Paige knew they weren't finished, not by a long shot.

Thankfully, though, it wasn't Marcy at the door. It was Tristan.

Paige spun around, her mouth still full of food, to find her former boss and friend standing there all tanned and freckled with a big smile on his face.

As happy as she was to see him, she still had a bone to pick with him as well. Once her mouth was empty, she would do just that.

"Didn't mean to scare you," Tristan said, stepping into the kitchen, his arms open wide for a hug. "But when Jill told me you were finally opening up your own place, I had to fly back up and see it for myself."

Chewing as she walked, Paige stepped into the arms of her friend. Her family.

Once they'd hugged for a few seconds and she'd chewed and swallowed her food, she pulled out of his arms and swatted him on the chest. "What the hell, man? You couldn't have called and told me you were leaving?"

Regret stained his face, and his amber eyes tilted downward toward his shoes. "I know. I fucked up."

"Yeah, you did. You were fired by the she-devil, and you didn't even call to tell me. Didn't even call to tell me you were taking off down to Mexico to lick your wounds. I thought we were closer than that. I thought we were *family.*"

He nodded, lifting his head and fixing her with a look that said he knew he'd fucked up and was currently beating himself up repeatedly for it. "I know. I just ... when she fired me, I went into a dark place. I loved that restaurant. It was my family. My blood, my sweat, my tears, and in the blink of an eye, it was gone. A buddy of mine owns a restaurant down in San Felipe, and he invited me to come down for a couple of months to bartend for him. I just needed to get away, regroup and figure out where I want to go from here."

She lifted an eyebrow. "And?"

He ran a hand through his sandy-blond hair. "I want to come back and work in the restaurant industry in Seattle again. I miss the vibe. The camaraderie."

You'd never know that Tristan was on the upper end of his mid-forties. The man looked good for his age and took care of himself. It also helped that he had very few wrinkles and boyish freckles across his cheeks, nose and forehead that made him appear younger than his passport would reveal. Many a woman in the restaurant, both on the front end and in the kitchen, had lusted after him over the years. But as far as Paige knew, he'd never crossed the line, never abused his position as the boss.

His lips thinned into a flat line as he reached into the back pocket of his jeans and pulled out a piece of paper he'd folded in half lengthwise. He handed it to her. "Ms. McPherson, my name is Tristan Green, and I would like to apply for a job, if you have any openings."

Paige took his resume with a small laugh, not even bothering to open it. "I'm still looking for a restaurant manager, somebody to oversee my front-end staff, help with scheduling and booking catering gigs. I also need someone who can manage catering waitstaff. Do you have any management experience?"

The corners of his eyes crinkled, and he lifted one shoulder. "A little bit, but what I lack in experience, I make up for in enthusiasm and willingness to learn. I'm a great team player."

Paige grinned. "I like your can-do attitude, Mr. Green. When can you start?"

"How about right now? You look famished. Eat something and let me finish plating these things." He stepped around her and went to the big stainless-steel sink at the back to wash his hands. "I haven't managed to try anything yet, just got here, but I can only imagine they're all incredible."

He dried his hands and joined her at the counter, where she had already shoved another two canapes into her mouth. He picked one up and took a bite, his eyes going buggy and his full mouth splitting into a big grin. They both had full mouths, but his nod and thumbs-up said he approved.

Paige rubbed his back as a thank you, her mood bolstered even more than before by the return of an old friend. She knew that Tristan was going to be the perfect addition to their growing Lilac and Lavender family. His management skills were incredible, he had loads of contacts, and he was a damn hard worker. With him on their team, they couldn't lose.

She was about to pop one more canape into her mouth when Jane's voice at the door had her pausing her bite and turning around. "Uh, Paige. You might want to get out here. An *uninvited, unwanted* guest has just arrived."

"Who?"

"One guess."

And *drop* went the other shoe.

PAIGE SHOVED DOWN ALL the other emotions clamoring for attention inside of her, releasing the only emotion that truly mattered—pity.

Careful not to put too much of a *march* into her step, she made her way toward Marcy, her head high, shoulders back, nerves somewhat under control.

This wasn't high school anymore.

Marcy wasn't her boss anymore.

Marcy had no power over her.

Marcy had no power.

"Paigey," Marcy said, her lips, the color of fresh blood, turning up into a sneer. "What a *cute* little party. You had to throw your own because you were never invited to any in high school. Poor little Paigey McFatson, always excluded from what the popular kids were doing."

Paige smiled back. "Thank you, but it's *Paige.* You will call me *Paige.* And you know my last name, so use it properly if you're going to use it at all."

Marcy's back went ramrod-straight, her glare ferocious, but Paige wasn't backing down. Paige's daughter was here. She needed to show Mira that her mother didn't buckle to a bully, didn't let herself be walked all over. Mira needed to know that her mother was a strong woman, a woman she could be proud of.

She cocked her head to the side and studied Marcy's face. The woman was painted up and decked to the nines in designer clothes and accessories. She probably sported nearly ten thousand dollars' worth of apparel on her slight frame.

"You can put a dog turd in a Tiffany's bag, doesn't make it a diamond ring," her father used to say.

Marcy Thibodeaux was living proof of that.

Finally, after enjoying the slight tick of unease to Marcy's smoky-shadowed left eye, Paige spoke again. "This party was invitation-only, Marcy, and you were most definitely *not* invited. I'm going to have to ask you to leave."

Marcy's cold blue eyes narrowed at Paige. "Was it now? Huh." Ignoring Paige, she began to wander around the gallery, the look on her face unreadable as she took in all the photos of Paige blown up and hung on every wall. "Photographer a fan of yours? Did he run out of models? Or was he just too cheap to pay them and you offered to do it for free? Anything for attention, right?"

"You need to leave," Paige repeated again, this time throwing a bit more edge to her voice.

Marcy stopped where she stood, turned and pinned her gaze on Paige, her face smug. "No."

Heat at Paige's back and a hand at her waist told her Mitch was behind her. "You've got this," he murmured.

Once again, Marcy's mouth slid up into the smile of an evil queen. Only the difference was Marcy only *thought* she was a queen.

She needed to be enlightened.

She needed to be dethroned.

"Marcy," Paige started, causing the woman's already hard eyes to turn to stone. "This is not high school, and I no longer work at Narcissus. You are not the popular girl making my life difficult. You are no longer my boss making my job unbearable. You're a nobody."

Marcy made a scoffing sound at the back of her throat.

Paige cut her off. "I suggest you leave quietly to save yourself some humiliation before you do something you're going to regret. I'm not afraid of you. I don't even hate you. You have no power over me. You have no power."

Rage flashed in Marcy's eyes, and her mouth opened just slightly.

Paige kept going. "What I do, however, is pity you."

Marcy's eyes went wide.

"I pity that you feel even now, nearly twenty years later, that you still need to bully people. You still need to put people down to make yourself feel better. That this is how you go about each and every day, looking to victimize in order to legitimize yourself."

She didn't need to see them to know that she had more than just Mitch at her back now. She felt their strength, their support, their power. The entire studio had also gone dead quiet.

"I'm sorry that you hated me all through school because I had parents who loved me, who were there for me and supported me. I'm sorry that you hated me because I worked hard and got good grades, that I earned the praise I received from teachers. I'm sorry that people liked me because I was nice to them, because I treated them like human beings with feelings and heart. Most of all, I'm sorry you felt the need to torture me every day to make yourself feel better. That humiliating another person was the only way you could feel happy inside. I'm sorry that you were and continue to be that broken."

A few murmurs behind and around them made Marcy's eyes dart up from Paige's and scan the room. Heat had flooded the woman's high cheekbones, and her nostrils began to flare.

Paige wasn't finished. Marcy had come to Paige, and Paige was finally going to let her have it.

"You made my life a living hell for twelve years. I had to leave the country to escape your torment and the rumors you started about me. But that was also a very long time ago, and we've *all* changed." She lifted an eyebrow. "Well, at least *most* of us have. Most of us are no longer stuck in the past, desperate to hang on to the status and fear we once demanded. What you haven't seemed to learn is that fear makes power brittle. Those who feared you also loathed you. You were not popular because you were well liked; you were popular because people feared you. Well, not anymore. Nobody fears you. All they do is pity you. I pity you. I pity you and your inability to grow and evolve and let go of who you once were and become somebody better. You had that chance over the last fifteen years, and you wasted it.

"This is my place of business, a celebration with family and friends. Of which you are neither. I don't owe you a damn thing. So unless you would like to be forcibly removed by the authorities, I suggest you turn around and leave through the same door you came in."

Paige had been wrong. That wasn't rage she saw glimmering in Marcy's eyes earlier. No, that was nothing compared with the sheer loathing she was regarding Paige with now. Everything inside Paige screamed at her to turn and run. Everything but her heart. Her love for herself.

She loved herself too much to let this woman break her down again.

Paige had had enough.

"I came here to let you know you'll be hearing from my lawyers," Marcy muttered through gritted teeth.

Of course, on all the days she could ambush Paige.

What a bitch.

Paige fought back a laugh. "On what grounds?"

"You poached four of my staff members."

"I'm Ms. McPherson's attorney," Liam said, having somehow emerged at Paige's side. "And you can have your lawyer send all correspondence my way."

Oh, snap!

Marcy had not been expecting that.

It paid to have friends in high places.

Paige kept her smile in check before turning to Liam. "Thank you, Liam, but that won't be necessary. If Marcy bothered to check my very detailed contract, she would see that there is no mention of a noncompete clause in there. I was free to bring any staff members I wanted along with me whenever I left. It wasn't my fault the staff members were more loyal to me than they were to their new boss. It's not my fault that Marcy here is—"

"Up shit creek without a paddle," Paige's father finished.

Oh, Dad!

"Precisely."

Marcy's face resembled a pomegranate. The woman was about to explode.

"I've called the police," came a voice behind them. "They're on their way to escort the trespasser off the premises." Paige turned around to find Jane waving her phone in the air, a giant smile on her face.

All eyes turned back to Marcy. The woman looked like she was going to be sick.

"This isn't over," she growled, her eyes flicking around the room to all the people that had Paige's back, all the people that loved her and that she loved.

Paige took a step toward her and did a small happy dance inside when Marcy took a step back. Paige got right up in Marcy's face, enjoying the unease in the woman's once-fierce eyes. "Oh, but it is over, Marcy. I'm over you. I'm done with you. Your reign as queen has finally come to an end. Now leave before you're made to leave." Then she turned around and showed the woman her back, never turning around, never even caring how she left, whether it was on her own or by police force, because Marcy Thibodeaux no longer mattered.

Marcy Thibodeaux was nobody.

22

A FEW HOURS LATER, only the stragglers remained. Paige's parents had taken Mira and Jayda home so the girls could have a sleepover, Violet and Adam had left as Violet was exhausted and feeling gross, and most of the invitees had thanked Mitch and Paige and then made their exit.

All that remained was the kitchen staff; their bartender, Mitch's friend from high school and soon-to-be-father, Mason; and a bunch of The Single Dads of Seattle.

"Did you call the cops back and tell them they were no longer needed?" Mitch asked Jane as they all sat around the studio on chairs drinking beer and listening to Mason strum his guitar.

Jane's smile was devious. "I never called anybody, but that dumb bitch didn't know the difference. The look on her face when I said the police were on their way will forever be one of my all-time favorite moments. I should have taken a picture of it and made it the wallpaper on my phone." She looped an arm around Paige's shoulder. "Of course getting hired by *the* Paige McPherson to work at her new kick-ass restaurant is *the* best moment in my life, but getting the best of Marcy Thibo*dumb* was a close second." She tipped back her beer and finished it, then wiped the back of her wrist over her mouth. "I'm going to bolt. The mean boss lady wants us here tomorrow at a ridiculous oh nine hundred, so I need to get my beauty rest." She pulled Paige in and planted a kiss on the top of her head. "Love you, mean boss lady, to the moon and fucking back."

Paige rolled her eyes and laughed. "Love you too, Janey Boo."

Jane pulled her arm away and fixed Paige with a mock glare. "It's *Jane,* and you will call me *Jane.*"

The room erupted into laughter as Jane and the other three staff members gathered their things and bid their adieu.

"You've got some great employees," Mark said, his arm casually draped around Tori's shoulder. "They were all very professional and friendly the whole night."

Paige smiled and snuggled into Mitch's side. "Thanks. I think they're pretty amazing too."

"What have you decided on for your logo?" Tori asked. "I know your name is The Lilac and Lavender Bistro, but are you putting those flowers on all your stuff?"

Paige nodded. "I'd like to. I haven't found a graphic designer I like yet, which is stressing me out because we open really soon. I have these ideas percolating around in my mind about what I'd like the logo to look like, and when I explain it to the designers, they say they get it, but when I see what they mock up, I don't care for it." She shook her head with a big sigh. "I'm probably just overly picky. Or what I want is impossible."

"My sister is a graphic designer," Tori said. "She's amazing. Reasonable too, as she's just trying to get her business up and running."

Paige sat up. "Really? Can you give me her contact info?

I'd love to help out a local artist and a fellow start-up. Us entrepreneurs need to stick together."

Tori brought out her phone, and seconds later Paige's phone vibrated in her pocket. "I just sent you all of Isobel's contact info and her website. Ignore the stuff on the side about her dog-walking business. She's also a nanny, though her family just bailed on her last week, so she's looking for another gig."

"A real Jack of all trades," Mitch said with a chuckle. "Or I guess *Jacklin* of all trades."

Tori nodded. "The girl has always had three or four jobs on the go. Never sits still, works her ass off. I don't know the last time she had a full day off. But she likes it that way."

Liam, who had been unusually quiet in the corner, given how chatty he'd been with Paige earlier in the evening, suddenly sprang up from his seat and plastered his phone to his ear. "Hello?" He wandered off to the other side of the gallery, a worried look on his handsome face.

All the single dads in the group exchanged concerned looks.

Scott, Liam's brother, stood up and wandered over to Liam but made sure to stand back a touch, as Liam's eyes were suddenly teeming with tears.

The mood in the room shifted, and everyone grew quiet and still. Mason stopped playing his guitar, and they all just sat there, watching Liam and Scott.

Finally, Liam hung up. His mouth was in the saddest, deepest frown Paige had ever seen.

"Fuck," Mitch murmured beside him, "I hope nothing happened to Jordie."

Scott and Liam spoke with their heads drawn down. Scott's eyes went wide, and then he brought his brother in for a hug. It was odd to see the Dixon brothers looking so serious. For the entire night, they'd been chatty and kept everyone in stitches.

Once again, everyone exchanged curious and concerned glances across the studio.

Without a word to anyone, Liam left, his head hung low and his whole body shaking.

Scott rejoined the group, his own eyes a touch watery.

"Jordie okay?" Mark asked, standing up and approaching Scott.

Scott swallowed. "Yeah, he's fine. It's just a friend and colleague of Liam's just died."

Mark hung his head. "Oh no."

Murmurs of sorrow and condolences filled the room.

"He's got to go deal with a bunch of shit now. They were like best friends."

"Fuck." Zak ran his hands through his dark red hair. "It was Dina?"

Scott nodded.

Zak blew out a breath and hung his head, shaking it. "She belonged to the gym."

"Liam is her in-case-of-emergency person, seeing as her brother was a SEAL and often away on a mission. Liam's gone to call Aaron now."

Silence fell among everyone as they took in the gravity of the situation. They didn't know the woman that had died, but it was the friend of a friend, and given how much loss Adam, Violet, Mitch and Paige had been through over the last few years, the news of any death was jarring.

That was the cue for their night to end.

Slowly, the studio emptied, leaving just Mitch and Paige to clean up.

Mitch locked the front doors and turned up the music, and Paige put a doorstop between the studio and the restaurant so that she could come and go between the two, and then they went to work.

They worked in a companionable and comfortable quiet. Once in a while, he'd stop her mid-stride as she carried a tray back to her restaurant and plant a kiss on her lips or grab her butt cheek. It was these small touches of intimacy that meant the most to her, that she found herself craving and looking forward to, each time they caught each other's eye across the room.

She was excited for the days when they worked next door to each other and he would pop by for a kiss or she would bring him lunch and they could cuddle up on his couch and eat together.

The countdown was on, and she couldn't wait.

It was nearly eleven o'clock by the time they finished tidying up, and both collapsed on the couch, limp-limbed, tired-eyed and pleased as punch. Mitch handed her a glass of white wine and then grabbed her legs and draped them over his lap, pulling her shoes off and running the pad of his thumb up the length of her instep.

"Holy mother of God." Paige shut her eyes and melted into the couch. "That feels incredible."

He kneaded her heel and the ball of her foot, working his long, nimble fingers in between each of her toes and working out the aches and cramps she didn't even know she had.

"You did it, baby," he purred, trailing one hand up her ankle and calf to massage those tight muscles. "Everyone loved your food. There was nary a crumb left over."

She didn't bother to open her eyes. She wasn't sure if she could. She simply hummed a reply. "Mhmm. I'm glad."

Mitch's warm, throaty chuckle swept over her. "And the way you stood up to—"

She cut him off. "Don't say her name. She's *Voldemort*. She who must not be named."

"But then you give her power."

"You can't give power to nobody. I just don't want the discussion of her to harsh my buzz right now. Her name is a total downer. I'm close to an orgasm from what you're doing right now, the wine is flowing through my veins, and I just successfully completed my first catering gig. Let me enjoy this."

The rumble from his laughter vibrated through his fingers and into her feet. She was closer than ever to coming. How did he do it?

"You earned every orgasm, every buzz, every bit of happiness flowing through you, baby." He switched to her other foot and delivered the same exquisite torture he'd given to the other one.

Unable to control the moan that slid up her throat and past her lips, Paige let her hand wander until she felt Mitch's hard-on beneath her thigh.

"Do you have a condom?" she asked, rubbing his length and enjoying the feel of him growing beneath her palm.

"Feeling like we need to keep this celebration going?"

"Mhmm."

"Front pocket."

She didn't open her eyes. It was more fun going on a blind hunt in search of the treasure. In search of the golden foil packet.

She was scheduled to meet with her doctor shortly after Labor Day to finalize everything for her surgery. Once it was done and she was through the recovery period, she and Mitch could throw away the condoms and go without.

Now *that* would be a day to celebrate.

She couldn't wait to feel just him inside her. No barrier, no protection. Because the last thing she needed protection from was Mitch. Mitch would never hurt her. Mitch had done nothing but save her. He taught her how to love herself again, how to go after her dreams and face her nightmares.

She wanted him to come to her doctor's appointment with her, be her rock, an extra set of ears and the hand she knew she'd need to hold.

He released her foot, and she suddenly found herself beneath him. She pressed the condom to his chest at the same time she finally opened her eyes.

His smile stole the oxygen clear from her lungs.

"Be proud of yourself, Paige." He wedged her knees apart and settled himself between her legs. They were both still fully clothed, but she knew they wouldn't be for long. Besides, there was something erotic and fun about making out on a couch completely dressed. It wasn't just the extra layers of fabric between them but also the anticipation, the frustration, the tease of slowly undressing the other person to reveal another patch of bare skin.

His lips fell to her collarbone. "Be proud of yourself and *all* that you've accomplished. And I'm not just talking about opening up the restaurant or the successful catering gig tonight. Be proud of *everything* you've done." He lifted his head and stared directly into her soul. "Since meeting you, I've watched a transformation like nothing I've ever seen. It was a privilege to see you regain your confidence, to see you find your footing, find your zest and passion again. I love watching you with Mira. You're an incredible mother, and you spoke up for yourself and asked for shared custody. You're moving out of the pool house, and you faced your demons. Or should I say *the* demon. You put Voldemort in her place."

A tear slipped down the side of Paige's head into her ear. "I love myself again," she whispered. "And it's because of you."

He shook his head. "It wasn't me, baby. It was all you, and

don't you forget that. All I did was show you the way the world sees you. Your beauty, your confidence, and everything you have to offer. It pained me when you couldn't see it for yourself, when you viewed yourself with such blinders on."

"But you pulled off the blinders. You saw something in me that I thought was lost, that I didn't think anyone else could see anymore."

He pulled at the fabric on the shoulder of her black T-shirt and planted a kiss on her bare skin. "And now the world can see it. Now the world can see how much you are loved and how much you love."

She brought his mouth down to hers, but before they kissed, her tongue stole out and slid across his lips. "I hope the world can see how much I love you. Because I do love you, Mitch. So much."

She felt him smile against her lips. "It can, and so can I. But right now, let's keep the world out and just focus on us."

"Sounds good to me."

23

PAIGE'S DOCTOR stopped typing on her laptop and leveled her gaze at Paige. "How did your consultation with the surgeon go?"

Paige nodded. "It went well."

"He went over everything you're to expect? Your recovery time, how to take care of the incision?"

They'd been through all of this. Why did they have to rehash it all? Sighing, she nodded again. "He did. But I *have* been through two cesarians, so I know how it goes."

Dr. McKinnon's head bobbed. "Right. Okay, well, a tubal ligation *is* different than a cesarian. Similar recovery time but very different surgeries."

"They're removing something either way," Paige said blandly, frustrated that they had to keep talking about this.

Dr. McKinnon didn't seem fazed in the least with Paige's impatience. She just kept talking. "You're on the list for the surgery, but Sandy in reception said she's having issues with your insurance company. Could you please update her with any new information before you leave?"

Paige nodded and frowned. "I switched insurance

providers because I left Narcissus. This new insurance company is putting me through the wringer." She growled. "It's ridiculous."

The doctor's eyes turned worrisome. "You quit your job?"

"I was fired, actually."

The doctor paused from where she'd bent her head to type something on her laptop again, and a look of confusion but also worry passed behind her dark gray eyes. "Well, this is new news since the last time we spoke. What's changed?"

"I've started my own restaurant. I'm renting a small space. We've been open for less than a week, but we're already really busy."

Dr. McKinnon's mouth drew down into a small frown. "Are you going to be able to take time off for recovery? New businesses can be hard."

Ever since that night where she'd told ol' Marcy *Voldemort* Thibodeaux to take a hike, Paige hadn't let a damn thing fluster her. She was like a new person. Confident, calm and in control. She glanced at her lap, where Mitch's fingers were laced with hers. "I have hired incredible staff. My manager will take over where I need him to, and my kitchen staff are like family. They have my back one hundred percent. I'm not worried at all." She lifted her eyes back to Dr. McKinnon's. "I *need* this surgery."

Dr. McKinnon pressed her lips into a thin line. "I understand. Just know that it has a long recovery time, so you may have to miss work."

"No, she doesn't," Mitch blurted out.

Paige spun in her chair and faced him. What on earth was he talking about?

Dr. McKinnon said it for her. "Excuse me? What are you talking about?"

"She doesn't have to get the surgery," he said.

Paige pulled her hands free from Mitch's just as frustration flooded her veins. She thought she had his full support. They'd been through this. He was on board. Why the heck was he switching gears now?

"That's not your decision to make," Dr. McKinnon said slowly, her gray eyes turning hard as they lasered in on Mitch. "Perhaps you should step outside if you're not going to be supportive of Ms. McPherson's decisions."

Mitch shook his head. "No, that's not what I mean." He turned his body and reached for Paige's hands again. Reluctantly, she let him take them. "What I mean is, you don't have to make the choice. Let *me* make the choice."

Paige's eyes darted to Dr. McKinnon. Neither of them was following his train of thought, though neither of them was a fan of the direction it was heading, either.

Mitch let out a sigh. "Let me get the procedure."

Dr. McKinnon's face split into a big smile. "You want a vasectomy?"

Mitch pinned his gaze on her. "I'm willing to get one, yes."

The doctor's eyes softened, and her smile grew wide. "That's quite generous of you."

Paige could feel her hackles beginning to rise. Was the doctor flirting?

"You do realize that there is a bit of a recovery time," Dr. McKinnon said.

Mitch nodded. "Yes, but it's like three or four days with a bag of frozen peas on my nut sack and a jock strap keeping my balls from swinging, right? Nothing like what Paige would have to go through."

Dr. McKinnon stifled a chuckle. "In a manner of speaking, yes. Your recovery time is far less. It's also an in-office, non-invasive procedure. No scalpel, just a bit of freezing and then pain medication afterward. More and more men are choosing to go this route to save their partners from having to have major surgery or continue to take hormonal birth control. If you're finished having children, it's a very safe and effective way to prevent pregnancy."

Paige's mouth opened in awe, and her eyes were wide. She lifted her head and fixed Mitch with a look she hoped he interpreted right. "You don't have to do this," she said softly. "I would never ask you to go through with something like this."

He was all smiles. "Baby, I am happy with Jayda. And now I also have Mira. Two perfect little girls. That's all I want. That's all I need. I'm done having children."

She stroked her thumb over the back of his hand. "You might change your mind later."

"I won't. I don't need any more kids. But what I do need is you. You're it, babe. You're my forever. And if you want me for forever, I'll hop up on the doctor's table right now and pull my pants down. I'm not afraid to get it done."

"Uh, that's not how it works," Dr. McKinnon said quickly. "I'll need to send in a referral."

Mitch rolled his eyes. "I'm aware of that." He turned back to face Paige. "My dad had one. A few of my friends have had them. It's no big deal. Hashtag real men get vasectomies."

Paige snorted. "Is that a trending thing?"

He was all smiles again as he lifted her hand to his mouth and planted a small kiss to the inside of her wrist. "No, but it should be." He turned back to the doctor. "Fire up your referral machine and send it off. I'm done with my swimmers. They've swum their final lap." He made the *snip-snip* motion with his fingers. "I'm ready to go out in the rain without a coat on."

Dr. McKinnon's bottom lip dropped and her mouth opened, but no words came out. Mitch had rendered the poor woman speechless. Paige fought down the chuckle that threatened to flee up in her throat.

She was speechless too, but for a different reason.

Mitch was saving her from surgery, from recovery, from

missing work and compromising her new business, saving her from getting pregnant again, saving her from heartache. Mitch was saving every part of her.

Because he loved her.

He wanted her and only her. Wanted her for his future, for forever.

A tear trickled down her cheek. "You're sure?"

"One hundred and ten percent. Why would I put you through that if I didn't have to? I love you, Paige, with my whole heart, and I want you to know that I'll do anything for you."

She choked back a hard sob. "I love you too."

"Enough to let me do this for you? For us? For our family?"

Our family.

"Because that's what we are. You, me, Jayda and Mira. We're a family."

She nodded. "Okay."

He leaned forward and wiped away her tears with the pad of his thumb, leaving his hand gently cupping her jaw. "I couldn't save Melissa, but I can save you. Save you from more heartache, from surgery and pain."

Her throat burned from fighting back the tears. She couldn't fight them any longer, and she collapsed against him, the sobs wracking her entire body as she cried against the soft cotton chambray of his shirt. She heard light footsteps and then the opening and soft click of the door. Dr. McKinnon was giving them a moment.

"Let it out, baby," Mitch whispered, rubbing her back. "Let it out. You put on such a brave front, but you don't have to with me. Let me take care of you. I could see it in your eyes this morning that you were nervous about the surgery, even though you refused to admit it."

She pulled away from him. He already knew her so well.

Something had been eating at her for days, and she couldn't quite put her finger on it. But now that Mitch said it out loud, she realized he was right. It was fear. She was afraid of the surgery. Afraid of the recovery and taking time off from the restaurant. She'd just been so hell-bent on getting her tubes tied that she refused to acknowledge the fear of everything that came with it.

With more hot tears running down her cheeks, she shook her head. "How do you know me so well?"

"I know what I love," he said with a simple shrug. "And I love you."

EPILOGUE

Eight LONG months later ...

PAIGE WAS JUST CLOSING the door after putting Jayda and Mira down for the night when her phone in her back pocket began to ring.

It was Mitch.

He'd been away for the last three days on a photo shoot in San Francisco and was due home in less than an hour. While the girls were at school yesterday, Paige had run out and gotten a bikini wax, eyelash extensions and her brows threaded. The lingerie she'd ordered online had also arrived that morning, and she was wearing it beneath her clothes, just in case.

"Hello?" she answered in the sexiest voice she could think of on the spot.

"It's official!" he hollered into the phone so loud she had to pull it away from her ear.

"It is?" Her whole body turned to molten lava from those two little words.

"Damn straight, baby. I'm sterile. No more sperm. No

more condoms. We can raw-dog it for life." He let out a *whoop whoop*.

She rolled her eyes. "Such a romantic."

"You better be naked when I get home, and I want to see that box of condoms in the garbage," he said with humor in his tone. "I've waited far too long to feel nothing between us." He grunted. "Fuck, I'm hard as a goddamn rock."

Paige's pussy clenched and her nipples pebbled beneath her corset. She'd waited far too long as well.

"How far are you from home?"

"Fifteen minutes tops. Just left SeaTac."

She made her way into their bedroom and lay down on their bed, letting her hand slowly make its way beneath her yoga pants and into her G-string. "I can't wait. I may have to start without you."

Mitch groaned on the other end. "You can start, but don't you dare finish."

She flicked her clit with her thumb, and her eyes fluttered shut. "Deal."

The call disconnected, and she pulled her hand free, stood up and got undressed.

As he'd so gallantly offered, Mitch had gotten a vasectomy six months ago. Only the man must've had super sperm, because after the mandatory four-week waiting period between the procedure and the test, he still had quite a healthy count of active swimmers. They had to wait another month to re-test him. And when they did, the poor guy still had a count. There were less viable sperm this time, but there were still enough little Mitches doing the backstroke in the specimen cup for the doctor to caution them. So they had to remain vigilant and keep their condom supply stocked.

They were now six months post-procedure and Mitch had submitted his third sample to the lab right before he left for

San Francisco. They'd been impatiently waiting for the call, for the all-clear. And now they finally had it.

They were safe.

Safe from pregnancy.

Safe from miscarriage.

Safe from heartache.

Sure, nothing was one hundred percent, but nobody got out of life alive, so there was no sense dwelling on odds and probability when the time they had on this earth could be enjoyed to its fullest. Mitch had taught her that.

Mitch had taught her a lot.

Mitch had saved her.

He'd saved her from herself. From the downward spiral she'd been so caught up in for much too long. From the negative thoughts she couldn't tune out, from the self-deprecation and feelings of failure.

Mitch had shown her the beauty inside her and all the amazing things she had to offer the world. He reminded her that contrary to what the voices in her head said, she was a good mother, an amazing chef and worthy of not only self-love but love from others as well. She had lost a lot in the last few years, and because of that, she nearly lost herself. But Mitch had shown her a way to climb out of the well. He'd helped her find the footholds and the crags to hold on to. Sure, once in a while she'd slip, lose her footing and let a negative thought or a negative person impact her day and drag her down into the dark. She knew now, though, that Mitch and the girls were always there to throw a hand over the edge and haul her back up into the light, to bring her out of the bleakness and despair and remind her of all the good in her life, all the incredible things she had going for her.

Once out of her clothes, she reclined back on the bed in her black and cream corset, thigh-highs and G-string. She'd never felt so sexy in all her life.

She wasn't sure what had come over her the day she ordered the set online. But when the ad popped up in her newsfeed, she hadn't been able to get the idea of surprising Mitch with the outfit out of her head. It had bombarded her thoughts for an entire day, even disrupting her sleep. So at three thirty in the morning, unable to close her eyes without the image of her in the satin and lace out of her mind, she'd reached for her phone and ordered the lingerie.

It had arrived yesterday, and she'd been itching to try it on.

It fit like a dream.

With the remote, she dimmed the bedroom lights and hit the button for the automatic blinds to go up. It was dark outside, the moon was out and full, and they had no neighbors. Why not make love under the light of the moon? Just like their first night together in the backyard.

It was too chilly outside to go lay in the hammock in the backyard, even though it was April. The weather had been particularly damp and cold this spring. But she looked forward to warm evenings in the coming summer spent swaying in the hammock, drinking wine and making love.

At such a thought, she pushed her hand back beneath her G-string and rubbed her fingers over her clit. She was already wet, and her pussy throbbed for more attention.

She heard the garage door go up.

He was home.

MITCH TOOK the stairs two at a time.

His cock throbbed in his jeans with each stride.

But none of that mattered.

What mattered waited for him just down the hall. Just beyond the closed door.

Muted light peeked beneath the door, and he could hear a faint buzzing sound as his hand landed on the latch.

He pushed down a groan and adjusted the crotch of his jeans before he turned the latch and swung open the door.

Holy fucking hell.

Paige, on the bed, in black satin and lace with her hand between her legs and the purple end of a vibrator sticking out the top of her G-string was the most incredible thing he'd ever seen.

His woman.

His.

Her red lips parted just slightly, and her stunning eyes remained closed. She'd obviously heard him thundering up the stairs, if she hadn't heard the garage door open and close directly beneath their bedroom. Yet she hadn't stopped. She was continuing to take care of herself.

Fucking hot.

Mitch was about to tear his clothes off and pounce, spread her luscious thighs and sink into her sweet heat when the snap-happy photo geek in him elbowed his way forward. He pulled his camera bag off his back and retrieved his lens, fixing it to the front and turning on the camera.

Paige's eyes fluttered open, and she smiled a lazy, sexy smile. "Welcome home," she purred, not bothering to stop.

His mouth split into a big grin as he brought the camera strap over his neck and played with the settings.

"You're not taking pictures of me masturbating," she said, pulling the vibrator free from her pussy and turning it off. "I'll pose for a lot of things, but I draw the line there."

He took a practice shot, studied it on the screen, then adjusted the settings once more. "Wouldn't dream of it. But I would like to take a few of you dressed like that." He released the snap on his jeans and pulled the waistband down just enough to reveal head of his cock. Her eyes lasered in, and she licked her lips. "For my eyes only, of course," he said.

"Just like that is for me and only me?" she whispered.

He nodded. "Only you, baby. Now just lie there and do your thing. Be your natural, beautiful self. Let me do all the work." He began snapping photos of her, moving about the room to get different angles and work with the lighting. She moved a little here, a little there.

She was a natural.

The camera loved her.

Mitch loved her.

"Enough," she breathed, licking her lips and pinning her light brown eyes on him. The gold around her pupils seemed to glow in the soft lamplight. "We've waited a hell of a long time for this," she said, pushing herself up against the pillows, spreading her legs and propping up her knees. Inviting him in. "Don't make me wait any longer."

She didn't have to tell him twice.

Mitch pulled the camera strap over his head, tossed the Canon down onto the chair in the corner and was naked in less that three seconds. He leapt up onto the bed, prowling toward his woman on all fours, admiring the way her dark, curly hair brushed the tops of her breasts as they practically heaved out of her tight corset.

He hovered above her, his body between her legs. "Where'd you get this?" He ran his fingers gently down the front of the bodice, then up again, dipping a digit beneath the cup and pulling out a dark, taut nipple.

"Online," she breathed, arching her back and pushing her breast toward him.

He obliged and took the crimson bud between his lips and into the heat of his mouth, swirling his tongue around and around, pulling on it with his teeth until he earned the sharp intake of breath and then a satisfied moan from the woman beneath him.

Paige's hands traveled down his back, her nails scraping against his skin. She'd leave marks. She always did. He loved it.

"We've waited so long, baby. I can't wait to be inside you," he murmured against her breast, lifting his head and circling her nipple with his tongue.

"Less talk, more action," she panted, cupping his butt and digging her nails into the flesh of his ass.

He hissed from the pain. But that didn't mean he didn't like it.

He liked the pain.

Liked the way it made him feel.

Alive.

Energized.

Propping himself up on one arm, he pushed the fabric of her flimsy G-string to the side, drawing his fingers up between her plump, damp folds. As much as he wanted to taste her, he wanted to feel her wet heat surrounding him more.

"Mitchel ... " she moaned.

He plunged two fingers into her and pumped. She squeezed her muscles around him, drawing him deeper inside her. The ridges of her channel pulsed against his fingertips.

Pain sprinted down his spine as two hands were thrust into his hair and fingers tugged hard on the roots.

"For fuck's sake, fuck me," she demanded, heaving hard on his hair until he was forced to lift his head and their eyes locked. "We've waited so long for this. Stop messing around."

A smile tugged at the corner of his mouth. Her impatience was adorable.

One eyebrow drew up half an inch on her face. "Don't you

smirk at me. Either fuck me or fuck off so I can finish the job you interrupted." He could tell she was struggling not to smile, which only made his grin grow wider.

She threw her head back on the pillow and laughed, tugging harder on his hair. "Don't laugh. I'm serious here."

"Blue ovaries?" he joked.

Her hips jumped off the bed. "Something like that."

"We can't have that, now, can we?" He kissed her, slow and lazy. Taking his time, he pried her lips apart with his tongue and pushed inside, exploring the contours of her mouth, tangoing with her tongue, sucking on it and nipping her bottom lip. And only once he knew she was caught up in the kiss did he slip inside her.

Her reaction was everything he hoped for. She paused the kiss, went still beneath him, then melted into the mattress and let out a sigh into his mouth. Her fingers relaxed in his hair, her lips and tongue stilled, and she squeezed her muscles around him.

"That's it, baby," he purred, beginning to move, lifting his head to look at her. "I'm not going anywhere. I'm right where I want to be. Forever."

Paige's arms flew out to the sides of the bed, and her fingers bunched in the sheets. Her eyes squeezed shut, and her mouth slightly parted.

Fuck, she was beautiful.

Stroke after stroke, he watched her body climb the mountain, watched her bite her lip, scrunch her face, gasp as he hit that sweet spot deep inside her. He wasn't going to last much longer. The anticipation for the last several hours, fuck, of the last several months had pushed away all his stamina.

Paige's eyes fluttered open, and what he saw staring back at him damn near made his heart explode.

Never in a million years did Mitch think he could ever love again. Ever love a woman as fully as he loved Melissa.

But Paige had changed all of that. What he'd had with Melissa would forever remain special and unique. She was his first real love, the mother of his child, and he would never stop loving her.

But he and Paige had something unique too.

Paige had given him exactly what he needed and when he needed it the most—hope.

She let him in, let him show her that she wasn't broken, that she was a good mother, an amazing chef and a wonderful person. He brought her out of the darkness, and she brought him out of his. Together they held the light. They had a future. A future together.

"Marry me."

Mitch stilled.

"Marry me," she said again.

His mouth split into a big smile before he said, "I'm the one who's supposed to do the asking."

She lifted her hips to meet his, her impatience at his sudden pause coming across in how hard she squeezed him. He started moving again but struggled to concentrate on his rhythm.

"It's the twenty-first century, Mitchel," she breathed, clearly enjoying the way he'd slowed right down and languidly slid across her slick channel. "We're raising women. Get with the times. Besides, I'm not asking." She squeezed her muscles around him again, and something primal flashed behind her eyes. Neither of them was going to last long. "Marry me."

Her strength. It was one of the things he loved most about her.

Even when she appeared to be circling the drain, at her lowest, there was a hidden strength inside her that was unparalleled. She was the epitome of *what doesn't kill us makes us stronger.* Paige was the strongest woman he knew.

"Mitch ... " Her hands wrapped around the back of his neck, and she pulled his mouth down to hers, tracing his lips with her tongue. "I want to be your wife."

A groan rumbled at the back of his throat as he supported himself on one elbow and leaned over to his nightstand. He was determined to stay inside her, so it took a bit of effort, but he got the drawer open.

"We don't need a condom," she said, impatience thick in her tone. "And you still haven't answered me."

He found what he was looking for and grabbed it, shut the drawer and returned to her. "What's a proposal without a ring?" he asked, opening the box with as much finesse as he could muster given how close he was to an orgasm and that he was trying to balance on one elbow.

Now it was her turn for her mouth to drop open.

"This was not how I'd planned to give it to you, but you have a way of surprising me."

Tears welled up in her beautiful brown eyes.

"Yes," he said softly, pressing a light kiss to her lips. "Yes, I will marry you." Then he took her hand from around his neck and released the cushion-cut diamond solitaire from its velvet bed and slid it onto her finger.

Just like Mitch inside Paige, the ring fit perfectly.

"I love you," she said, holding the ring out beside his head to get a better look.

"And I love you."

Then he took her mouth, took her body and together they came undone, with nothing between them ever again.

LIVING WITH THE SINGLE DAD - SNEAK PEEK

SINGLE DADS OF SEATTLE BOOK 4

Chapter 1

His feet were made of fucking concrete.

His heart the same.

People visiting babies in the NICU shouldn't have to pay for fucking parking. They shouldn't have to pay for squat. A human that weighed less than a fucking house cat was fighting for her life in a plastic box, hooked up to only God knows how many electrodes and monitors, and they were charging him to go and see her. They would also charge him to keep her there, to keep her alive.

And if he couldn't pay?

Would they pull the plug on a one-month old?

This country was so fucked up.

Pay to live. Pay to be kept alive.

Hippocratic oath his fucking left nut.

You were only worth saving if you could afford it.

Thank Christ he could pay.

Dina made good money as a lawyer. She'd made sure Sophie would want for nothing.

Except her mother.

She'd want her mother.

She'd need her mother.

Fuck.

Aaron needed his sister.

Grief ensnared him, digging its razor-sharp claws into every cell of his body and shaking him like a ragdoll. He pounded his fists on the steering wheel, hollering at the top of his lungs until tears rolled his cheeks and his throat was raw.

How?

How could this have happened?

He'd spoken to Dina on the phone not two days ago. He was on his way back from a wedding in the South Pacific and couldn't wait to go see Sophie. Dina said that they were getting ready to take her off the ventilators and that if her glucose stayed steady and she could breathe on her own then they might be able to bring her home soon.

Home.

To Dina's condo.

To the nursery his sister had spent hours decorating. Where the crib he'd built for his niece sat waiting for her to sleep in.

The home his sister had created for a child she'd longed for her entire life, and then finally decided to go it alone when she knew her clock was ticking and she hadn't found the right man yet.

They were going to raise Sophie together.

She would be the mother. The world's best mother, and he would the cool uncle who spoiled his niece rotten. He would be the one to buy her her first tutu, her first horseback riding lessons, her first phone, her first car. He'd also be the tattooed muscle at the front door to intimidate the shit out of any boy that tried to mess with his precious Sophie.

From the first moment he laid eyes on her after Dina had her, he'd fallen in love and had vowed to protect her with everything that he was, everything that he had. He would gladly lay down his life for his niece.

He'd also said all that when he knew Dina would be doing the majority of the child raising. When he knew she'd be doing all the hard stuff, like diapers and discipline.

But now, he was all Sophie had.

He was her everything. Mother, father. Uncle, aunt.

There was no *cool* uncle status anymore. Just the overwhelming responsibility of being everything she needed.

Sophie wouldn't be running to him when her mother brought down the hammer, pissed her off and she needed somebody to talk to. Now he was going to have to be the one to bring down the hammer. Who would she run to?

Two days.

Two days ago his sister had been alive. She'd been happy, madly in love with her daughter and both excited and scared to embark on her new role as a mom.

"Give her a kiss for me," Aaron had said, as he stood in line with his boarding pass in his hand. He'd been out of town for ten days his buddy Rob's wedding in French Polynesia and was just heading back to the States. "I can't wait to see how much she's grown and changed."

"She's doing so well. Gained nearly a pound and half, her jaundice is gone and she's starting to nurse a bit. Which is amazing, because I fucking hate pumping and my boobs are constantly sore. I look like a porn star."

"Not an image I want to conjure up about my sister, thanks."

Dina chuckled into the phone. Aaron had always loved his sister's laugh. It was so big and loud and full. You knew she put her whole soul into her laugh. "Whatever. One day you'll have a wife or whatever and she'll be complaining of the same shit."

Aaron made a noise in his throat that said he wasn't sure he agreed. He couldn't see himself settling down anytime soon—if ever. "We'll see." He approached the desk before the jet bridge and handed the attendant his boarding pass and passport. "But listen, sis, I'm about to board. I can't wait to see the little monkey ... and Sophie too."

"Ha. Ha." He could practically see her eye roll from across the globe.

Then they'd said they loved each other, like they always did before they said goodbye on the phone, and they hung up. And that was last time he spoke to his baby sister before she was gunned down during a mass shooting in a mall as she was busy picking out preemie baby clothes for Sophie.

His baby sister, the only person he'd ever loved, his best friend in the entire fucking world was gunned down in a goddamned shopping mall while buying baby clothes for her premature daughter who was back at the hospital breathing via machine.

It would never sink in.

Never.

How did shit like this happen?

How?

Still unable to move from behind the driver's seat of his black Chevy pickup truck, Aaron Steele, retired Navy SEAL and special operative stared straight ahead at the sign for hospital parking and how much it would cost him an hour to go and sit with his one-month old niece who'd been born one month premature. To stare at her little body as it struggled to live, knowing that she would never see her mother again. Knowing that she would never know the sound of her mother's voice, the feel of her mother's lips on her soft baby cheeks, her arms around her.

Sophie was in there fighting for her life, and in the blink of an eye her mother's life had ended.

How in the fuck did this make any goddamn sense at all?

How was Aaron supposed to get out of the truck, walk into the hospital and go be a father to Sophie? He had no idea how to be a father. He'd never had a father to know how to be one, let alone a good one. He could hardly take care of himself. He wasn't even sure he ever wanted kids.

Cool uncle had been fine with him.

Love them until they're annoying and then pass them back to their parents.

Win-win for everyone. Mainly him.

But all that changed in a fucking instant, and now he was a dad. He was a single dad with a one-month old daughter who would never know her mother, and he had no fucking clue where to start.

A knock on his window had him reaching for the gun on his hip. Only he wasn't carrying a gun today. He hadn't carried a gun in two days and he wasn't sure he ever would again.

The only thing that stops a bad guy with a gun is a good guy with a gun.

Yeah, fucking right. He called bullshit. Where the hell had the good guy with the gun been when his sister was in the baby boutique bleeding out?

The only person who should have a gun is a fucking sane person with proper training and a fucking permit.

You needed a license to own a dog, to drive a car, to catch a fish, why the fuck didn't you need one to own a goddamn weapon?

Another knock on the window and a confused face brought his thoughts back to the present.

Liam stared at him through the window, his brown eyes as hollow as Aaron's heart. He'd been one of Dina's closest friends and colleagues. He was Dina's *in case of emergency* person because Aaron had been a SEAL for so long and not always around. It was Liam who'd called Aaron with the news about Dina.

Aaron rolled down the window.

Liam's throat undulated on a hard swallow. The man looked like complete shit. Dark bags under his eyes, messy dark blond hair, days and days worth of scruff.

He looked how Aaron felt.

"Hey."

Aaron nodded a hello.

"Going in?"

"Hoping to."

Liam scanned the parking lot. It was late August and hot as fuck. You could probably fry an egg on the blacktop. "I just left."

Aaron lifted his head and narrowed his eyes at Liam. "You saw Sophie?"

Liam nodded. "Yeah. I've been going as much as I can since she was born. Whenever Dina had to leave, she always made sure someone else was with Soph. Someone besides a nurse or doctor. Like a friend."

Aaron's heart ripped in two. His sister was the best fucking mom in the whole fucking world. And of course she would be. She knew what a shitty mother was like, they both did. Having grown up in foster care their entire lives, Aaron and Dina had bounced around the system for years. They never found a home or family they could really call *theirs*. But at least they had each other.

When Aaron turned eighteen, he left the system, or more accurately was *kicked out* of the system, left to his own devices to either flounder or flourish in the big cruel world.

Thankfully, he flourished. The day he graduated high school he got a job in construction. Walked right on to the site and refused to leave until the foreman gave him a job. And at 4:58 pm, right before quitting time, he was handed his very first hard hat.

Over the next six months he proved himself and his boss at the construction company offered to pay for Aaron to go to carpentry school while he worked. He earned his journeyman ticket in carpentry, and obtained all of his necessary apprenticeship hours by the time he was twenty-one.

Shortly after getting hired, his boss—who became more of a father figure than anything else—helped him petitioned the courts to get legal custody of Dina—and he won. She was fifteen and he was eighteen, and he was so happy to get her out of the shit show house they'd been living in before that. Eight foster kids, one foster mother, one bathroom and barely enough food to feed a family of rabbits.

Though, he and Dina didn't live like royalty, at least they were together. He found them a modest little two-bedroom apartment in a questionable part of Seattle, but it was clean, it was safe and most importantly, it was theirs and they were together.

He worked and went to night school for his journeyman ticket, she went to high school and worked a part time job at a movie theater on the weekends. They made ends meet— just barely, but they did. They never went to bed hungry, were never late on a rent or a utility bill. Somehow, by Grace and by God, Aaron even managed to save a small sum by the time Dina's senior prom came around, and he surprised her with the dress she'd been dreaming of for over six months.

She was his person and he was hers.

Because they're all the other ever had.

Sure, he had his brothers in arms. He had Rob and Colt, Wark and Ash. They were his brothers.

They were his team.

But they weren't blood.

Dina was his blood.

She was the only blood he had. His only connection to his past.

They didn't know their parents, their grandparents or whether they had more siblings out there. It was just the two of them. Aaron and Dina Steele taking on the world.

When she graduated high school, he made sure she got into college before he enlisted in the Navy. He knew she'd be safe and make friends at college. She wouldn't be alone. He put her through four years of school and then law school, sending her money whenever he could. Even if they went months without seeing each other, he wanted her to know that he was always there for her. Always supporting her.

He'd never cried so much in his life—up until recently— than he did the day his sister accepted her diploma at her law school graduation. And he didn't give a flying fuck who saw him bawling his eyes out. His baby sister was a mother-fucking lawyer and he would shout it from the rooftops and sob until his eyes were empty, he was so damn proud.

"I can go back in with you." Liam's voice drew Aaron out of his thoughts. He'd been spacing out a lot over the last two days. Jet-lag and grief will do that to a person. "If you're not ready to go face Sophie alone, I can go back in. She knows me. Seems to like me."

Aaron pursed his lips together before rolling the window back up in his truck, turning off the ignition and opening the door. "Thanks, man. Right now I'm not sure how to face her alone."

He locked the truck and dug into his pocket to grab his wallet so he could pay for parking.

Liam's hand slapped his shoulder. "Don't worry about it, man. I got ya. I'll go enter your license plate number and get your parking. Go see your niece."

Swallowing down the razor blade that had lodged in his

throat, Aaron did nothing but nod, murmur a thanks and then head in the direction of the hospital main entrance, the ache in his heart feeling more like an anvil on his chest as he approached the main doors.

He wasn't cut out to be a dad.

He was going to fail Sophie, fail Dina, fail them all.

Just like he'd failed in Colombia.

IF YOU'VE ENJOYED THIS BOOK

If you've enjoyed this book, please consider leaving a review.
It really does make a difference.
Thank you again.
Xoxo
Whitley Cox

ACKNOWLEDGMENTS

There are so many people to thank who help along the way. Publishing a book is definitely not a solo mission, that's for sure. First and foremost, my friend and editor Chris Kridler, you lady are a blessing, a gem and an all-around amazing human being. Thank you for your honesty and hard work.

Thank you, to my critique groups gals, Danielle and Jillian. I love our monthly meet-ups at Starbucks where we give honest feedback and just bitch about life. You two are my bitch-sisters and I wouldn't give you up for anything.

Andi Babcock for her beta-read, I always appreciate your attention to detail and comments.

Author Jeanne St. James, my alpha reader and sister from another mister, what would I do without you?

Megan J. Parker-Squiers from EmCat Designs, your covers are awesome. Thank you,

My Naughty Room Readers Crew, authors Jeanne St. James, Erica Lynn and Cailin Briste, I love being part of such a tremendous set of inspiring, talented and supportive women. Thank you for letting me learn, lean on and join the team.

My street team, Whitley Cox's Curiously Kinky Reviewers, you are all awesome and I feel so blessed to have found such wonderful fans.

The ladies in Vancouver Island Romance Authors, your support and insight have been incredibly helpful, and I'm so honored to be a part of a group of such talented writers.

Author Cora Seton for your help, tweaks and suggestions for my blurbs, as always, they come back from you so sparkly. I also love our walks, talks and heart-to-hearts, they mean so much to me.

Authors Kathleen Lawless, Nancy Warren and Jane Wallace, I love our writing meetups. Wine, good food and friendship always make the words flow.

The Small Human and the Tiny Human, you are the beats and beasts of my heart, the reason I breathe and the reason I drink. I love you both to infinity and beyond.

And lastly, of course, the husband. You are my forever. I love you.

ALSO BY WHITLEY COX

Love, Passion and Power: Part 1
The Dark and Damaged Hearts Series Book 1

Love, Passion and Power: Part 2
The Dark and Damaged Hearts Series Book 2

Sex, Heat and Hunger: Part 1
The Dark and Damaged Hearts Book 3

Sex, Heat and Hunger: Part 2
The Dark and Damaged Hearts Book 4

Hot and Filthy: The Honeymoon
The Dark and Damaged Hearts Book 4.5

True, Deep and Forever: Part 1
The Dark and Damaged Hearts Book 5

True, Deep and Forever: Part 2
The Dark and Damaged Hearts Book 6

Hard, Fast and Madly: Part 1
The Dark and Damaged Hearts Series Book 7

Hard, Fast and Madly: Part 2
The Dark and Damaged Hearts Series Book 8

Quick & Dirty

Book 1, A Quick Billionaires Novel

Quick & Easy

Book 2, A Quick Billionaires Novella

Quick & Reckless

Book 3, A Quick Billionaires Novel

Hot Dad

Lust Abroad

Snowed In & Set Up

Quick & Dangerous

Book 4, A Quick Billionaires Novel

Hired by the Single Dad

The Single Dads of Seattle, Book 1

Dancing with the Single Dad

The Single Dads of Seattle, Book 2

Saved by the Single Dad

The Single Dads of Seattle, Book 3

Upcoming

Living with the Single Dad

The Single Dads of Seattle, Book 4

ABOUT THE AUTHOR

A Canadian West Coast baby born and raised, Whitley is married to her high school sweetheart, and together they have two beautiful daughters and a fluffy dog. She spends her days making food that gets thrown on the floor, vacuuming Cheerios out from under the couch and making sure that the dog food doesn't end up in the air conditioner. But when nap time comes, and it's not quite wine o'clock, Whitley sits down, avoids the pile of laundry on the couch, and writes.

A lover of all things decadent; wine, cheese, chocolate and spicy erotic romance, Whitley brings the humorous side of sex, the ridiculous side of relationships and the suspense of everyday life into her stories. With mommy wars, body issues, threesomes, bondage and role playing, these books have everything we need to satisfy the curious kink in all of us.

YOU CAN ALSO FIND ME HERE

Website: WhitleyCox.com
Twitter: @WhitleyCoxBooks
Instagram: @CoxWhitley
Facebook Page: https://www.facebook.com/CoxWhitley/
Blog: https://whitleycox.blogspot.ca/
Multi-Author Blog: https://romancewritersbehavingbadly.blogspot.com
Exclusive Facebook Reader Group: https://www.facebook.com/groups/234716323653592/
Booksprout: https://booksprout.co/author/994/whitley-cox
Bookbub: https://www.bookbub.com/authors/whitley-cox

JOIN MY STREET TEAM

WHITLEY COX'S CURIOUSLY KINKY REVIEWERS
Hear about giveaways, games, ARC opportunities, new releases, teasers, author news, character and plot development and more!

Facebook Street Team
Join NOW!

DON'T FORGET TO SUBSCRIBE TO MY NEWSLETTER

Be the first to hear about pre-orders, new releases, giveaways, 99 cent deals, and freebies!

Click here to Subscribe
http://eepurl.com/ckh5yT

Made in the USA
Las Vegas, NV
10 November 2022

59152183R00163